Who Cat Loved

A novel

She had only one life left.

CHELSEA WILSON THAYER

Contact the author:
www.chelseawilsonthayer.com

Editing by Victoria Gracia'a
Book cover and interior design and typesetting by Lisa Von De Linde of LisaVdesigns
Cover photo credit: Dewberry Photos and Design
Author headshot credit: Dewberry Photos and Design

ISBN: 978-1-7355117-3-3

Published by Write Now Press, LLC

Printed in the United States of America

First Edition, 2021

So I wait for you like a lonely house,

Till you will see me again

and live in me.

Till then my windows ache.

—PABLO NERUDA

CHAPTER ONE

LUKE PUT THE LAST OF HIS PAINTINGS IN THE CRATE, STAMPED 'Handle with Care' on the side, and stepped back to examine the contents of his life neatly packed, stacked, and waiting for transport in his beat-up truck. It's a little daunting to view all of your belongings like that.

Luke tried not to think about how snugly his possessions had fit into the back of an old Silverado. He tried to focus on the fact that he was about to accomplish something that for so long he had only dreamed of. He was about to intern at a gallery, a gallery in New York City in fact. He had even been offered the rare opportunity to show his own work in the new artist series the gallery would be doing the coming year.

He smiled as the thought crossed his mind. His work had been chosen the previous spring, his junior year of college, to be showcased in an exhibition in New York with other young rising artists.

At the time, he realized the significance of such an honor, but had no idea what would become of it. The last nine months had been a whirlwind. He ended up selling more pieces than any other artist had during the exhibition. His success had drawn supporters from all walks of life. Of course, they all shared one common attribute—they were filthy rich. Luke had never been around people of that culture before, unless you counted Cat.

He didn't.

Luke had worked very hard to bury that brief period of his life. And most of the time, he went about his business without the slightest thought of her. Most of the time.

"Is that everything?" Luke's father asked from the entrance to the barn.

"Yes, sir," Luke looked back at the barn, which looked emptier than Luke had ever seen it.

"Still don't know why yer drivin' all yer' stuff up to New York on yer' own," his dad spoke with a mouth full of chewing tobacco.

"Don't trust anyone but yourself to get the job done right. Isn't that what you always said, sir?" Luke smiled at his old man.

His father mumbled something unintelligible and followed with, "Them yahoos up in New York got enough money to give a gallery to my son, then they got enough money to fly him first class."

"Well, they offered to fly me," Luke shrugged, "I told them I'd rather transport all the paintings myself. And it's not my gallery … it's just a senior internship, remember?"

His father just nodded. Usually a man of very few words, Luke assumed he'd reached his quota for the day.

"Well," Luke said, shaking his father's hand firmly, "I'd better get going before the snow comes in tonight. Tomorrow morning, I'll be watching the sun rise over the Hudson."

Luke started to climb into the cab of the truck when he heard his father call out his name. Luke sighed. He knew what was coming. They'd been going round and round about the same things since he declared himself an art major his sophomore year. He was tired of explaining his career choice, his dreams of owning a gallery, the purpose of a gallery, why he loved painting, and insisting that he was, indeed, straight. Though when his father asked how many girls he'd slept with, Luke never quite answered honestly. Twenty-two and a virgin. *I deserve a damn medal*, Luke thought to himself before his dad called his name again and forced him to turn around.

"Sir," Luke called back.

"Luke," his dad walked up to where he stood beside the truck. There was an awkward moment of silence before his dad reached around and wrapped him into a quick hug. "I'm proud of you, son. And your mama, well, she would be proud, too."

Luke nodded. He didn't let himself tear up until he was in the truck and his father was well out of sight. Best not give him any reason to think I'm a "fruitcake," Luke swallowed the lump in his throat and wiped his eyes with his sleeves.

He had ten hours to go to New York City. His new home. He popped open a Red Bull and downed it in a few gulps. A long drive by himself would mean a lot of time to think. Luke narrowed his eyes on the road ahead. He didn't allow himself time to think alone. He filled that time with painting. It kept his mind busy. Busy was good.

He synched his iPod to the truck's radio to distract himself with music. He put it on shuffle to hear a good mix of songs. The distraction worked. He found himself thinking of where in the world he had gotten half the songs from and promised himself he would clean out his music files once he settled in New York. Then a Lupe Fiasco song came on, the same one that had been playing over four years ago on the way home from a cross country meet. The same song that he had listened to when Cat had sat curled up beside him.

Cat. Where was she now? Was she still that broken soul he had fallen for all those years ago? Did she still have the fire in her eyes? Was her temper still unpredictable and utterly amusing? One question continued to come back to him—*does she still love me?*

He thought about New York City and the eight million people that lived there. For all he knew, she would be one of them. For the first time in four years, they would be living in the same place. He knew it was highly unlikely that he would run into her on his own. He couldn't even imagine what he would say if he did. Sorry didn't even begin to cover it.

No, he decided. He would have to start with 'I love you.' That would be the only place to start. If he ever saw her, of course. All this hypothetical thinking was foolish to begin with, he told himself. After all, it was highly unlikely.

CHAPTER TWO

LUKE TIGHTENED HIS GRIP ON THE GROCERY BAGS HE WAS CARRYING back from D'Agostino. His Bank Street studio apartment was only four blocks away. He was learning the hard way that you never buy more groceries than you can carry in New York City. He was also remembering why you shouldn't go grocery shopping when you are starving. He hadn't really thought about how the groceries were getting home until he was in the midst of checking out with his cart full of food. At least his cupboards would no longer be bare.

He squeezed the bags tighter as the numbness spread from his fingers to his hands. New York City was brutal in January. He knew it would be cold, but growing up in Boone, North Carolina made him certain he could handle it. He looked at his gloveless fingers that had now turned as red as a cherry tomato. *Next time I'll wear gloves*, he promised himself.

When he finally climbed the four flights of stairs and was safely inside his apartment, he let the bags drop to the ground with a thud. He popped open a can of honey roasted peanuts to munch on as he put the food away. While he was in a working mood, he continued on to unpacking the last few boxes he had shoved into the corner. In less than two hours he was finished.

His apartment was by no means spacious by North Carolina standards, but the 600 square foot studio apartment suited him just fine. Not to mention the fact that he had managed to sublet it for seven-hundred dollars a month, an unheard-of price for New York, let alone in the West Village. One of his new backers was letting him rent it from him at cost while he was in Europe for the year. Thank you, rent-stabilized apartments. His trip to Ikea the previous Saturday had been quite successful as he had been able to purchase just enough to make the space feel like home. Except drapes. Luke didn't do drapes, not that his windows needed them. They were enormous, causing your eyes to travel up to the skylights overhead. No drapes needed here.

The wonderful light the room provided made it an excellent studio. Luke had gotten a futon in place of a bed and was using the alcove space in the apartment as a makeshift studio. He knew he would be moving his work into the gallery at the end of April to begin setting up the first exhibit, but he wanted to create a few more pieces before the summer opening. His collection was complete, as far as his patrons were concerned, but Luke couldn't help but feel that it was lacking … something.

His blackberry began to buzz happily in his pocket. He couldn't help but grin at the name flashing on the screen.

"Hello there, old friend," his voice boomed through the empty space.

"Who are you calling old, Luke Presnell?" Rachel's voice said with amusement.

"Or should I say 'Bonjour, mon ami?'" Luke inquired jokingly, "Aren't you in Paris!?"

"It's actually 'm'amie,' Luke, because I'm female."

Luke smirked to himself as Rachel continued. She always did have to correct him … and everyone else.

"And, no. I've just moved to New York," Rachel said excitedly, "And a little bird told me you just moved here, too!"

"Finally took the plunge," Luke nodded to himself.

"What do you think?" Rachel asked.

"Too cold!" Luke laughed. "But, seriously, I don't know why I didn't do it sooner. I think this will be good for me."

"And your art," Rachel added.

"Well, that too," Luke smiled. "A little exposure couldn't hurt."

"Yes, well, I doubt that the mice in that old barn were very big supporters to begin with," Rachel joked.

"There were a few stray cats there, too," Luke's reflection in the floor-to-ceiling windows beamed genuinely back at him.

It was so easy to joke with her. She was like the sister he had never had. And now she was in New York, too. What a small world.

"So, tell me Luke," Rachel said, "I know, you're on your way to becoming a big shot artist and all. But, do you think you could squeeze me into your schedule for dinner one night this week?"

Luke could practically hear Rachel grinning as she talked. He blushed with embarrassment. Sure, he'd landed himself a pretty sweet deal with his internship and upcoming show at the gallery. A feat that rarely, if ever, happens for newcomers. But, 'big shot artist' was a title he wasn't ready to claim quite yet.

"My schedule?" Luke replied, "I think I'll have a harder time making it into your date book, Ms. Fashionista."

"All right, all right. We're both on the way to becoming fabulous," Rachel laughed. "We're tied. So, how about dinner at Mighty Quinn's? You're in the Village, right? They have the best barbecue in the city."

"You free tonight?" Luke asked.

"Eight o'clock?" Rachel replied.

"Eight? For dinner? A little late don't you think?"

"Oh, Luke. Darling, Luke. You have so much to learn about New York City."

Luke could easily picture Rachel shaking her head at him. He could have sworn he heard her clucking her tongue through the cell phone.

"See you then," Luke chuckled to himself as he hung up the phone.

At least I have one friend in the city, Luke thought to himself. It felt good knowing he wasn't entirely alone. As he looked forward to catching up with Rachel, he wondered who else she'd caught up with. Cat? He stopped himself. Even if she had, it wouldn't mean anything. He would never go and find her. Bringing up the past would be too painful for both of them. It had been over four years; some things are best forgotten.

CHAPTER THREE

"SO?" LUKE SMILED AT RACHEL AS HE TOOK A SWALLOW OF HIS THIRD oatmeal stout. "You still have never taken a sip of alcohol?"

Rachel sipped happily on her virgin cocktail, "Nope. Not that I have anything against it. I have just never felt the desire to try it. I'm content with my virgin daiquiri."

"You are something else, Rachel McKinney," Luke shook his head.

"That's exactly right," Rachel said, pleased with Luke's assertion.

After catching up about family and their lives the last few years, it felt like they had never been apart.

"So, I'm going to be crazy busy through the end of February with fashion week, and lining up our fall styles. But it will be totally worth it!" Rachel exclaimed, giddy about her new internship.

"It sounds like what you always wanted," Luke was genuinely happy for her. He couldn't think of anyone who deserved it more.

"What about you Luke?" Rachel's voice shifted. "Do you have everything you've always wanted?"

Luke paused; he could sense the hidden message behind that question, but he wasn't ready to address it quite yet.

"As close as I'm going to get," he finally answered with a smile. He was being honest.

"Have you tried to find her?" Rachel's voice was quiet now.

"Have you?"

"No."

An uncomfortable silence fell between them.

"I'm going to try to get her phone number from Mimi, though," Rachel munched on a celery stalk.

"If you do … I don't want to know," Luke spoke briskly. "I wish her well and all, but I don't want to know anything. And I think it's best if she doesn't even know I'm here."

Rachel looked down at the table, this was clearly not the response she had been hoping for.

"Rachel?"

Finally, Rachel sighed and nodded, "Alright, Luke. If I talk to Cat, when I talk to Cat, I won't tell her that you're in New York."

"No matter what," Luke added.

"Promise," Rachel nodded, "She won't hear it from me."

Luke finished his beer.

"Luke, I know you still think about her," Rachel began.

It was clear from Luke's reaction that she had said entirely the wrong thing.

"Oh, you do, do you?" Luke snapped back. "You know? I haven't seen you in nearly three years, Rach. We talk every once in a blue moon. What makes you think you know anything that I think about?!"

Tears welled up in Rachel's eyes, "I shouldn't have said that, Luke. I'm sorry. Maybe you have moved on. That's fine. If that's what you want?"

"It is!" Luke's voice was drowned out by the noisy bar, despite the fact that he was practically shouting. "I have moved on."

"Good."

"Good."

Rachel sighed, "I won't bring her up again."

"I think that's a good idea," Luke agreed. His reply was curt.

Rachel's gaze drifted to watching others around the bar. A wave of fresh guilt covered him, and suddenly, a memory surfaced from their childhood. It involved a pig pen and Rachel in a new Sunday dress she was keen on showing off. Luke shook his head and smiled to himself. He was no better at controlling his temper at twenty-two than he had been at age five.

"Sorry I snapped like that. It was uncalled for."

"Luke, I've known you since we were in diapers," Rachel turned her attention back to the table. "I'm entirely used to your temper by now."

"Yeah, well," Luke straightened up in his chair and motioned to the waitress for the check. "I guess I'm still working on it."

"Good luck," Rachel laughed.

"Ha, ha," Luke said dryly as he threw some cash on the table.

Rachel tried to protest his generosity.

"Get me next time," Luke smiled. "Hey! You want to see my apartment?"

"Luke Presnell, are you trying to take me home with you?" Rachel joked as they donned their winter coats and stepped out into the night air.

"Well, if I were, you would be the first," Luke said plainly, as he wrapped his scarf around his face.

"No way!" Rachel shouted aghast. "Oh, Luke! I'm so proud of you!"

Luke offered her his arm as they set out in the direction of his studio.

"What a strange thing to be proud of! The fact that I'm still a ... well, that's hardly something to gush over," Luke blushed under his scarf.

"Well, you should be proud," Rachel put her arm through his

as they walked. "It's not like you couldn't have, if you wanted to. You chose not to. That's what makes it pretty awesome."

"Yeah," Luke rolled his eyes. "Awesome."

True to her word, Rachel had not mentioned Cat again. They had gotten together three times since their initial meeting—twice on the weekends and once on Rachel's lunch break. Luke couldn't help but wonder if Rachel had made contact with Cat, if they were hanging out, if they talked about him. Despite his efforts, Luke was finding it impossible to forget her. Moving on should have been easier by now. It's not like he hadn't dated girls in college. He had dated plenty ... but always found it easy to break up with them when the relationship began to get "serious." But dating here, in her city, he felt like he was cheating on her somehow. Every time he turned a corner, he could swear that he caught a glimpse of her. He had nearly run over a dozen people in the subway when he thought he saw her get off the train. This only ended in him getting completely lost for an hour in Soho.

Then, when he was on his way to meet Rachel for coffee, he walked by Fresh and caught a whiff of her perfume. It nearly killed him. It was time to take drastic measures, he decided, and quickly.

"Rach," Luke wasn't sure how to begin on this particular coffee date, "do you have any other friends?"

Not the right thing to say, Luke quickly realized, before Rachel could respond.

"What I meant was," Luke revised, as Rachel's hurt expression faded from her face, "do you have any friends ... for me? You know, to set me up with?"

Rachel smiled, "There are several girls I work with that I'm sure would love to go out with you."

"What makes you say that?" Luke feigned disinterest as he pretended to read the paper.

"Luke. Honestly?" She pushed the paper down to get a better look at him. "You're a good looking, southern gentleman who's about to become a very famous artist."

Rachel continued with her hand held aloft to halt his protest, "A straight artist. You're manly, yet with a sensitive side; every girl's dream," she batted her eyes at him, as if to make her point.

"I don't see you chasing after me," Luke countered.

"Yeah, well. I know you," Rachel teased.

"Nice," Luke laughed.

"That's not mean. I know you … and I know I'm not the one for you," Rachel added. "And you're not the one for me. We're meant to be friends."

"The 'one' for me," Luke repeated, sipping his coffee, "Everyone only gets one."

Rachel changed the subject, "I think I'll set you up with Cara first."

"First," Luke raised an eyebrow. "What if things work out with this Cara?"

"Oh," Rachel smiled, "They won't. But you'll have a *really* good time. She'll be a good one to introduce you to the world of New York City dating."

"Why does this sound so scary to me?" Luke rubbed his palms together, they were starting to feel sweaty. Maybe this was not the best idea.

"Because it is," Rachel nodded. "Good Lord, Luke. I was only kidding. Sort of."

"Okay," Luke took a deep breath, "Cara first. Tell me a little bit about her."

"Have you ever seen *Sex and the City*?" Rachel tilted her head.

"I think I may have caught parts of an episode here and there," Luke wasn't sure where this was going.

"She's a Samantha," Rachel nodded knowingly.

"The whore?" Luke's eyes widened. "Rachel, why would you set me up with a Samantha?"

"Because you need to have some fun," Rachel's eyes twinkled mischievously. "And then, I'll set you up with a Miranda, so you can see what sarcastic northern women can be like …"

"Rachel," Luke hissed.

"No one's listening," Rachel shushed him and glanced around before lowering her voice. "I like Yankees now. I'm not being mean. Just honest. Where was I? Oh yes, then I'll set you up with a Charlotte."

"So, that's the one for me?" Luke nodded. "A Charlotte."

"No," Rachel sounded very sure of herself. "You need a Carrie. Someone witty, yet sweet. Someone fun, yet grounded. Someone with a little fire in them."

Someone like Cat, Luke thought. He knew Rachel was thinking the same thing.

"That sounds about right," Luke coughed.

"Are you free tomorrow night?" Rachel asked as she typed furiously into her phone.

"Let's see," Luke checked his Blackberry calendar. "Saturday, I have to stop by the gallery around six to inspect the new lighting, but free after that."

Rachel nodded and continued to type furiously. Her phone beeped at her. She typed again. Seconds later, her phone beeped once more.

"Perfect," she exclaimed.

"You arranged all that in less than a minute?" Luke was impressed.

"She will be meeting you at the gallery at seven o'clock," Rachel winked at him, "She's really excited."

"She'll be disappointed," Luke muttered.

"Are you kidding?" Rachel laughed. "Withholding sex will drive her crazy … in a good way. She'll think you're a gentleman. And there's nothing sexier than that."

"Since when did you become such an expert on sex?" Luke was learning a lot of new things from his old friend.

"Luke, I was stealing Cosmo from the doctor's office since I could read," Rachel laughed.

"That's just sad," Luke shook his head ruefully.

"But true," Rachel nodded shamefully.

"So, Cara. Tomorrow night at seven," Luke confirmed, as he typed into his blackberry.

"Get ready for a wild night," Rachel grinned.

CHAPTER FOUR

LUKE DECIDED TO WALK THE TWELVE BLOCKS NORTH TO THE GALLERY in Chelsea. His internship had only just begun, but he found himself coming in to work even on his off days. It felt comfortable. Surrounded by the work of fellow creative minds and those who appreciated it, it felt like coming home. Only not to a home he'd ever had the privilege to be a part of before. He felt welcomed here, understood, appreciated, even admired for his own meager contributions to the world of art. He couldn't get used to that part. Humility would always be his default.

The gallery was on the western most edge of Chelsea, only a block and a half from the river. The owners, Marc Whitson and Jonathan Plum, who had awarded him the internship, had assured him that it would be the perfect locale for his artwork. Luke had to agree with them. As he walked north, store windows and lighting became more vibrant, and it was clear that there was a lot of nightlife in the neighborhood. It was perfect for lots of exposure to his paintings. He made a mental note to keep the gallery open late on weekends. He was going to be responsible for the day to day operation, along with Nicolas, the gallery manager. The owners were keen on hands-on learning. It was sink or swim. Luke knew he had one shot and prayed it would be enough to make it in this industry.

As he approached the front of the gallery, Luke was a little relieved to see that Cara had not arrived yet. He was running nearly an hour late to check the lighting and knew she could be showing up at any moment. He had been dreading this date, almost since the moment he had agreed to it. He took his time opening the series of locks at the entrance. As he slid up the storefront security gate and moved to unlock the front door, he heard someone clear their throat behind him. It was distinctly female.

Turning around, Luke forced himself to smile, "You must be Cara."

The young woman was attractive. Very attractive. Her blonde hair was cropped short and messy; it was swept to one side in a tousled, yet utterly alluring manner. She wore ankle boots, black opaque tights, burgundy velvet shorts, with a metallic tank top. Her long fur coat was worn open; Luke wasn't certain if that was meant to show off her outfit or her curves. She was a knockout. He didn't realize he was staring at her until she spoke.

"And you must be Luke," she purred.

Her perfect white teeth were blinding.

"Would you like to come inside?" Luke stammered, as he opened the door for her.

"Love to," she flashed him a brilliant smile as she stepped through the doors. "Rachel has told me so much about you."

"Oh, dear," Luke laughed.

"All good things," Cara laughed, "I swear."

Her laugh threw Luke off a bit. Her voice was so sultry, but when she laughed, it sounded like a shrill little girl. It reminded him of Clarissa, whom he had dated in high school. He didn't care for it. He gritted his teeth.

"I'll just be a few minutes," he said as he started turning on the lights, "Sorry, you had to come here first. They just installed new lighting today that I needed to take a look at."

"Not at all," said Cara, as she draped herself suggestively over a lounge chair in the center of the room.

Luke found it difficult to stay focused on his task, as he moved the ladder about the room and adjusted the lights. It was quite obvious Cara had practice at putting on a show. First, she bent over in front of him to adjust her boots. It was clear she wasn't wearing a bra.

"This is the last one," Luke cleared his throat again, as he adjusted the final light. His mouth felt like cotton. Was it his nerves? He suddenly felt like he could drink a gallon of water and still be thirsty. He glanced down at her again and quickly back at the light he was adjusting. Luke wasn't opposed to silence, but this awkward silence was killing him. What do you say to someone you don't know and have stupidly agreed to spend the evening with?

"This is a great space," Cara admired, as she led herself around the gallery. "Just one question, though."

"Shoot," Luke said.

"Where's the fabulous artwork I've heard so much about?" she winked at him.

"Oh," Luke laughed as he looked at the bare walls. "My artwork will go up last, after we finish setting up the new exhibits. I just moved it into the basement today."

"Mind if I take a peek?" Cara asked sweetly as she approached him.

He did. Luke had given very few people a private showing of his artwork. He had always been private about it. It was a habit he'd held onto. Showing to hundreds of people at once didn't bother him. He could disappear into the sidelines, watch their expressions, and listen to comments as they observed his work. Usually, they didn't even know he was the artist. But showing it to one person … there was pressure there.

"It's a mess down there, and it's awfully dark," Luke side-stepped the question. "I think it's probably too dim to really see."

"Are you scared of the dark, Luke?" Cara teased, "I can hold your hand."

Luke found that she was leading him towards the back doorway that led to the basement. With a sigh, he took the lead and consented to show her his work. But only a few pieces.

"The stairs are a little steep." He took her hand as they descended. "Just watch yourself in those boots."

"Oh, I'm fine." Cara squeezed his hand. "I run in stilettos daily."

"You run in stilettos?"

"Oh, you know what I mean. To catch a cab or get on the train before the doors close. Or, when I'm trying to snag the perfect Marc Jacobs suit jacket at the Barney's sale … I run."

"I didn't realize running was required in shopping."

"Well then, I'll just have to take you shopping with me next time. It's my competitive sport."

Yep. Luke thought to himself. This would be the first and last date with Cara. He reached along the wall until he found the light. His neatly wrapped canvases lined the wall.

She "ohh'd" and "ahhh'd" over each canvas as though it was the best thing she had ever seen. Luke wasn't sure how much of it was put on, but it made him feel good. It was becoming obvious that she had intentions for later in the evening, her friendly pats and squeezes were becoming more like caresses. As much as Luke wanted to protest, he couldn't think of a single excuse as to why he shouldn't allow himself to have a good time. Even if only for one night. It had been four years since Cat. It was about time he moved on.

After Cara's private showing of Luke's artwork, they made

their way to Lotus in the Meatpacking District. Chelsea's art district gave way to the cobblestone streets and lively nightlife of this see and be seen neighborhood. A celebrity must have arrived at The Gansevoort Hotel across the street judging from the blinding flashes of what seemed like a thousand cameras. Cara had taken the lead and seemed to be pulling Luke along in her bouncing wake.

Luke immediately felt underdressed as he descended into the club. He smoothed his shirt down several times, though the wrinkles remained.

Cara seemed oblivious to Luke's marked discomfort. Luke wasn't used to the big city style. Nor did he see the appeal of large, noisy clubs. He would much rather go to a wine bar where they could relax and talk.

Cara glanced back and gave him a blinding smile as she pulled him to the dance floor.

"Oh, Cara," Luke began to pull back, "I really don't dance."

Cara stuck out her bottom lip.

"Are you sure you can't make an exception this once?" she pleaded.

Decision time, Luke thought to himself. *Either I refuse and she thinks I'm a jackass. Or I dance and I look like a jackass.*

"This won't be pretty," Luke warned her, as he followed her onto the dance floor.

Cara moved against him to the music, as Luke stood in place and bobbed along. He had no experience dancing. The only place people 'dance' in Boone is at Klondike, which is a trailer so tightly packed with drunk college students, that nobody can even tell whether or not you can dance.

Cara could dance; Luke recognized that. Luke commenced his white-man shuffle as she turned circles around him. She dropped and scooted her rear against his pants leg in a way that Luke had mostly seen in music videos. What was he supposed to do? Pat her on the back and say, 'Good job?' Smack her ass? He froze in place and looked awkwardly around him.

"See," she whispered in his ear, "this isn't too bad is it?"

"I guess not."

"What about now?" she moved even closer against him as she shimmied.

"I- uh," Luke laughed out of embarrassment. "No, it's not too bad."

"Can I buy you a drink?" she asked.

"No," Luke said bluntly, "But, if you'll allow me to buy you one ..."

"Martini," she cut him off, "Apple martini."

"Apple martini it is," Luke smiled and weaved his way in and out of people towards the bar.

After fifteen minutes of attempting to get the bartender's attention, Cara appeared at his side. Immediately, she was served a brightly colored concoction that looked far too sweet for Luke's taste, but Cara appeared content, downing the contents of her martini glass in one gulp.

"I should have had you come over sooner," Luke smiled at her as the bartender mixed her another drink.

Cara laughed that shrill little laugh that threw Luke off.

"Want to try a sip?" She offered her drink to him when the bartender handed it to her.

Luke had never tried an apple martini before, and he was pretty sure he wouldn't like it, but he didn't want to be rude. He eyed the green mixture suspiciously.

"Why not?" he shrugged, and took a large swallow. It tasted like liquid jolly ranchers. Not at all what he preferred.

"You don't like it?" Cara laughed, taking in his expression.

"Not my cup of tea," he admitted.

Cara motioned the bartender over for the third time so Luke could order a scotch, neat.

"Neat," she giggled. "You mean it's like, nifty, or something?"

Luke choked on his drink. "No," he stammered, trying not to laugh in her face. "It's a way of ordering a drink. It means 'without' ice."

Cara cackled, making Luke take a deeper sip of his scotch and start plotting his exit strategy. She may be nice to look at, but Rachel should've known better than to set him up with a cackler.

He was still working out an escape route when she led him over to a booth along the wall where they could watch the action on the dance floor. It was perfectly positioned for people watching. Or, in Cara's case, fashion narrating. She commented on the different designers she noticed women were wearing. She pointed out the B-list celebrities scattered through the room. Worst of all, she elbowed Luke each time a fashion faux-pas passed their way. He was beginning to wonder if he would still have all of his ribs after tonight. Thankfully, the nudging subsided as she began to talk about her job, her love of fashion, and her desire to be head buyer someday. Luke nodded and responded at the appropriate places, but beyond that, he didn't have much to say. Her priorities were so different from his. She got a thrill by getting into a particular club, or from the new Alexander McQueen coat she had just found at a 'fabulous' price. Sure she was pretty to look at, but where was the substance?

"So, where are you from?" Luke changed the subject, after she'd been blathering on for the better part of an hour.

"Huh?" Cara looked confused.

"Oh," Luke chuckled, "Sorry to change the subject like that

… I was just wondering where you were from. Where's your family?"

"They're in Connecticut," she already looked bored by this new topic. "But I've been in the city since I was eighteen. New York is my family now." She cackled again.

Her tone suggested she was only kidding, but the look on her face told Luke she was quite serious. His phone buzzed in his pocket, shaking him from his thoughts.

"I'm going to get another drink," Luke said suddenly standing up. "Want another?"

"Of course," she winked at him, "Don't be gone too long."

Luke faked a chuckle.

When he got to the bar, he fished in his pocket for his phone while he waited on the bartender. It was Rachel. Her text read, 'Totally Samantha, right?'

He shoved his phone back into his pocket with a grimace, without responding to the text. How was he supposed to end this date, if he knew he felt nothing for this girl?

He mulled over several options as he headed back to the table with the drinks.

Cara downed her martini in a few swallows. Luke decided to follow suit.

"You want to get out of here?" Luke inquired, realizing a little too late that this seemed like an invitation to move the date to the next level and not his opportunity to end it. Whoops.

"I thought you would never ask," Cara hissed in his ear as she leaned across the table and kissed him.

Luke had no warning, whatsoever. Perhaps he should have expected it, given the signals she had been sending him all night. But, not being accustomed to sudden and intense kisses on a first date, Luke nearly fell out of his seat.

"I'll get our coats," he coughed, standing up.

"Alright," she sighed, skimming her hand down his body as he stood up.

By the time they were in a cab, she was all over him. Luke was walking a fine line of mildly returning her affection and ripping her clothes off. Not that he cared for her. But part of him, the part that had never had sex, wanted to have a crazy night for once in his life. What was he holding out for anyway? The glances from the driver kept him in control of himself.

He pushed Cara back down when she tried to straddle him.

"We're not exactly alone," he whispered in her ear.

This seemed to be news to her. It took her a second to figure out what he was talking about.

"Oh, him?" she brushed it off, "People do this in cabs all the time. They're used to it."

With that, she attempted to mount him a second time. This time, Luke scooted away, his back now pressing against the cold window.

"I'm not really comfortable with this," Luke said firmly. "Sorry."

"Fine," she sighed, visibly annoyed, "When we get back to my place, I'll make you very comfortable."

Luke could see the driver smirking in the rear-view mirror. Luke made his decision at that moment.

"There's going to be two stops," Luke piped up.

The cabbie nodded.

"What?!" Cara sounded horrified.

"I'm going to head back to my place when we drop you off." Luke said bluntly. "This wouldn't work. I just don't see a relationship between us, Cara. We're very different …"

Cara began to laugh, "A relationship? Luke, we don't have to have a relationship. I don't care if you want to go out again or not. But … tonight … we're here. Why not enjoy it?"

The cab pulled over to the curb.

"And I promise you … you would really, really enjoy it," she hissed in his ear.

Luke felt conflicted. The voices in his head were at war with each other.

"I'm sorry, Cara," he finally said after a long pause. "I just can't."

She looked legitimately hurt, but mostly surprised, as she stepped out of the car and slammed the door much harder than she needed to.

Luke could tell she was not used to getting turned down.

The cab driver turned to look at him before shaking his head and muttering something that Luke was rather glad he didn't understand.

He lowered his head into his hands and massaged his temples. He wasn't going home. Not now. He needed some release. He gave the cabbie the address to the gallery. Painting would be the only way to achieve that now. He would paint and work up a good sweat. He would feel better about what he had done in the morning. He turned his mind to Rachel's matchmaking adventure. Maybe the next date would be different. Maybe he would actually meet someone. But all the "maybes" in the world wouldn't drown out the biggest one of all—maybe he would never care for anyone the way he had cared for Cat.

CHAPTER FIVE

LUKE CREATED TWO PAINTINGS THAT NIGHT—MORE THAN HE HAD ever completed in a twenty-four-hour period. The fact that he had finished both paintings in four and a half hours still baffled him.

"I can see a sense of urgency in this one," Nicolas commented knowingly, while Marc and Jonathan nodded appreciatively, each examining his new pieces.

Nicolas had become one of his most enthusiastic supporters; he was also the gallery manager and would be working with him and the other emerging artists to prepare for the upcoming exhibit. He had an impeccable taste in art and was a prominent figure in the neighborhood. He was the JFK Jr. of the LGBTQ society in New York. His interest in Luke's art began at his first art show in the city. And, after Luke was certain Nicolas's interest in his work was strictly professional, they had become quite good friends.

Marc and Jonathan, co-owners of the gallery, were ardent philanthropists, suave entrepreneurs, businessmen, and life partners. They had an eye for art, but particularly, what would sell. They gave each other knowing looks and nodded towards Luke as though he was their new golden goose.

"I'm glad we convinced you to come here." Marc winked at him, as he and Jonathan turned to leave.

"Want to join us for brunch, boys?" Jonathan called back towards him and Nicolas.

"I'm good," Luke waved them on. "Thanks, anyway."

"Sure?" Marc asked. "We're going to Extra Virgin, best brunch spot in the village, if you haven't tried it yet."

"The BEST," Jonathan nodded and added jazz hands to emphasize his point.

"Brunch seems to be a big thing here," Luke laughed. "I've never been to brunch before."

Jonathan clutched his heart, "Tell me you're joking."

The others began speaking in unison. The general disbelief that Luke had never been to brunch seemed to be as shocking and unacceptable as though he had never brushed his teeth. How horrifying!

Luke threw up his hands in surrender, "Alright, alright! I'll come to brunch. Just let me clean up first and I'll meet you there." He was covered in paint from his more recent project that morning and needed to rinse his brushes before he could run off to brunch.

"Am I right, though?" Nicolas tilted his head towards Luke, when Marc and Jonathan had exited.

"About what?"

"The painting. The sense of urgency ... the tension?"

"Again," Luke smiled. "You are only the second person I've met who is able to tell me more about my paintings than I am."

"Am I?" Nicolas glowed, "Well, oh-la-la! Aren't I special? Who was the first?"

Luke brushed aside his question, "I think we should be able to open by July 1st if the electrician doesn't cancel on me again."

"Ahhh," Nicolas nodded. "So, these are the questions we avoid. The ones that remind you of someone—mystery girl. The one who got away."

"Nicolas," Luke sighed, he hated dodging questions like this, but he couldn't bring himself to talk about Cat.

"Say no more," Nicolas waved his hand. "We won't talk about her. Let's talk about you. Are you seeing anyone special?"

"No," Luke said bluntly. "But I am seeing a lot of very un-special people."

Nicolas raised an eyebrow.

"My friend, the one from North Carolina you've heard me talk about."

"Rachel," Nicolas interrupted.

"Yes," Luke affirmed. "She's on a sort of quest to expose me to dating in New York City."

"How exciting!" Nicolas's eye twinkled. "Do tell. Or should we save this story for brunch?"

"No, we shouldn't," Luke laughed, "and, not exciting at all. Two weeks ago, I turned down an offer for a wild night of sex and whatever else, no strings attached, with a beautiful woman. And last week I got stood up."

"What happened?" Nicolas looked concerned.

"She emailed me the next day to tell me something came up at work," Luke shrugged.

"No, not with that one," Nicolas shook his head, "the sex goddess."

Luke didn't know what to say.

"Does it have something to do with the girl we don't talk about?" Nicolas asked, understandingly.

Luke didn't respond and began wrapping the paintings back up.

"Forget it," Nicolas patted him on the shoulder, "I didn't say anything."

"Good," Luke replied.

"You know what you need?" Nicolas told him, opening up the little black book he kept in his jacket pocket.

"I'm not going to let you send me a hooker, Nicolas," Luke stepped back.

"I'm not," Nicolas smiled as he flipped through the pages.

"No cross dressers or drag queens, either," Luke wagged a finger at him.

"As amusing as that would be," Nicolas smirked, "I'm going to do something much better. I'm going to set you up with Paulo's little sister, Gabi."

Paulo was Nicolas's partner of eight years. He was, Luke was sure, what most women would consider a Latin hottie. Luke couldn't help but wonder what his sister would look like.

"He and Gabi could be twins," Nicolas smiled as if reading his mind. "And she's the sweetest girl you'll ever meet."

Luke thought it through in his head, "What does she do?"

"She's a student at Columbia and a nanny a few days a week," Nicolas spoke, as he dialed her number on his phone.

Luke just nodded, she sounded normal. Normal was a good thing, compared to what he'd been dealing with lately.

"I'm taking your thoughtful look as permission to call her," Nicolas smiled.

Luke shrugged, "Okay. Sure, I guess."

He suddenly felt nervous.

He was half listening as Nicolas chatted away with Gabi.

"How about tomorrow night?" Nicolas mouthed to him.

Luke shook his head and whispered, "Already have a date planned. But next Friday or Saturday."

Nicolas talked quietly for a few more minutes.

"You are set," he said triumphantly as he hung up the phone. "Next Friday at seven o'clock. You are meeting her at her apartment on the Upper West Side."

"Sounds good," Luke nodded.

"So, who's the date with tomorrow?" he asked. "Another set-up?"

"Another set-up," Luke sighed. He was already sick of dating in this city and he'd only had two dates. Though the second date might not count, since she didn't show up.

"You'll find her, Luke," Nicolas said knowingly. "New York is the best place in the world to be in love. You'll find her."

"Yeah," Luke said sarcastically. "Best place in the world to be in love, worst place to be lonely. I'll be along in a few."

Nicolas nodded and left him alone to tidy up his workspace at the gallery.

With any luck, maybe he wouldn't be lonely for much longer.

CHAPTER SIX

HIS CLOCK READ 6:58 PM AND HE STILL HAD ELEVEN BLOCKS TO GO to reach The Boathouse. Traffic was at a standstill and he knew, even though he was still learning the layout of the city, that he would not be there on time. After watching a mother with her toddler walk past faster than the cab was moving, he decided to go the last half-mile on foot. He could run there in under three minutes, but given his dressy attire, he opted for a brisk-paced walk.

Louisa-Ann Mortimer was a perfect lady, Rachel had assured him. She was raised in Westchester, heiress to God-knows-how-much-money, and always flawless in everything she did. Luke shuddered as Rachel's description of her re-played in his head. She didn't sound anything like his type. She sounded snobby and boring. He couldn't remember what had made him agree to this. Oh yes, he did—Rachel. After his first date, Cara, had disclosed his unwillingness to bed her to all the ladies at work. Ever since then, Rachel had a never-ending line of girls at her desk, waiting to be set-up with the infamous gentleman. Louisa-Ann was at the top of the list because, according to Rachel, she was sweet, beautiful, classy, and most importantly, she was Rachel's boss.

Luke sighed. He hoped she wasn't one of those people who always showed up early. If so, he was not making a good first impression. It was nearly ten after seven when he finally arrived, a little disheveled, but present nonetheless. Taking a quick glance at himself in the foyer mirror, he straightened his tie and smoothed down his hair.

"She's waiting for you at the bar," the maître d informed him, when he gave his name for the reservation.

Luke nodded and headed in that direction. He wished he'd asked Rachel to describe what she looked like. He only knew she was supposedly beautiful and very classy. Those words would have described several of the young women sitting alone in the bar area. What was he supposed to do? Walk up to each one and ask until he guessed it right? He swallowed hard and resisted the urge to turn and bolt.

He felt someone tap lightly on his shoulder, "Are you Luke?"

Turning, Luke looked down on a woman so pint-sized she could've been mistaken for a child. She was, as Rachel said, quite pretty. No more than five feet tall, long blond hair pulled back with a headband, and a short yet classy black cocktail dress. Her style reminded him very much of Cat. He pushed the thought to the back of his mind.

"I am and I'm terribly sorry to be running late," Luke extended his hand to her, but not before wiping it on his pants. His palms had already started to sweat.

When she held her hand out to him, he wasn't sure if it was appropriate to kiss it or shake it, as he was accustomed to doing. Someone needs to write a rule book for dating in New York City, he thought to himself, as he awkwardly shook her hand while half bending forward as though he was going to kiss it.

She giggled, which made him quickly stand upright.

"So, Louisa-Ann, should we find our table?" Luke asked, as he offered his arm to escort her.

"You can just call me Lulu, Luke," she smiled, "and yes, I

reserved one of the patio tables if that's alright?"

"Fine with me. You sure you'll be warm enough eating outside?" Luke was impressed that she would consider eating outdoors on such a cool evening.

"It's winterized," she smiled. "They have it enclosed and have the heaters out until it warms up."

"Ahh," Luke nodded.

He didn't have anything else to say. It was clear that Lulu dined there frequently, as she led the way to their table. Waiters nodded in her direction, and as soon as her bottom touched the seat, she was brought a bottle of Pellegrino and lime wedges.

"Thank you, Paul," she smiled warmly before turning her attention back to Luke.

"So, Luke," she raised an eyebrow, "Rachel has told me all about you. What do you want to know about me?"

Her professional tone and poise suddenly had Luke feeling as though he was being interviewed. He cleared his throat as he adjusted his tie unnecessarily.

"Well, I have to say Rachel has said nothing but wonderful things about you," Luke tried his best to sound as refined as she looked. "Though, I am wondering how someone so young is a head buyer at a major department store like Bloomingdales? It's pretty impressive."

"I'm not as young as I look," she winked.

"No?" Luke didn't believe her. She looked like she could be twelve.

"A lady never tells her age, Luke," Lulu laughed with a mock offended look on her face, "but I will say I am closer to thirty than twenty."

Luke took a sip of the wine Paul had just placed before him, after showing the bottle to Lulu. That meant she was three years older than him, at least. He'd never dated anyone older before.

"And as for how I came to my position," she sipped her wine, "a lot of hard work, paying my dues, and having an uncle who's the VP doesn't hurt." She winked in his direction with a laugh.

"I'll say," Luke smiled.

"But don't worry," Lulu continued, "Rachel's job isn't riding on this date. I just wanted a chance to meet the gentleman I've heard so much about."

Luke felt himself blushing, "I don't think rejecting a woman qualifies for being labeled as a gentleman."

"You're too modest," Lulu smiled, "You didn't just reject any woman. You turned down Cara. I think she's still grieving."

Luke wasn't sure how he was supposed to react to all of this, so he took another sip of wine.

Lulu, deliriously happy over Cara's rejection, showered him with compliments for the remainder of the evening. Luke listened with interest to Lulu's stories of growing up in such a privileged upper-class family. To his surprise, she seemed keenly interested in Appalachian culture and what it was like to grow up in such a rural area. Luke wasn't particularly attracted to her, despite her good looks, but she was enjoyable and carried conversation well. As he hailed a cab for her at the end of the night, Luke pleasantly decided that it had been a fairly successful evening. From the way she was holding his hand, he was quite certain Lulu considered it a success, as well. They continued their conversation in the cab, all the way back to her place on the Upper East Side.

Luke stepped out of the cab to let her out when she caught his hand.

"Come in for coffee," she insisted, waving the cab driver to go on. "I just love hearing about what it was like growing up in the mountains and working on a farm. It's like a completely different world … so different from anything I've ever experienced. Honestly, I could listen to your stories all night. Especially if they involve Rachel falling into a pigpen. She will die when I tell her on Monday!"

She continued on as she opened the door and ushered him into her luxury apartment building. Luke couldn't hide his amusement. Here was a woman who had grown up with every available opportunity, and yet she was mesmerized with his childhood on a farm. It was flattering to have someone paying him such interest. To have someone listening intently, and not just looking at him like some piece of meat, it was a nice change since his last date.

He sat himself in front of her floor-to-ceiling windows that overlooked the park while she went to make coffee.

"Would you rather have wine?" She called from the kitchen, "I have a bottle of Stag's Leap I've been holding onto for just the right conversation."

"Umm, sure," Luke called back.

This girl is something else, he thought happily. *She wants to talk, get to know each other.* Suddenly, Luke found himself relaxing. The sweaty palms had subsided, at last. Maybe she was someone he could actually date.

She handed him a glass of wine poured all the way to the brim.

"Tell me about your family," she smiled.

Luke hesitated, "My father's quiet. I don't feel like I really know him very well …"

"And your mother?"

"She, she passed. Quite a while back, actually," Luke never spoke about that. He didn't know why he suddenly felt compelled to open up about her now. "We were really close. She was the one who supported my artwork. I didn't paint for a long time after she died."

They sat in silence for a while, sipping their wine.

Luke looked up to see Lulu misty eyed, wiping away tears. He grabbed a tissue from the box on the side table and raised it to her cheek.

"You've had to go through so much," she sighed. "It just breaks my heart." She reached up and caught his hand as he began to lower it. "But I have no doubt that those trials have made you into the strong, thoughtful, and sensitive man that is sitting in front of me."

She leaned into him and Luke suddenly understood what was about to happen. Though a voice in his head told him he had just been very well played, he couldn't help but hope all the interest she'd paid to him tonight was genuine. He leaned in, too.

"Ahh," she shrieked, as red wine went flying all over both of them. "Oh, Luke! I'm such a klutz. Forgive me!"

"Oh," Luke stammered as he tried to get his bearings, "It's fine. I should go anyway."

"Go?!" she looked shocked, "You can't leave like that. If you don't treat that stain right away, it will never come out."

Luke was confused, "You want me to wash my pants here?"

"Of course not," she smiled, "I spilled the wine on you. I'll wash your pants. Here, give them to me."

It wasn't a request as much as a demand. Luke was becoming more certain by the minute that this entire scenario had been planned. But the kindness she had shown him all evening, the interest in his childhood, the thoughtful questions, the way she looked him in the eyes when he was speaking, he still had to hope for the best from her. He stood up and stepped out of his pants, as she'd commanded.

"I'll just be a second," she smiled, as she dashed off to her laundry room.

She hadn't eyed him like a piece of meat. She had hardly looked at him at all, Luke realized in relief.

Maybe it was all in my head after all? When did I become so skeptical of people? Is that what living in New York does to people?

"Luke," she called from a distant room, her voice causing his thoughts to vanish.

"Do you need something?" he called back.

"I seem to have gotten red wine all over my dress, too!" she called, "Can you come get the stain remover down for me? It's on the top shelf. I can't reach it!"

"Sure," he said as he stood up.

Walking down the hallway, Luke became aware of the fact that he didn't really have any clothes on other than a button up shirt, a tie, and boxers. A shiver of nervousness ran down his spine. Turning the corner, he saw Lulu bending over to take off her heels, wearing nothing but a bustier and matching lace thong.

"Whoa!" Luke shouted automatically, covering his eyes.

"What?" she shrugged, "I told you my dress was stained, too."

"Yes, I know, but, well," Luke felt his cheeks growing red, "you're not wearing any clothes. And, and I, I hardly know you."

Lulu interrupted him with a sultry voice he was surprised to hear coming from her, "Would you be more comfortable if you were in nothing but your underwear, too?"

Luke was dumbfounded. Wasn't Louisa-Ann Mortimer supposed to be a high-class lady? Lulu seemed to take his lack of response as the okay to start unbuttoning his shirt.

"Hey there," Luke pushed her hands down with more force than he intended. "What are you doing?"

"What does it look like I'm doing?" she asked coyly.

"It would appear that you are trying to seduce me," Luke replied, as Lulu slowly backed him to the wall.

"You are so perceptive," she purred in his ear.

Luke couldn't take it anymore. First Cara, now Lulu.

"Am I wearing some sort of sign?!" Luke shouted at her.

Lulu was taken aback, "What?"

"Seriously! Why are you women trying to jump my bones on the first date?" Luke said exasperated.

"You women?" Lulu's voice filled with offense.

Luke didn't care enough to take notice, "Yes. First Cara, now you. What happened to getting to know someone first?"

"Are you putting me in the same category as Cara?" Lulu asked, clearly affronted.

"Yes! But you're worse. Cara might be a slut, but she was upfront about what she wanted from me the whole night. I actually thought you were interested in getting to know me. But all you were interested in was making me your conquest," Luke ran out of air as he spit out the last words.

Lulu's laughter made his cheeks burn with anger, "Wow … you know what you sound like?"

Luke glared at her in silence.

"A girl!" she laughed again. "You sound like such a girl."

Luke refused to respond and, instead, turned on the spot and walked to the door.

"Where are you going?" Lulu laughed, "You can't leave like that! You don't have pants on!"

"Watch me," Luke snapped as he wrenched the door open.

He didn't feel uncomfortable until he was in the elevator, descending to the lobby. He wished he had just grabbed his pants. At least he had the sense to snatch his wallet off the couch on the way out the door. There was no way he was going back up there now. He knew Louisa-Ann-Lulu-whatever-the-hell-her-name-is was furious at him, but it was nothing compared to the frustration he was feeling. He was angrier about tonight than he was about getting stood up last week, and even more annoyed than after his date with Cara. Lulu had deceived him. He had opened up to her and shared things that he wished he could take back. So much for trying to find love in New York City. He would be better off locking his heart away for good.

I would be better off wearing pants, he thought, as the elevator doors opened and he dashed out. He walked with determination and his eyes on the door.

"I better be able to find a cab," Luke muttered to himself as he stepped out into the chilly night air.

A few catcalls and the stares of passersby made him wish he could slink out of sight, or perhaps into the nearby manhole. A yell from above caught his attention. Lulu had thrown his pants off her penthouse balcony, and they flapped in the air, as they fell down to the street. Whatever words had accompanied their dismissal were lost in the wind. Luke was rather grateful she had the decency to toss them down … that is until he bent down to retrieve them from the sidewalk and saw white letters hastily scrawled across the backside with a marker that said, "PUSSY."

He groaned as he wadded them into a ball and threw them into the nearby trash can.

Launching himself off the curb, he hailed a passing cab that thankfully had its light on. It screeched to a halt. He slid in, ignoring the raised eyebrow of the cab driver. Luke was going home. And when he woke up in the morning, he would deal with Rachel. As furious as he was with her for setting him up on such ridiculous dates, he was more upset with himself for allowing it. He only hoped that tonight's events wouldn't jeopardize her job. He didn't know what she would do with herself if her career in fashion was over. A career in matchmaking seemed very unlikely.

CHAPTER SEVEN

LUKE SAW CAT RUNNING AHEAD OF HIM. SHE WAS SO FAST, HE couldn't catch her. Her wavy hair bounced behind her as she darted behind another Christmas tree. He darted one way and she the other, and so their game continued—laughing, tickling, touching, until they fell to the ground, arms wrapped so tightly around each other.

"I love you," he breathed into her neck. "I've always loved you, Cat. I'm so sorry for everything. For all the pain I've caused you."

She was quiet. Her hands stroked his face, his hair, their lips brushed. It felt the same as it always had between them.

"Say something," Luke nudged her playfully.

Cat smiled and opened her mouth to speak.

BUZZ

BUZZ

Somewhere, a million miles away, Luke heard his apartment door buzzing. It seemed as though he was descending through a fog, back to New York City, back to his studio apartment, back to the futon where he had fallen asleep the night before.

BUZZ

BUZZ

Luke opened one eye. The sun was shining directly into his eyes, reflecting off the windows from the building across the street like a mirror. It had to be close to noon.

BUZZ

BUZZ

"Good Lord," Luke grumbled, as he pushed himself up and stumbled to the door. Slamming his hand onto the button, he nearly shouted into the speaker, "Who is it?"

"It's Rachel," a voice chirped.

Luke pressed the button to unlock the door below.

Looking down, he realized he wasn't exactly presentable. All he had on was an old pair of boxers. He scrambled through the nearby hamper to retrieve his track sweatpants and pulled them on hastily, just in time to hear the knock on the door. Rachel didn't knock like normal people, she knocked in a rhythm, like it was a part of announcing her presence. If Luke hadn't been friends with her since childhood, he might find this annoying. Instead, it was endearing, only not today. Today, it announced the arrival of the world's worst matchmaker.

"Hey," he mumbled as he opened the door to let her in.

Rachel stood there with a sheepish grin on her face, holding an aluminum foil-covered platter in her hands of what smelled like homemade blueberry pancakes.

"You're forgiven," Luke smiled, as he took the platter from her. "But, only if you brought syrup, because I don't have any."

Rachel's grin turned into a beaming smile, as she pulled Aunt Jemima's finest out of her Marc Jacobs handbag.

"Well," Luke took the syrup from her with a wink, "it's not real maple syrup, but it'll do."

Luke pulled out plates and napkins as Rachel recounted her phone conversation with Lulu and apologized profusely to him, over and over again.

"I will set you up with the perfect person on the next date," Rachel began, before Luke cut her off.

"Oh, no you won't," Luke said, his mouth almost too full to understand what he was saying, "Your matchmaking days are over. Three strikes and you're out, Rachel."

"But," she began.

"No way," Luke swallowed his food, "The last three dates I've been on have been nightmares. I'm giving someone else a chance to set me up."

"What do you mean?" Rachel looked offended at this.

Luke informed her of his upcoming date with Gabi and everything he knew about her, which Luke realized, wasn't very much at all.

"She sounds," Rachel paused, "nice, normal."

"That's what I'm counting on," Luke nodded, as he helped himself to another pancake.

"She sounds like someone you could really fall for," Rachel sighed. She opened her mouth to speak before closing it again and snagging a bite of pancake off his plate.

"Why would that be so bad?" Luke asked.

"I guess I thought," Rachel sighed, "You know, after these dates, you'd be ready to find Cat. You still love her and …"

"Whoa, whoa, whoa," Luke held up his hands and pushed back from the table, "Did you set me up on all those dates expecting them to go bad?"

Rachel's face turned red and he noticed she started fidgeting with her charm bracelet. Classic Rachel.

"Why the hell would you put me through something like that, Rachel?" Luke stood up in anger and began pacing the small space. "Who are you to take charge of my love life like that? Who are you to tell me who I still love or don't love?"

Rachel's eyes watered up, "I just want you to be happy again … and I thought …"

"You thought that the only way I will be happy is if I realize that I still love Cat and go after her," Luke shouted at her.

Rachel nodded.

"Did you ever think about Cat?" Luke's voice continued to rise. "What if she's not even in the city? What if she's dating someone? Or … if she doesn't want to see me? What if she's forgotten about me completely?"

All of the secret fears Luke had imagined spilled out of him.

"But what if she still loves you?" Rachel retorted, "Luke, you'll never know until you try."

Luke froze, fists clenched, but he couldn't bear the thought of trying and never finding her. Or worse, finding out that she's moved on. Finding out that she's happy without him. He couldn't bear it.

"Tell me you didn't go looking for her for me, Rachel," Luke said quietly.

Rachel looked up sheepishly, "I have her number."

"And have you …," Luke began.

"No, I haven't called her yet," Rachel quickly interrupted. "I thought you might want to call her."

Rachel dug into her purse for a moment and pulled out a napkin with a phone number scribbled in the corner.

"Mimi finally caved and gave it to me," Rachel smiled slightly.

Luke felt his hand tremble slightly as he reached out to take the napkin and he willed it to be still. He prayed that Rachel couldn't see his true feelings. He worked so hard to bury these emotions from everyone, even from himself.

"Are you going to call her?" Rachel sounded so hopeful as he took the napkin.

Luke took a deep breath, "No."

The sound of the ripping paper napkin and Rachel's gasp

filled the room for a moment.

"I have to let her go, Rachel. Do you understand that?" Luke felt his voice fill with emotion and he shouted in an attempt to play it off as anger. "I can't let the memory of what Cat and I once had haunt me forever. I made a mistake; I failed her. She wouldn't want to see me again. I wouldn't want to put her through that."

"What mistake, Luke?" Rachel stood up.

"It's over, Rachel," Luke nearly knocked her over as he turned and strode towards the door. Opening the door, he gestured for her to leave. "Thanks for the pancakes."

"Luke," Rachel's tears spilled over again, "I'm sorry. I-I thought I would help things, but—I'm sorry."

Luke stood in silence as Rachel gathered her things. He knew he wouldn't be seeing her again anytime soon. Part of him felt sadness, but most of him was still furious at what she had put him through during the last two months. Above all, he felt betrayed.

"Rach," he said as she brushed past him, "when you contact her ... cause I know you will, leave me out of things. Okay? Please?"

Rachel looked at him with such clear annoyance, "You are both so damn stubborn! When will you just give in to what you want? You know you wa—"

Luke slammed the door in her face before she could get out another word. She was right, though. He was stubborn, only Cat was worse. Maybe if one of them had given in, or if they had just found each other sooner, things would be different. Too much time had passed now. It was too late. The time for reconciliation had come and gone. Now was the time for moving on. Now was the time for new beginnings.

"Whatever our souls are made of,

his and mine are the same."

—EMILY BRONTË,
WUTHERING HEIGHTS

CHAPTER EIGHT

PANT. PANT. PANT. Cat focused her mind on the road ahead. Her feet hit the pavement in a fixed rhythm. She ignored the burning in her thighs. Having entered the lottery to run in the New York City marathon, she had miraculously snagged a spot. Cat had entered the previous two years with no luck. Attempting to buy her way in on Craigslist had also been unsuccessful. Apparently, she hadn't offered enough money. Good things come to those who wait, she reminded herself with a smile, as she forced herself to run uphill, passing a few fellow runners in the process.

She loved running on early Saturday mornings like this one. The city was still sleeping, whether it was struggling with hangovers from the night before or enjoying their cozy beds, it was hard to say. The brunch crowd would eventually rouse itself around eleven o'clock and head to Sant Ambroeus or Café D'Alsace for endless Bellinis or Bloody Marys garnished with blue cheese stuffed olives. Leave SaraBeth's for the tourists; the true New Yorkers had their own go-to brunch spot. Brunch was a religion in Manhattan. A weekly high holy day that was revered and honored by Manhattanites, regardless of their status or the neighborhood in which they dwelled. Suddenly, Cat found herself famished and decided that some eggs benedict would be the perfect reward for the long run she was getting in this morning.

Central Park was the New Yorkers' backyard and the 6.75 mile loop within it was a magnet for avid runners. Cat glanced at her new Fitbit One; she was closing in on 13 miles. Not much further. Returning her gaze to the road ahead, she eyed a lamppost in the distance. She narrowed her eyes in focus; she would sprint to the lamppost.

"Ready, set, go!" Cat breathed aloud.

Like a six-year-old at a playground race, saying the words seemed to make her go faster. Logically, she knew the idea was ridiculous. But her feet picked up speed each time, so it hadn't failed her yet. She could lose herself in her stride, her breathing, the sounds of her feet on the pavement, and forget the busy city around her. Cat pushed herself harder. Grunting loudly as she tore past the finish line—the lamppost, she slowed to a jog once more. She loved these heavily wooded areas of the park. Some parts around the northern edges were so dense that they completely obscured the sights and sounds of Manhattan; she almost forgot she was in New York City.

If she really wanted to feel isolated, she could veer off the road onto one of the many trails into the woods. She did this on very rare occasions though, as it almost always reminded her of the wildness of North Carolina, or seemed the ideal spot to be molested, take your pick.

She didn't like to be reminded of that place, despite it being her favorite place on earth. Strange that such a brief time in her life could be so impactful. She shook her head to clear the memories and pressed onward. The vibration of her iPhone in her pocket caused her to slow down and catch her breath.

"Cathleen Rhodes," she breathed noisily into her phone. The

unavailable number meant it could be anyone, likely a telemarketer.

"Is this Cat?" a familiar voice spoke cautiously.

She hadn't gone by Cat in years. Four years to be exact. Her breath caught in her throat.

"To whom am I speaking?" Cat said in confusion. One hand on her lower back, she stretched to one side and then the other as her breathing slowed to a somewhat normal pace. Cat's breath came out in short puffs of steam on this cold, late March morning.

"Cat, this is Rachel. Rachel McKinney. I got your number from your grandmother—from Mimi. I hope that's okay?" Rachel's voice sounded apologetic, even a little nervous.

"Oh, Rachel," Cat beamed. "Of course, it's okay. Oh, wow! Great to hear from you! Where are you now—is, is everything okay?"

Cat couldn't help the latter part of the question. After four years with hardly any contact, it seemed that a call could mean very few things. If something had happened to Luke … her thoughts began to veer.

"New York City, actually," came Rachel's bubbly voice through the phone. "I moved here in January and have been meaning to call you since I arrived."

"You're kidding!" Cat laughed as she lowered herself onto the nearby bench. "That's great. You're finally where you always wanted to be—so, how does it feel to be a New Yorker?"

Laughter came from Rachel's end. Cat had forgotten how warm her laughter was. It was like a blanket on this chilly morning, covering her with comforting memories. She blinked rapidly to keep the unexpected tears at bay. How dare they betray her like that, coming without warning. Cat chalked it up to her wandering thoughts of North Carolina, the woods, and the fact that she was starving. Doesn't everyone cry when they're famished? *No, no they don't, Cat*, a little voice in her head snarked.

"Honestly—crowded," Rachel chuckled. "But I'm loving it. Even though I'm working around the clock."

"What are you doing?" Cat asked.

"Assistant buyer for Bloomingdales," Rachel sighed dreamily, "My boss is a bitch and makes me do half her work, but I honestly don't care. It's my dream job."

"Mimi told me you did your internship in Paris with Christian Louboutin last year. I am so proud of you! Doesn't it seem like yesterday that we said we would do anything for a pair of those heels?" Cat's mind took her back to her and Rachel's first meeting.

She smiled at the image of herself, sitting on the quaint front porch of Rachel's house, reading Vogue, and covered in those ghastly hives. Then she pursed her lips together and wiped the bothersome tears away as other images immediately followed. If at all possible, she tried not to think of the time she spent with Luke. That's probably why she and Rachel lost touch over the years. Cat was never very good about returning her calls or writing her back. Rachel was a link to a life that was far behind her, a life she tried to forget.

"Oh, Cat! We have to get together soon and catch up," Rachel spoke up again, interrupting Cat's thoughts. "When are you free?"

Cat searched her mind for excuses not to see Rachel, but she couldn't suppress the desire to connect with an old friend, no matter the memories it might bring with it.

Taking a deep breath, Cat smiled, "How about dinner tonight?"

"Great!" it sounded as though Rachel had been holding her breath in anticipation. "I'll text you this afternoon and we can make plans."

"Can't wait," Cat replied.

As she hung up the phone, she realized that this would be the first time she would be seeing Rachel in over four years. They'd spoken over the phone a handful of times and emailed occasionally in the months after she'd left Boone, but they had eventually lost touch when they went to college. Then Cat got a new cell number, and intentionally, failed to transfer the contacts over. It was easier that way, she reasoned. Besides, that's what happens when people go to college, Cat had told herself. But deep down, she knew that had not been the real reason for breaking ties with Rachel. She had a feeling that Rachel knew that, too.

CHAPTER NINE

CAT WRAPPED HER SCARF AROUND HER NECK AND SKIPPED DOWN THE steps of her nondescript, mid-rise apartment on the Upper East Side. Her junior one-bedroom apartment was modest, but chicly decorated and suited her just fine. Her father had attempted to bribe her with a darling little brownstone in the 70's, but in an effort to piss him off, Cat insisted on paying her own rent for her quaint little space on 88th Street between 1st Avenue and York. She succeeded, as she almost always did, when it came to the many little matters her father attempted to exercise his authority over her. However, when it came to larger matters, she was still less successful. She twisted the ring on her left hand until it loosened and finally slid off.

Matters like David Randolph. She loved David, of course. But would she have agreed to a date with him had her parents not badgered her into it? She wasn't certain. No matter. Her life would unfold exactly how they had always planned and Cat was content with her current circumstances. She reminded herself daily of just how happy she should be.

She examined the perfectly round 2.3 carat diamond cushion setting in platinum. Though it wasn't precisely what Cat would've chosen for herself, it was what most would describe as perfect. She unclasped her necklace and slid the ring on it for safekeeping. Re-clasping it around her neck, she glanced at the time on her phone. *Shit*. Running late, per her usual.

She shivered as the wind blew against her and she struggled to snap up the buttons of her Burberry coat, which was a gift from her mother last month for no particular reason. Cat sighed. Her mother's "just because" gifts had become more frequent the last half decade. Cat pretended not to know why.

The late March wind sent shivers down her spine. She thought of ducking into the nearby Starbucks to grab a latte on her way to meet Rachel, but she reminded herself she was already running about five minutes late.

Rachel had suggested that they meet at Brother Jimmy's, a completely unpretentious and equally southern barbeque joint with several locations in the city. Cat stifled a giggle. The fact that Rachel spent a year in Paris, then moved to New York City, a city with as nearly as many restaurant choices as people, and then chooses to dine at a place that serves fried green tomatoes and sweet tea was beyond her comprehension. It made Cat love her even more.

Rachel had also informed her that North Carolina would be playing tonight, so she should wear Carolina blue. Cat frowned at her navy sweater and pearls; this was as close as she would get to being a Tar Heel fan tonight.

The bar area was packed when she arrived, a sure sign that March Madness was in full swing. She carefully maneuvered her way through the rowdy crowd towards the back dining room, still crowded but not quite as bad. She instantly spotted Rachel, wearing her Carolina Championship tee shirt from 2009, holding her diet coke, and cheering at the t.v. along with the crowd. She looked even more stunning than in high school, but with the same girl-next-door charm. Cat chided herself for running away from their friendship for so long.

"Cat!" Rachel spotted her, and would have rushed to her had

the crowd not been between them.

Cat waved at her through the dozen young men that stood between them. When she finally reached the table, she began to sit, but realized that Rachel had her arms open wide for a hug. Cat felt fresh guilt wash over her as she indulged her friend in a long overdue bear hug.

"You look exactly the same," Rachel said, pulling back to look at her. Then, brushing a haphazard curl from Cat's face, she smiled. "You're still too thin, though."

Cat laughed. Yes, Rachel was exactly the same.

"You look amazing, Rach," Cat nodded. "Honestly, it is so good to see you."

"Can you believe it's been over four years?" Rachel raised an eyebrow at the scantily clad waitress passing their table. "Way too long. You are one hard chickadee to keep up with."

Again, Cat tasted the sourness of guilt. "I'm sorry. I've been such a terrible friend. I should have called you more and responded to your emails. After I left I just … well." Cat was at a loss for words.

"I know," Rachel reached across the table and patted her hand. "We don't have to talk about any of that … unless you want to."

Cat opened her mouth to speak.

"She'll have Cheerwine," Rachel shouted over to the waitress. "I'm sure you haven't had that in a long time.

Cat laughed, "Too long."

Two Cheerwines, a barbeque sandwich, and an hour and a half later, the two friends had fallen into comfortable conversation. It felt just like old times.

"And that was when I decided my French was far too poor for me to remain in Paris any longer," laughed Rachel, concluding the story of her decision to return to the states and take the job at Bloomingdales.

"Well, at least you got some fabulous shoes from the experience," Cat laughed as she lifted her glass in a toast.

"Seven glorious pairs," Rachel sang as they clinked glasses.

"Cat, I feel awful. I've been rambling for almost two hours about me and what I've been up to. What about you?" Rachel inquired.

"Oh, well. I don't know where to start," Cat fumbled with her glass.

"How about when you left North Carolina?" Rachel began cautiously.

Cat took another swallow of her Cheerwine to finish it off and put the glass down slowly.

"Another Cheerwine?" the waitress asked, swooping in to clear their empty plates.

"I think I need something a little bit stronger," Cat smiled. "How about the-," she quickly scanned the drink menu, "-Carolina Cooler."

"Why don't you bring a pitcher?" Rachel added to the waitress, who nodded and left them in silence.

Cat turned to Rachel with a smirk and clucked her tongue in feigned disappointment.

"The daughter of a southern Baptist preacher? Well, I never!" Cat said in her best southern drawl.

"I thought if we were finally going to go down this road, a little vodka might make it smoother," Rachel smiled knowingly.

Cat had never spoken to Rachel about what happened. Not really. She especially had never mentioned Luke. It was too painful. He betrayed her. Whatever her father had said to him that day, she didn't care—he had deserted her. He had walked out of that hospital room and didn't look back.

The waitress brought their pitcher, complete with two mason jars, and filled them to the brim.

Cat took a swig. It was dangerously delicious. Lemonade, vodka, and blue curacao—a deadly combination.

"Well," Cat began, "My parents took me straight from the airport to Emma Willard. It's the boarding school upstate I told you a little bit about. And … they left me there, until I graduated, that is. Then, I spent the obligatory summer in Europe traveling. Just as everyone in my family does after high school graduation. My mom chaperoned the entire trip, so it was mostly art museums and high tea. I mean, not that I'm complaining—it was Europe, after all. When I got back, I enrolled in Columbia, in their Art History program. I did my internship with Musée d'Orsay in Paris last summer, which was incredible. I still think it's so crazy that we happened to be there at the same time and never knew it!" Cat inhaled deeply. Had she said that spiel all in one breath?

She paused to draw another deep sip from her blue concoction and avoided Rachel's gaze. "But now I work for The Children's Museum of Manhattan on the Upper West Side."

"Wow," Rachel looked impressed. "I'm sure your parents are very proud of you."

Cat felt as if a knife had been jabbed into her side. She knew Rachel hadn't meant it that way, but it stung nonetheless. Mainly because she knew she was right. They were proud of her. She had done everything they had asked of her. Ever since that fateful day in the hospital in Boone, she had stuck with *their* 'plan.' She could get away with making a few decisions on her own here and there, like her apartment, but if she ever veered too much off course, her father would crack his whip and she would fall in line.

Cat filled the glass again.

"Cat?" Rachel looked at her seriously.

"Hmm?" Cat responded as she swallowed another gulp.

"Now, why don't you tell me about you? What's been happening since you left North Carolina?" Rachel asked quietly.

Cat knew what she was getting at, but she played the confused card out of habit, "Isn't that what I just told you?"

"You told me what you've been doing. But you didn't tell me a thing about you," Rachel said pointedly.

Touché, spoke the voice in Cat's head.

"Good Lord, Cat," Rachel's mountain accent was beginning to come through more and more with every sip she took from her mason jar glass. "I know I haven't seen you in forever and a day, but you were my best friend senior year. You left without a word. Luke wouldn't speak to a soul for at least two months. I have no idea what really happened."

Cat bit her lip. That was the first time either of them had spoken his name. She opened her mouth to speak and hesitated. She downed the remaining contents in her glass and inhaled deeply. She prepared her words carefully. She planned to tell Rachel that this story was far too painful and private to share, but when she looked up at Rachel's eyes, different words began to spill out. All of it. The snowy day by the river. The truck stuck on the bank. The endless walk through the falling snow to the barn. Laying with Luke under the quilt with nothing between them, just to stay warm. And, of course, being found that way the next morning and the disaster that had subsequently unfolded.

When the story was finished, so was the pitcher between them. Normally, Cat would be dancing on tables at this point, but instead, she felt unusually calm, collected, and for the first time in a long time, she felt like a weight had been lifted off her shoulders.

"He still loves you," Rachel slurred her words slightly.

"I don't think so," Cat shook her head. Her heart began pounding and she fought furiously to settle it. "If he did, he would have contacted me by now," Cat reasoned.

"Maybe he thinks it's too late," Rachel nudged her.

"Isn't it?" Cat asked honestly. If there was one thing life had taught her, it was how to be realistic.

"Is it ever too late to reconcile with the one person you were meant to spend your life with?" Rachel asked sleepily. Her droopy eyelids told Cat that consuming this much alcohol was not a habit for Rachel. She'd only been in New York City a couple of months, after all.

"I think your Carolina Cooler has gone to your head," Cat laughed as she shrugged off Rachel's painfully accurate words. "Let's get you home."

Cat hailed a cab while Rachel puked in the nearby trash can.

"I can't believe this had to be my first experience with alcohol," Rachel moaned, as she slid into the backseat.

Cat was dumbfounded, "What?!"

"You heard me," Rachel's words came out garbled, "I've never had alcohol till tonight. Never." She leaned her face close to Cat's until they were eyeball to eyeball as though to emphasize her point.

"Rachel, are you telling me that you are twenty-three years old and have never had one sip of alcohol?" Cat asked wide-eyed; even the cabbie had his eyes on them in amusement.

"Well, I have now," Rachel groaned and then began to laugh. "That was fun."

Those were the last words Rachel spoke before she began snoring on Cat's shoulder. Cat had to laugh. She gave the cabbie her own address, since she didn't know exactly where Rachel lived. Good thing tomorrow was Sunday.

They would be having an impromptu sleepover tonight Cat decided. She couldn't help but wonder if Rachel's return to her life would bring anyone else back to her.

Cat looked out the window, best not to get one's hopes up.

CHAPTER TEN

CAT WAS PREPARED WITH TWO ADVIL, A FULL GLASS OF WATER, AND a piece of toast when Rachel stumbled into the kitchen the next morning.

"I think last night was the first and last time I'll ever drink," Rachel groaned and accepted Cat's hangover cure with a forced smile.

"You'll find yourself saying that every time you have a hang-over," Cat laughed and handed her the glass of water, "And then, before you know it, you'll be saying it again. Trust me."

"No, no, no," Rachel shook her head again, "never again."

"For your sake, let's hope not," Cat laughed. "You wanted to swan dive off the balcony when I got you back."

"What?!" Rachel shrieked.

"Look," Cat gestured to the couch pushed against the French doors that led out to the balcony, "that's the only way I could keep you from going outside. And then, when I finally got pajamas on you and forced you to lay down on the couch, you kept telling me that you were going to fall into the ceiling fan."

"I did not!" Rachel covered her mouth in disbelief.

Cat simply nodded.

"I. Am. SO. SORRY," Rachel said slowly, emphasizing each word.

Cat shrugged her shoulders as though it was something she saw all the time and smiled at Rachel.

"Coffee?" Cat offered.

"Oh, no thanks, Cat. Ugh. I just feel so bad," Rachel continued to apologize.

"Rach, look at me," Cat took her friend's shoulders, "you were fine. It was nothing."

"Um, trying to swan dive off your balcony is not nothing," Rachel shook her head, "It's embarrassing."

"If only you'd gone to Spence with me," Cat shook her head, "the behavior at those parties was embarrassing. You were fine."

Rachel watched Cat scurry around the kitchen, getting ingredients down, mixing bowls, cutting boards.

"What are you doing?" Rachel asked curiously.

"Making you breakfast," Cat said, as though it was obvious.

"Cat," Rachel laughed, "I can have cereal. And since when do you cook?"

"You are my guest," Cat smiled, "I had to learn to cook sometime, right? I've actually taken some French cooking classes at Alliance Française with … um, a friend."

"A friend?" Rachel asked, attempting to sound nonchalant.

"Rachel," Cat paused, "How much of our conversation last night do you remember?"

Rachel wrinkled her nose in thought.

"I remember when you ordered the pitcher of something blue," Rachel grinned, "And I remember that it tasted like fruit punch."

"I ordered a drink," Cat corrected, "and you changed it to a pitcher."

"Oh," Rachel giggled, "Oops."

"Well, our conversation after the pitcher was finished," Cat sighed, "was mostly about Luke. About how I felt when he left, about how I have no idea why he left, or where he is or what he's doing …"

Cat paused, "And that's when I decided that I had to move on. I had to let myself move on. Luke's moved on obviously, or else he would have come back into my life by now."

"Did I say anything … in particular, during this conversation, Cat?" Rachel asked timidly.

"Yes," Cat snapped, "You kept saying 'oh, I wish I could tell you something!' And it was driving me crazy!"

"Ugh," Rachel put her head in her hands.

Rachel looked up at Cat, staring at her impatiently.

"So," Cat leaned forward, "Now that you are sober, are you going to explain what the hell you were talking about?"

Rachel shook her head, "I really have no idea why I would have said that."

"Really?" Cat was disappointed. In her mind, she had envisioned Rachel divulging some juicy secret, like why Luke had walked away. Or maybe that he was still secretly pining away for her after all these years. Not that it mattered, of course. Cat's hand reached automatically for the ring that still hung around her neck. Suddenly, it felt heavy.

"I'm sorry, Cat," Rachel sighed, "There's really nothing I can tell you about Luke."

Cat nodded, "It's probably better that you don't. Easier to really move on this way. And I have moved on."

Unclasping the necklace, she carefully slid off the ring. Rachel watched with wide eyes as Cat returned it to her ring finger and held out her hand for Rachel. For the life of her, Cat couldn't remember why she had not told Rachel the night before. I mean, when you have good news to share, shouldn't that be the first thing on your lips? She should've said, 'Oh Rachel! It's so good to see you … and look, I'm engaged!'

Rachel grabbed her hand and pulled it close for a more

thorough inspection. She nodded appreciatively as she took a moment to examine it from each angle. Cat half expected her to pull out one of those special diamond magnifying glasses.

"Impressive." Rachel tilted her head, and glanced back at Cat. Her expression gave nothing away. "Do you love him?"

"David is great." Cat smiled convincingly and nodded enthusiastically at her old friend. She even attempted a coquettish giggle when glancing at the small ice-skating rink on her hand.

Rachel forced herself to share in Cat's joy, "I'm so, so happy for you, Cat."

They hugged. Cat breathed a sigh of relief. She had such anxiety about telling Rachel this morning, especially after having poured her heart out the night before. She had been heartbroken for so long over Luke. But the time had come for her life to move forward. Cat only hoped that Rachel would understand and support that decision.

Rachel pulled away and looked at her mischievously, "So … this David? How is he … you know?" She winked.

Cat laughed in spite of herself, "Oh my, you haven't changed a bit!"

"What?!" Rachel began laughing too, "What did I say?"

"It's the way you said it," Cat shook her head, "I know what you are dying to know!"

"Which is?" Rachel leaned in, playing along.

"No!" Cat huffed, "No, okay. There's your answer. No, we haven't."

They stared at each other for a moment.

Cat looked down, slightly embarrassed, "No, I haven't had sex with my fiancé. Oh my gosh … does that sound terrible? That's terrible, isn't it? It's not that I was waiting for Luke … I was just waiting for anyone I cared for as much as I did for him.

And now I've found David, of course. It just feels like we might as well wait until the wedding night at this point," Cat looked away from Rachel as she began soaking thick slices of challah bread into the egg batter. "He's really traditional," she lied as she focused her eyes intently on making the French toast, lest they betray her. Cat was never good at lying.

"You really don't need to explain yourself to me, Cat" Rachel's voice softened. "If you're happy, then I'm happy for you."

Cat didn't know why she suddenly felt so uncomfortable. Or why the ring on her left hand suddenly felt like it weighed a thousand pounds. She had this sickening sensation of guilt. As though she was cheating on Luke by getting engaged, which was pure insanity because he was the one that walked out on her, and over four years ago at that!

She felt nausea climbing in her throat. Whether it was the heartache creeping in, or the pitcher of Carolina coolers from the night before, she wasn't sure. She just knew she needed fresh air. Leaving the French toast sizzling on the stove, she turned abruptly and made a beeline for the balcony. With the couch stretched in front of the sliding doors, it left Cat having to reach over to open the door and then clamber over the couch while her friend watched in confusion. Cat's bare feet landed on the balcony just as her stomach betrayed her and she spewed vomit onto the concrete patio floor and over the railing. She prayed no one was walking on the street below. What an unwelcome surprise that would be. She couldn't bring herself to look over the edge to check, and she was mortified that Rachel was scrambling over the couch behind her to hold back her hair.

"Don't, Rach," Cat held up her hand. "I'm fine. Really. You should go."

She held back tears as she watched Rachel retreat into the

apartment and was surprised when she reappeared moments later with a wet paper towel for Cat and some dish towels to clean up the mess.

"Oh, please don't clean up after me," said Cat, mortified, as she accepted the wet paper towel and wiped her mouth and chin, but Rachel was already on her hands and knees.

"Don't be ridiculous, Cat," Rachel sighed. "Let someone help you for once. Also, you might have forgotten that I am the oldest of four. I practically have a degree in diaper changes and vomit clean up."

"Well, thank goodness I don't need a diaper change," Cat laughed.

She then joined her friend in the repugnant task. Rachel handled the task much better than Cat, who kept gagging. Eventually, Rachel told her to hand over the Clorox and get out of the way. Cat couldn't help but laugh at herself in that moment, which sent the two of them into giggles. It felt like old times, except that they were hungover and cleaning puke.

Suddenly, the smoke alarm started blaring behind them. Cat was reminded of the French toast that was now blackened and flaming in her kitchen.

"Shiiiiiiiit," Cat leapt to her feet as Rachel hurdled past her, over the couch, and tossed the pan into the sink, flipping on the water, and extinguishing the flames in a matter of seconds. Visions of Rachel on the high school track practicing her hurdles flashed in her mind. She hadn't lost her touch.

"What would you do without me?" Rachel turned to her with mock exasperation and a shake of her head. The alarm continued to torment them. "Now, how do you turn that damn thing off?"

Cat scurried over the couch, much less gracefully, grabbed her broom in the broom closet, and jabbed at the button on the alarm, hoping she had gotten to it before the alarm system was triggered for the entire building. This had already happened twice before and she did not want to experience the wrath of her building's super again. Thankfully, it seemed that she was quick enough. Cat let out a long sigh of relief. The friends locked eyes and shook their heads.

"There's never a dull moment when you're around," Cat laughed.

"I was thinking the same about you," Rachel retorted.

When the smoke had cleared and the kitchen clean-up was complete, Cat showered and changed into fresh lounge clothes. She felt completely embarrassed by the series of unfortunate events, but thankful that if anyone had to be there in that moment, it was Rachel. Reentering her kitchen, she found Rachel sitting at the counter with two cups of coffee waiting for them.

The friends sat with their coffees in silence for a moment.

"So," Rachel, ever persistent, broke the silence between them, "I feel like I need to ask. Are you happy with ... um?"

"David."

"Yes, David." Rachel looked at her closely. "Are you happy, Cat?"

Cat paused, "I thought so."

"Until?"

"Until, I started thinking of Luke last night." Cat looked into her mug. "I hadn't thought of that day in a long time, Rach. And telling you ... remembering ... it was harder than I thought it would be."

"I'm so sorry, Cat," Rachel took her friend's hand and gave it a reassuring squeeze. "What do you think that means?"

"I wish I knew," Cat laughed and wiped a tear that was threatening to break free from the corner of her eye. She blinked and pushed them back. She glanced at her ring. The ring David had presented to her on Valentine's Day. The ring she had been so happy to accept. But had she? Thinking about it now, the overwhelming thought that came to her mind was how happy she knew her parents would be. Was she mistaking their happiness for her own?

"How did you meet him?" Rachel asked.

"That part was easy," Cat laughed. "My father had a never-ending list of successful, handsome men in the finance world. But David was the one he continued to mention to me … and finally, in October I agreed to being set up on a blind date."

"Ah," Rachel nodded knowingly, careful not to give her own thoughts away, "Your dad is welcome to send some of those guys my way!"

Cat laughed, she knew Rachel was trying to lighten the mood, "I am happy to set you up anytime. But I'll warn you, most of the men are so absorbed in their careers … I wouldn't really consider them marriage material."

"Oh, I'm not looking to get married anytime soon," Rachel shook her head. "But I wouldn't mind a nice dinner and you know …"

"Rachel McKinney! I'm shocked," Cat feigned offense, but was truly relieved to know her friend had relaxed a little since their high school days. Back then, even the mention of seeing a guy naked, in-person, would send Rachel into hysterics.

"So … your blind date with David?" Rachel returned to their previous topic. She shifted uncomfortably in her seat, Cat noticed. "Would you say there was an instant attraction? Are we talking about love at first sight?"

Cat looked down. On her ring finger was the ostentatious engagement ring. She twisted it on her finger, remembering the twisted wires that Luke had placed there over four years ago which he had fashioned into a promise ring of sorts. She twisted it on her finger till it slid off. Cat placed it on the counter and glanced out the window. She could feel Rachel watching her and wondered if she knew or remembered what ring used to be there.

"Do you still have it?" Rachel asked, as though reading her mind.

Cat shook her head and swallowed to keep the tears at bay. She was not ready to talk about what had happened to that ring. Not yet.

Rachel nodded.

"You know," she said slowly, "Love will be different now. You're older. You've gone through some really difficult seasons, Cat. I think it's okay if you don't feel all the tingles down your spine. You're not some hormone driven teenager anymore."

Cat wasn't sure if Rachel believed what she was saying or was simply endeavoring to make Cat feel better. Either way, it was working.

"You're right, Rach." Cat slipped the ring back onto her finger before she could give it a second thought. "I am so grateful for your friendship, you know that?"

Cat squeezed her hand.

"Likewise," Rachel returned the squeeze, all the while wishing she could tell Cat a thousand thoughts. *Do not intervene, Rachel. Do not meddle.* Her mind willed her to keep her smile fixed in place for Cat. But she knew she couldn't maintain it much longer without the truth bursting out.

"I'm so glad we got to catch up, Cat," Rachel smiled as she finished her coffee, "I wish I could stay longer, but I have some errands to run this morning."

"Oh," Cat took her empty cup from her, "of course. Let's get together again real soon. Okay?"

"We'll plan on it," Rachel gave her a quick hug before gathering her things and darting out the door.

Cat felt a sudden sadness after Rachel left. She wasn't sure if it was due to the absence of her friend, or the thoughts of Luke, or suddenly and desperately missing her old ring, or maybe it was brought on by the thoughts of David, and the five hundred and twenty-six questions that seemed to be swirling in her mind like hungry sharks, circling their prey. Cat's hands started to shake.

CHAPTER ELEVEN

"SO, YOU'VE SET THE DATE, RIGHT?"

Cat heard Rachel's voice coming to her over the noise of the shower.

"Uh huh," Cat called back to her, as she turned off the water and gently patted herself dry with the towel.

Cat had just received her first airbrush tanning session and would be livid if she messed it up ... especially considering how much it cost. Trying on wedding dresses that afternoon meant she needed to look the part of the glowing bride.

Examining herself in the mirror, she was pleased with how it turned out. It looked like she had spent a week basking in the sun in Barbados. She had even gotten some balayage highlights in her hair to fit with the coming spring season. She felt refreshed and ready for a whole new Cat. The Cat that was the blissful bride to be with no unrequited love lurking in the shadows. She was determined to play the part perfectly. No, not play the part, because that would imply that she wasn't actually blissful. Cat frowned at herself in the mirror. Ugh. The thoughts that crossed her mind sometimes were enough to drive her mad. She had moved on. She was engaged. She was happy. End of story. Cat nodded decisively and gave herself a seductive wink in the mirror. She laughed and shook her head. It was a good thing no one could see her.

Eyebrows plucked, legs shaved, she was ready for her wedding dress appointment. She bit her lip nervously as she applied her eyeliner. Cat could hear Rachel rummaging through her tiny wardrobe and her dresser drawers.

"What are you doing out there?" Cat called to her.

"You should wear this," Rachel leaned around the corner with a long sleeved, high-necked navy dress.

"You can't be serious?" Cat raised an eyebrow.

"It's Donna Karen," Rachel inspected the label.

"It's my funeral dress, Rachel!" Cat laughed at her friend.

Rachel sighed and plopped herself on Cat's bed before patting the spot beside her for Cat to join her. Cat could feel some sort of a lecture coming on. She stifled a giggle and putting on a serious face, she seated herself beside Rachel.

"Cat, are you sure about this?" Rachel asked her seriously.

Cat blinked her eyes at Rachel and tilted her head slightly. She was so taken aback, she was speechless. She felt the blood rising in her cheeks.

"What do you mean?" Cat answered, "Am I sure that I want to go to the bridal appointment my mother practically sacrificed herself for … what kind of question is that?"

Rachel looked at her as though she had three heads.

"You haven't seemed entirely yourself since we talked about Luke. So many of those feelings you had for him are still there … I just want you to be sure."

Cat raised an eyebrow and turned away.

"I'm just saying— " Rachel began.

"Rach- " Cat interjected. "I knew this would be hard for you, but I really hoped that you could let me be happy."

"What does that mean?" Rachel snapped back. Cat had never spoken to her in such a tone.

"It means I don't think you should go with me to the appointment today."

Cat couldn't believe the words that were coming out of her mouth. Of course, she wanted Rachel to come. Rachel was a rock for her. She needed as much support as possible. Cat knew that … and somewhere, deep down, she knew Rachel's questions were warranted. She shushed those thoughts promptly.

Rachel stood and turned to leave, stopped herself short, and turned to face Cat.

"Cat, I've lost a friend before for telling them what I thought they should do and who I thought they should love. I'm not going to do that again. I want you to be happy, and if David makes you happy, then that's great."

Cat wanted to know what friend she was referring to, but forced herself not to ask.

"He makes me happy," Cat nodded, though she was beginning to doubt herself.

"Well … great," Rachel nodded. "I'm going to go ahead and leave. Let me know if you find a dress."

Cat fought the urge to burst into tears and apologize, which she knew she needed to do. Her conscience wouldn't let her rest until she did. Yet the stubborn side of her stayed rooted to her spot with her lips refusing to budge. *Why do I have to be so damn stubborn?* At that moment, she hated herself for it.

Instead, she nodded and watched Rachel walk out of her room.

"Rach-" Cat called out at the last moment, but it was too late. The slamming door echoed in the apartment.

Cat slumped onto her bed, feeling absolutely shitty for the way she had treated her friend. *As you should*, a voice chided.

"Shut up," Cat said aloud as she laid back onto the pillows.

She didn't have all day to wallow in self-loathing. Her mother and Lili would be waiting for her at the boutique if she didn't hurry. Infuriated with herself for sending Rachel away, frustrated that she didn't apologize in time, Cat sent a quick text to Rachel before exiting her apartment to hightail it to the bridal salon.

'Forgive me. I was an ass. I love you and I know you only want me to be happy. Xoxo'

The reply came seconds later as Cat skipped down the front steps.

'Follow your heart, Cat. All is forgiven. Love you, too.'

Follow your heart. Cat read the text again before shoving the phone into her jacket pocket. What does that even mean? That seemed easier said than done, but most things are.

CHAPTER TWELVE

"JUST THREE MORE BUTTONS," DARCIE RHODES BREATHED ON CAT'S neck. Cat could feel her mother's excitement radiating through her fingertips as she continued the arduous task of fastening the delicate buttons. Cat gave an unperceivable nod to her mother and kept her eyes down, focused on maintaining her balance while staying upright.

Damn four-inch stilettos. If only they would just agree to letting her wear fashionable flats. But it threw off the entire ensemble, according to her mother. The untold length of time it took to fasten 100 petite silk buttons had her feeling slightly dizzy.

"Done," her mother exclaimed, just as Cat became certain she would need to sit down.

Her mother stood back and smiled at Cat's reflection in the mirror. Cat tried to take a deep breath, but the dress, as beautiful as it was, was too constricting for deep breathing. Instead, she swallowed and attempted a smile.

"Isn't she stunning?" the stylist cooed.

"Oh, Cat!" Lili clasped her hands together and rushed around to the front to get a better look. "You look … pale. Are you feeling alright?"

"Of course, she's alright!" Darcie answered for her. "She's just found the perfect wedding dress. Look at her. Cathleen, I've never seen you look more perfect than you do right now."

"She is perfect," the stylist nodded and refilled their champagne flutes. "Absolute perfection." No doubt she was thinking about the *perfect* nine percent commission she would be receiving for a six-thousand dollar wedding dress.

Perfect, Cat thought, turning her gaze to the young woman staring back at her in the mirror. The dress was perfect. Too perfect. Too tight. Suddenly, she felt too tall. The mirrors surrounding her multiplied her reflection so that she was forced to look at some twenty-odd duplicates. She turned towards the right, arching her back to see those buttons that had forced her to stand still for too damn long. The mirrors seemed to rotate with her, spinning around the room. As the edges of her vision began to blur, she had just enough time to call out, "Lili!" as she tumbled off the platform and towards the wooden floor.

"She's fine!" her mother was standing over her and frantically fanning her with the latest issue of Bride's magazine. "She's fine! Everything's fine. Are you fine?"

"I told you she looked pale," Lili was on the floor with her, cradling her head in her lap.

"Be quiet, Lili" Darcie snapped towards her youngest daughter, before turning sharply back to Cat. "What happened, Cathleen? Why didn't you tell us you were feeling faint?"

"I don't know," Cat blinked and tried to push herself up. "I didn't realize it, I guess."

The form-fitting lace gown had proven to be difficult to maneuver. She noticed a slight tear in the side as she rose, which sent the stylist into a tizzy. Embarrassed, she turned towards the mirror to examine the damage, while her mother smoothed things over.

Cat felt the fire creeping into her cheeks, "Lili, help me out of these effing heels!"

"Language, ladies!" their mother snipped.

"Hey! I didn't say anything," Lili defended, before bending to help her sister out of the four-inch torment-inducing heels. She winked up at Cat, "Such language, Cathleen."

"I know. I'm awful," Cat smirked in her mother's direction. Thankfully, she didn't notice, as she was still entangled in a heated discussion with the stylist. "I just hope we don't have to pay too much for them to repair this. I can't believe I fainted."

"I can," Lili stood to look her older sister directly in the eyes, now that Cat had been brought down to her height. "Cat, it's your modus operandi. It's just what you do when you're overwhelmed."

"Thank you, Ms. Pre-Law," Cat quipped. "You can save your legal jargon for someone else, okay."

"It's actually a term used outside of law, as well," Lili smirked.

"Yes, I know that," Cat bent low to scoop the shoes off the floor, when she heard the dress rip further. "Holy hell!"

"Language!" Darcie turned from the stylist with a shout. Turning back, her voice softened, "We'll take the dress."

Appeased with the purchase, the stylist and her mother rushed around the boutique to gather any other must-have accessories to complete her look. This left Cat alone with Lili to be unbuttoned. Thankfully, this process was much quicker, thanks to her sister's small fingers and nineteen-year-old eyesight.

Cat was grateful to no longer be standing on display on the platform, but secluded in a dressing room. She leaned her arms forward to brace herself against the wall.

"Do you like it?" Lili asked

"Huh?"

"The dress. Is this THE one?"

Cat laughed, "Oh, Lili. Yeah … I guess it is now that I've ripped it; it has to be."

"Cat, don't pick it if it's not what you want?"

"It's a stunning dress."

"That's not what I asked," Lili's voice rose in volume.

"I know what you asked," Cat defended. "It's lovely. And," her voice faltered for a mere milli-second, but enough for Lili to catch it. "And, it's lace. Just what I've always wanted." She fixed her smile and looked back at her sister. "It's perfect."

Lili stared at her, clearly unconvinced, but at least she didn't press the conversation further. She knew by now that once Cat had fixed her, 'I'm fine' smile, she would not waver.

"Girls! Are you ready?" their mother's voice rang through the elegant dressing room.

"Cat's just getting her clothes on," Lili stepped out, taking the soon-to-be purchased gown with her.

Cat heard the gentle swish of the layers, the footsteps, and their voices trail down the corridor and back into the show-room. She waited until their muffled conversation disappeared entirely before she sank to the floor. She would not fall apart. Not here. Not in the dressing room of this 5th Avenue bridal boutique. Her mother had pulled so many strings to get an appointment. Normally, they were booked out six months ahead. But David wanted a December wedding, and December was eight months away. She was shocked that her parents had even considered the idea of marriage at her age. She had only just graduated from Columbia in December, a semester early thanks to her AP credits she brought with her from high school. But they adored David. Looking back over their whirlwind romance the last six months, it was clear to Cat that everything had happened according to their plan. Just as everything else that had transpired during the last four years.

David, eight years her senior, was ready to settle down. Ready for marriage. Ready for a life-long partner to shower with affection … and gifts. David loved giving gifts more than anyone Cat knew. She smiled at the diamond on her hand. It was truly stunning. Almost an embarrassing spectacle of a ring. Her mother had all but pulled Cat's hand off trying to get a closer look when she came home on Valentine's Day wearing it. She still couldn't believe she was engaged. The ring felt heavy and awkward. Cat hadn't told a soul, but she had taken to only wearing it when she knew she would see David or one of her family members. It just felt so cumbersome. She promised herself she would start wearing it more. Everyday even. Just like she had worn the sweet-sad twisted wire on that finger for all the years before. Cat suddenly missed it terribly. She desperately wished she hadn't thrown it into the Hudson River in an attempt to move on six months ago. But she had. No amount of wishing would return the ring to her, or Luke, for that matter. Cat blinked the tears away as she wiped furiously under her eyes. She had not worn water-proof mascara; and therefore, she would not fall apart. She glanced in the mirror to set her face accordingly. The blissful bride-to-be. Perfect composure-as always.

Yes, David was ready for marriage. And he was especially ready for Cat to give in already to his sexual advances. He had been so patient. He was so incredibly understanding when Cat told him that despite what 99.9% of twenty-somethings chose to do, she wanted to wait. He said that only added to his interest in her. Though it didn't stop him from trying to push things further a time or two. Cat found him nearly impossible to resist at times, but if they had managed for this long, they might as well hold out till the wedding night. Charming. Handsome. An excellent career in trading and quantitative measuring at Goldman Sachs with her father. He was exactly what her parents had always pictured for her life and, to some extent, what Cat had always pictured for herself. Until her time in North Carolina, that is.

Cat spun the ring on her finger. It fit a little too snugly and Cat made a mental note to take it to the jeweler for adjusting. She steadied her breathing and closed her eyes. Life moves on. Regardless of what you want, life just keeps going. Living in the past doesn't bring anything but heartache with a side of nausea. Cat was done pining away for someone who had walked out on her. She pushed herself off the ground with such enthusiasm that she surprised herself. Smoothing her caramel colored waves in the mirror, she smiled decisively at her reflection. Today was a victory and no deep unsettled feelings would declare it otherwise. She was Cathleen Rhodes and she had found the perfect dress.

CHAPTER THIRTEEN

CAT TURNED DOWN THE OFFER FROM HER MOTHER AND LILI TO HAVE the town car drop her back off at her apartment after their bridal appointment. The sun was shining. It was a glorious spring day and Central Park was calling her to stroll down The Mall. She loved seeing the street performers, the artists, and occasionally, a highly-skilled musician, along with the less-than-skilled. She would always toss some spare change into a guitar case when it came to music.

She slowly sipped the iced latte she had grabbed at the corner Starbucks on 63rd and Lexington. Turning the events of the day over and over in her mind, she heaved a sigh and slumped onto a nearby bench. She had begun the day so eager to find the perfect dress. Always prepared, Cat had been prepping for this day for the past two weeks. Hair appointment. Waxing appointment. Ouch. Spray tan appointment. And then, all of that preparation had come crashing down with Rachel's questioning and Cat's literal crashing to the floor of the bridal salon. What did it mean? Did it have to mean anything at all? Was all of this uncertainty simply a part of being an adult and in love? Things with Luke seemed so clear, so black and white. With David, there were fifty shades of grey and nothing seemed certain anymore.

But David was happy, and her parents were happy. And therefore, so was she, Cat reasoned.

She leaned back on the bench. The sun-dappled light cast

shadows across her face. She soaked in the warmth of the early-spring sun as she sat beneath one of the many colossal American Elm trees that lined the path. Her mind traveled back to her first date with David in October, near this very spot.

"I think that was the best steak I have ever had," Cat announced, as David held the door open for her to exit The Capital Grill.

"It was very good," David agreed. "Most certainly the best company."

Cat blushed.

He took her hand in his as they crossed the street.

"Where to next?" Cat asked with anticipation. David had insisted on planning every aspect of the date.

"How about joining me on a carriage ride?" his eyes twinkled. "We're not far from the Park."

"Believe it or not, I've actually never taken one before," Cat laughed, "Isn't that sad?! I've lived in New York practically my whole life and have never taken a carriage ride."

"That is sad," he tightened his arm around her waist and pulled her close to him.

Cat knew this was the moment. She prepared herself to kiss him. The whole evening had been a success. This moment would just be the cherry on top of a perfect first date. She prepared herself for fireworks. Their lips touched, parted, and suddenly, she felt like his tongue was trying to remove her tonsils. Then, he pulled away with a huge smile on his face. Cat smiled back.

Was that it? Maybe she was remembering everything with Luke much better than it actually was. Memories are funny like that. *That kiss was probably perfectly fine*, Cat told herself.

She scolded herself for not focusing, not trying hard enough.

Conversation came easily with David. They had such similar backgrounds. Both were from affluent families, though he grew up just outside of Philadelphia. His upbringing had mirrored hers in so many ways. They both had parents who were somewhat overbearing, and they wanted him to have the best and be the best at everything. It hadn't been easy for him growing up, he explained, as he had opened up over dinner. But, in the end, it had served him well. He had been offered a position at Goldman-Sachs, while still in their internship program, and had climbed the ladder steadily from there. Cat's father was certainly impressed.

As they crossed Central Park South, David reached over and took her hand in his. It was such a sweet gesture. Cat felt comfort, a steady reassuring presence. Isn't that exactly what she needed? Who needs fireworks when you have the steady warmth of a fire? David could be that. Cat beamed at him appreciatively. David whistled and flagged down a carriage driver who was all too happy for the business. Holding her hand aloft, he helped her up onto the plush, red velvet seat.

"I'll be right back," he winked at her and darted away.

Cat leaned her head back and closed her eyes. David was wonderful. She really did like him. Couldn't she just choose to love him?

"I just had to buy one for you," he said, interrupting her thoughts as he climbed into the carriage, extending a perfect red rose.

"Oh," Cat smiled, it was a cheesy gesture, but heartfelt. "It's beautiful, David. Thank you."

Taking the rose from him, she leaned in to give him a kiss. The carriage started to move, causing him to fall forward into her, bumping his head against hers.

Rubbing their heads, they laughed.

"Let's try that again, shall we?" David lowered his voice and moved closer to Cat once more.

This time, his kiss was more forceful than before. She tried to give into it, to let her emotions take control, to get lost in the moment. But all Cat could think about was how his arms had uncomfortably pinned down some of her hair. Or how his breath smelled like steak, foie gras, and asparagus. It wasn't entirely unpleasant, but why did it feel so contrived?

His hands moved from her shoulders down her arms. One hand went to her knee and slowly began to make its way up the inside of her thigh. Thankfully, his mouth moved from her lips, allowing her to breathe, and moved down her neck. Cat opened her eyes.

It was almost completely dark out now, if not for the street lamps.

Cat sighed. The night was lovely. The dinner exquisite. This moment on a two-hundred and fifty dollar carriage ride should be romantic. It was romantic. What was wrong with her?

Luke, her heart reminded her.

Luke.

It was as though the clop, clop, clop of the horse's hooves drummed his name louder and louder. Luke, Luke, Luke! There was a rhythm to it and an annoying increase in volume. Or was it all in her head?

She gently pushed his hand away, "I'm so sorry, David. I suddenly feel a little sick. I think it must've been dinner. Can we take a rain check on this? This moment is perfect. Truly. I just need to get out—stop the carriage!" Cat shouted to the driver, who pulled up quickly on the reins, making Cat lose balance momentarily and slide off the seat, before hopping up and jumping out.

"Um," David looked dumbfounded, "Okay. Do you want me to call you a cab?"

"No, no," Cat signaled to the driver to continue on, "I'll be fine from here. I'm really close to my place. This just came on so suddenly." Cat wrapped her arms around her abdomen as though to emphasize the point.

"I'll call you," she called behind her as she fled the scene.

She could only imagine what David was thinking of her now. But David was not the one on her mind. It was Luke. Maybe it always had been.

By the time she made it out of the park, it was dark. She hobbled back to her apartment in her four-inch heels. Had she been planning on walking this far, she would have decided on more sensible shoes.

Of course, it had been David to contact her first, after that disastrous ending to their first date.

Sweet, thoughtful David had shown up the very next day at her door with soup. Not homemade, of course. He didn't cook. But the fact that he had thought of her and wanted to see her again, in spite of the fact that she had deserted him in a carriage, that's what sealed the deal for Cat.

Yes, she reminded herself. *I am the lucky one.*

And with that thought, she whipped out her phone and quickly sent a text to Rachel, "Found the perfect dress! Xoxo," and pressed send.

CHAPTER FOURTEEN

"YOUR MOM SAID YOU FOUND IT," DAVID WRAPPED HIS ARMS AROUND her from behind and kissed her on the neck, making her jump slightly in surprise as she sliced the carrots julienne-style on her cutting board.

"You are lucky I didn't just slice my hand off," Cat raised her chef's knife and teasingly prodded it in his direction.

"Whoops, my bad," he raised his hands and stepped back slowly. "So, what are we having tonight?"

"Stir fry," Cat resumed slicing the carrots. "Is that okay with you?" She looked up at David who had already removed his tie and kicked off his shoes. She loved that he was so at ease at her apartment. "I'm sorry. I didn't even think to ask what you wanted for supper?"

"That's fine, babe," he said as he reclined on her couch and rested his eyes. "I was thinking we could order out, but stir fry is fine."

"I really enjoy cooking," Cat pulled the stir fry oil off the shelf and turned the stove on to high heat. "It saves money. We both know you would insist on paying, if we ordered out."

"That's alright by me."

"I know it is," Cat rolled her eyes. "But the whole point of me paying for my own place, and everything else, is to prove to my father that I can take care of myself."

"Well, as long as I get to start taking care of you in December, right?" David sat up and ran his hands through his honey-blond hair. It had just the slightest wave to it and was beginning to show specks of silver on the sides and above his ears. Cat thought it made him look distinguished.

Cat sidestepped his question and continued, "Besides, it relaxes me. Especially after shopping with my mother."

"That bad, huh?"

"David, I tore the dress."

"You didn't!"

"I absolutely did … I sort of, well, I fell off the platform in the showroom."

"Oh my God, Cathleen," David began chuckling as he rose and crossed to her. "Only you."

"I know, right?!" Cat turned and moved her hands over his shoulders and down his biceps as he stepped into her. It was very apparent that he was making use of the gym Goldman Sachs provided their employees. "Seriously," she squeezed his upper arm, "how many times a week are you lifting?"

"Oh, you know," David stepped back and started unbuttoning his dress shirt. "Like four or five," he pulled off his shirt and tossed it over the nearby bar stool and began to flex for Cat, who couldn't contain her girlish giggles.

"Stop that right now," she whacked him with the pot holder. "My kitchen is hot enough."

"Come here," he pulled her close and rubbed his five o'clock shadow against her cheek.

"Aahh," she playfully tousled his hair.

"Cathleen, the hair," he stepped back and finger combed it back into place, before replacing the smile on his face and stepping in for a kiss. She obliged.

She frequently forgot that he didn't like her, or anyone for that matter, to mess with his hair after it was gelled and in its proper place. Cat tried not to let it bother her, but for whatever reason, her desire to run her fingers through his hair seemed like such an automatic and natural response when they were close. She balled her hands into fists and tucked them behind her own back as they kissed, so she would not be tempted. *This is David, not Luke*, her mind reminded her. And at that thought, she pulled away and turned back to the stove.

"Oh, the oil!" The pan had begun to smoke during David's gun show and the kitchen had filled quickly with the stench of burning oil. Cat turned the fan on and David moved past her to open the window, but Cat knew it was too late. Her uber-sensitive smoke alarm began to blast and before she could grab the broom to hit the button, the building's alarm began to chime in unison.

"Ahhh!" Cat exclaimed. "I swear it usually doesn't make the building's alarm go off that quick."

She continued to jab the button with the broomstick, but it was pointless now. The fire department would soon be on their way.

"Damnit!" Cat frantically fanned the smoke with a dish towel, but she couldn't decide if it was making matters better or worse.

"How many times have you set this thing off, now?" David took the broomstick from her and tried unsuccessfully to shut it off. The alarm throughout the building was now in full effect, complete with flashing lights in the hallway.

"Since January? Or just this week?" Cat groaned. "The super is going to kick me out. I'm sure of it."

"Good," David winked as he slipped his shoes back on, "then you can just move in with me."

Cat shook her head, "Not yet, bud." She walked over to him and planted a kiss on the top of his head, while he was bent low adjusting his Johnson Murphy loafers, "We'd better get outside with everyone else."

Hand in hand, they walked down the eight flights of stairs with the other residents in the building. Cat had tried to take the elevator, knowing there wasn't a real fire, but it was locked due to the alarm. Several of the other tenants in the building gave her icy glares in the stairwell.

Her neighbor from 8b patted her back and whispered, "It could've been any of us."

Cat returned the smile, but didn't argue. It wasn't anyone else but her. *You are the expert screw-up after all*, the sarcastic inner voice piped up. She wanted to punch it in the throat.

"Your super really should replace your alarm," David leaned in and lowered his voice. "It shouldn't be going off for just a little smoke."

Only two flights remained till they would be on the street and out into the chilly night. They would have to wait there until the fire department gave the all clear. Hopefully, it would be quicker than last time. Cat didn't think she could bear the stares and whispered insults. Only four days earlier they had been left waiting fifty minutes in a cold drizzle before being let back in.

"Let's hop in a cab," David pulled her towards 2nd Avenue the moment they stepped outdoors into the crisp night air. Early April in NYC meant the temperature was still dipping into the thirties at night. Cat wished she'd had the forethought to grab her winter coat.

"Really?" Cat glanced at the apartment residents shivering, as the firemen ran inside. She caught the eye of her super who appeared to be making a beeline in her direction. "Yep, let's bounce."

Hand in hand, they took off towards the Avenue where they could catch a cab to eat somewhere. Anywhere. Cat was famished and exhausted. As much as she was looking forward to relaxing in her apartment, seizing the opportunity to be spontaneous was exciting. She felt butterflies. A rare feeling, these days.

"Where should we go eat?" Cat asked as she slid into the cab.

"I know the perfect place," David smiled. "356 East 80th Street," he nodded to the driver.

"Wait," Cat looked at him surprised. "Your place? You don't cook."

"Well, then," David nodded, "you'll just have to show off your cooking skills. Or we can order. Whatever you want. Your wish is my command." He picked up her hand to kiss it and frowned. "Where's your ring?"

"Oh," Cat pulled it back. She had forgotten to put it back on before David came over. "I took it to the jewelers, finally." She lied. "Didn't I mention it?"

"No," David's response was curt. "No, Cathleen. You didn't."

"It was just the slightest bit tight."

"Was it?"

"I thought I had mentioned it."

"No," David turned to face the front of the cab. "I bought the size your mother told me you wore."

"I'm sorry. It's really not your fault," Cat reached out to touch his shoulder. He shrugged away. "I just want it to fit perfectly. And it will. I'm sure it won't take them long to adjust." Cat made a mental note to take the ring immediately to the jeweler first thing in the morning. Guilt was positively dripping from her words, "Let's open some wine when we get to your place. Tonight is special. We should celebrate my shopping adventure. Torn dress and all. Everyone thinks it's the perfect dress.

And I have a stunning ring."

David softened, "That will fit perfectly as soon as it's resized."

"It will," Cat agreed wholeheartedly.

"And then, we can start our perfect lives together," he squeezed her leg.

Cat beamed at him before turning to look out the window with a smile, "Absolutely."

"A special night calls for a special bottle of vino," David emerged from his hallway closet that doubled as a wine cellar. He was an avid collector of fine wine and was ever eager to distribute that knowledge to Cat whenever they shared a bottle. "This wine has a wonderful balance to it. Full flavor with intense aromas of dark fruits and hints of incense and sandalwood."

"Wow," Cat was impressed. "Sounds … great."

"I'll open it and let it breathe for a bit." He walked confidently to his bar cart. His stride alone told her he was in his element. Confident. Knowledgeable. All without sounding cocky … or at least, not too much. This must have been what his co-workers saw everyday and the reason he was seeing promotions every year. Her own father was hailing him as the best trader he'd seen in twenty years, before she had agreed to their first date.

"What kind of wine is it?" Cat inquired, knowing his response would not mean much to her. She was woefully uneducated in the world of fine wine. Though David was doing his part to bring her quickly up to speed.

"Screaming Eagle Cabernet," he showed her the bottle. "Napa Valley. This bottle cost me nearly three-thousand dollars."

"That's insane," Cat's eyes went wide. She didn't know how

she felt about drinking a glass of wine that would cost her fiancé a cool seven-hundred and fifty dollars. "You know, David. I feel like you should be sharing this wine with someone who will truly appreciate it. Like, your brother maybe? Or Warren from work? He knows about wines."

"You will appreciate it," David winked.

"I'm sure I will," Cat agreed. "But, you know, wine is wine to me. I enjoy it, but I'm still learning."

"Let me be your teacher, in that case," David meticulously poured the wine into a decanter as he spoke. "Besides, you said yourself that you wanted tonight to be a special night for us. This will just get it started the right way."

Cat froze in her chair. She suddenly had the feeling that his intentions for this evening were very different from her own. "Actually, today was already special. I—I just thought we should celebrate it. No need to pull out anything extra for me …" her voice trailed off. David was clearly already set upon his method of celebrating. He simply nodded and mumbled a response as he continued to search for the red wine goblets he'd purchased in Napa this past fall. They would be perfect to bring out the bouquet of this vintage, he explained. Cat bit her lip in worry. This was not how she wanted the evening to unfold, but like so many other things in her life over the last few years, she felt like a passenger along for the ride.

CHAPTER FIFTEEN

CAT MADE THEIR DINNER WITH WHAT CONTENTS WERE AVAILABLE IN David's pantry and fridge. Which, other than alcohol, turned out to be sparse. She managed to make some banana pancakes with a past-its-prime banana and some Bisquick she found at the rear of the pantry. She knew it wasn't the best meal to compliment this fine vintage, but it was the best she could do.

David walked her through a full wine tasting after they'd wrapped up their meal. First, she had to swirl her wine vigorously in the glass to open it up. He further explained that this brings more oxygen to the wine, allowing the aromas to rise from the glass.

"Alright, Cathleen," he had his board-room voice turned on; she realized she did not care for it. "Keep your eyes closed and just smell."

"Just smell?" Cat felt so awkward sitting with her eyes closed, dissecting the many aromas of a glass of wine. Couldn't she just taste it already?

"Lift it to your nose and breathe it in."

"Like this?" she leaned in and took a whiff.

"Yeah, no. Not at all like that," he put his hand on the back of her head and practically shoved her nose into the glass. "Breathe it in deeply."

Cat felt the fire in her cheeks rising and she inhaled deeply through her nostrils.

"Better?" he questioned.

"Sure." Cat leaned back in her chair. "Can I open my eyes now?"

"Of course," he patted her knee. "So, tell me. What did you smell?"

"Well," Cat was reaching with her guesses, "Um … maybe chocolate?"

"Good!" he encouraged. "And …"

"And …" she hesitated. "David, I don't have a clue. You know I was just guessing at chocolate, right?"

"Well, you got it right." He turned his attention to his own glass and proceeded to swirl, sniff, and repeat.

"You know, hon," Cat paused. She felt her nerves tightening in her stomach. She had never stayed the night at his apartment and was suddenly feeling less inclined with the three-thousand dollar bottle of wine on the table. *Men don't open a bottle like that without some expectations*, a little voice continued to nag her. *Shut up, Cat.* Another voice piped up. *Maybe he just wants to enjoy the evening with you and a glass of fine wine. Is there anything wrong with that?* The voices continued their argument, leaving Cat suddenly exhausted and desperate for a cozy pair of pajama pants and maybe a red velvet cupcake from Crumbs Bakery.

"I really should catch a cab and get back to my place. I left the veggies on the counter and everything. Plus, I have an early meeting tomorrow."

"Really? An early meeting, huh?" David raised an eyebrow, amused. "What kind of early meetings do you have at the Children's Museum?"

Cat tried to ignore the sarcasm in his voice, "We are meeting about a new exhibit coming in next month." She straightened her spine against her chair. He was as bad as her parents. Getting a job at an art museum or gallery wasn't an easy feat when no one was hiring. She felt lucky that she had snagged a full-time position at The Children's Museum of Manhattan. So, she wasn't working with Picassos, but at least she was working at a museum and earning her own living.

"What's the exhibit on? Peter Rabbit?" David laughed, amused at himself with a slight slur in his speech. He had opened a new bourbon, presented to him at work after his last promotion, to enjoy with dinner. And had already enjoyed three pours over ice prior to their wine tasting.

Cat turned and stood half-way to leave before he caught her by the elbow. She didn't want to tell him that the exhibit was actually called "Grossology" and focused on all the bodily functions that children find so amusing.

"I'm sorry. I'm sorry," he said through his laughter. "I know you're enjoying your new job and all. But I wish you'd let me put in some calls for you. Or you could always come work at Goldman Sachs with your dad and I. We desperately need some administrative assistants. With a degree from Columbia they'd probably hire you."

"Well, it's not Harvard," Cat's voice had an edge that David did not pick up on.

"No," he agreed. "But it's still Ivy. Maybe not the top … but certainly not the bottom."

"Argh!" Cat removed his hand from her elbow and tried to respond politely. "I know you don't mean to offend me David, but you do. You, my parents, everyone has always pulled strings or shoved me in one direction or another. I'm tired of it. I can't do this anymore."

"What are you talking about, Cat? What does that even mean?" David stood, seeming alarmed, and moved his hands back onto Cat, but this time to her shoulders, turning her to face him. He failed to realize her frustration or the fact that she pulled away ever so slightly with his advances. He never noticed.

"Nothing," Cat suppressed the moment of fire that had ignited within her. There was no use explaining, she reminded herself. Some things were best to ignore, not ruffle feathers, move on, and just keep going. She looked up at him and managed an apologetic smile. He cared. He wanted what he thought was best. Just like her parents. For their sake and his, she would press on. It was all she knew how to do anymore.

"I really don't know what came over me," Cat placed her hands on top of David's and sat back down to swirl and sniff her wine like she'd been taught.

David sighed in relief as he sat, "You just haven't seemed yourself the last few weeks."

"Haven't I?" Cat was surprised he had noticed. She realized her mind had been elsewhere since the wedding planning pace had quickened, but she thought she had done a decent job concealing it. She had managed to conceal so many feelings for so long that sometimes she wondered whether she knew the truth about her emotions at all.

She recovered, "My mom is just taking charge of so many things. I feel a little lost sometimes."

He rubbed her hand sympathetically and she leaned into him. With her eyes closed, she could tell herself anything and almost believe it. She was happy. David loved her and, of course, she loved him, too. Who wouldn't? His hand slid suggestively up her arm to her shoulder. With her eyes still closed, he stroked her cheek, took her chin in his hand, and drew it closer to him for a long kiss. She smiled, returned the kiss with all the energy she could muster, and opened her eyes. She was staring at David; no amount of imagining could replace him with her eyes open.

She looked down at her practically untouched glass of wine.

"I should at least stay to finish my glass," she smiled sheepishly at him.

"At least," he agreed, pulling her into another kiss.

It was nearly ten o'clock and Cat knew she needed to get back, if she wanted a decent night's sleep before work the next day. She had finished her wine some time before, and David had poured them both another glass before opening up another special, though less expensive, bottle.

David stumbled slightly on his way to the stereo and Cat couldn't help but laugh at him and herself. This somewhat whirlwind of a day was ending sweetly after all. He rifled through his cd collection before turning to give her a somewhat mischievous look. Nora Jones' soulful voice filled the apartment and Cat felt herself melt as David extended his hand to her for a dance. This. This is why she would marry him. Just when she would find herself frustrated with him, he would redeem himself. Cat sighed as she leaned her head against his shoulder. Sweet, dependable David. So what if he was occasionally snobbish. Her parents were always snobbish and she loved them. David took her chin in his hand and lifted her head up for a kiss. Cat moved into him, letting her hands move down his back as she tugged at his dress shirt until it had untucked from his pants. He raised an eyebrow slightly before moving to kiss her with more ferocity than before. Cat closed her eyes and allowed herself to get caught up in the moment. She wasn't sure if it was the alcohol or an attempt to solidify the fact in her mind that she loved David, and no one else, but she found herself pushing him down onto the couch.

Her own take-charge actions had taken them both by surprise. David smiled broadly as he leaned back on the couch cushions and patted the space beside him that was no more than six inches wide. Cat knew that in joining him she would really be on top of him, but she couldn't think of any reason not to. In fact, she wanted to. They were engaged after all. Though they had messed around plenty, this time felt different. Things had never moved below the clothes, and Cat knew for a nearly thirty-year-old-male, this had to be torture and she commended him for submitting himself to it time and time again. Maybe she should give in and give them both the satisfaction.

She turned her body just so she fit narrowly on the couch with one leg draped over his body and her head resting comfortably in the crook of his shoulder. He caressed her hair while they continued kissing. Kisses that continued to grow in intensity. Fueled by his three rather large glasses of wine and the bourbon, his hands moved over her back, down to her waist, and back up again. Cat sighed and arched her body against him. Things were moving farther than they had on previous encounters and Cat was running out of reasons to wait any longer. Hadn't she waited long enough? Hadn't David?

Taking her sigh as a sign of contentment, David moved his hand further down to her rear and gave it a squeeze.

"Hey, now," she teased, lifting herself onto her elbow and leaning forward to kiss him.

"Hey, to you," he wrapped her in his arms and held her firmly against him. His kisses were sweet and Cat found herself lost in them. She closed her eyes and a series of images flashed in her mind. Luke. Luke kissing her. Luke touching her. Luke on top of her in the truck while the snow fell softly outside.

"Luke," Cat breathed in between kisses. Her eyes shot open.

Thankfully, David hadn't heard, but Cat on the other hand was washed in guilt. A sudden feeling of ickiness crept over her as she realized David was sloppily kissing down her neck, with one hand on her chest, and twisting as though trying to open a door. This was not working. Whatever moment they were having ended for Cat the moment she'd uttered his name. Luke.

While Cat waged a war with her emotions, David had rolled her under him. And though he was now kissing her sweetly with his hands cupping her face, she couldn't help but feel smothered. His hand slid down one side of her body and then up under her shirt. She tried to lose herself in the moment again. She had been thoroughly enjoying herself until that pesky Luke popped into her mind. *Well*, Cat thought, *he walked out on me once, he can walk right out of my thoughts.* Cat instinctively wrapped her legs around Luke's back. *David*, she chided herself, *David's back!*

Argh! Why can't I stop thinking of Luke? And why does it have to be now? Cat scolded herself. David's kisses began to grow uncomfortably forceful. Cat had to decide, and quickly, just how this was going to play out.

It wasn't until he began kissing her neck that she was able to take a breath, "David …"

"Hmmm" his mouth moved across her collar bone.

"David," Cat tried again. "Let's take this slow, okay?"

Somehow, in his male-sex-driven brain, David saw this as a green light to what he'd been waiting for, for the last six months. A smile spread across his face as wide as a child with a shiny new toy. "Oh, god! Yes! Cat, I will take it so slow for you. You have no idea how happy this makes me."

Cat felt her stomach drop. That was not at all what she meant. *Idiot*, she scolded herself. Why hadn't she just come right out and said 'stop?' Or, 'I was really enjoying myself until I started imagining you as my ex?' Or 'I'm not ready to have sex with you, yet, David?'

Or ever, another voice in her mind said pointedly. *You really don't want to have sex with David, ever.* She shouted internally at this know-it-all-voice. *If I don't want to have sex with David, MY FIANCÉ, by the way, who would I have sex with?!*

Luke.

She knew this voice was right. She knew it because it was the voice she tried so hard to suppress and submerge in the busyness of life the last four years. She knew if she threw herself into her studies, she could ignore it. But then college was coming to an end and where could she go to override the pain. And there was David. Sweet, safe David.

David. The David who was now undressing himself in the middle of the living room. And there was no denying that he looked good. Damn good. His muscles rippled and she could tell, as he pulled off his undershirt, he'd recently gotten another spray tan. No one is naturally that tan in April. She bit her bottom lip to keep from laughing out loud.

Cat swallowed her feelings and lack of desire and pushed herself to a seated position. Then, she did something that even shocked herself. She undressed. Hating herself for doing it, but hating herself even more for not wanting to be with David, Cat gave in to the one emotion she knew well—guilt. She would have guilt sex and that was that. *No.* She rebuked her thoughts. *This is not guilt sex. It's just sex with my fiancé and it will be great.*

She would have moved heaven and earth and all the spaces in between to turn back time. To go back for a moment nearly four and a half years ago when she stood like this, exposed, before some boy in a cold barn in Boone, North Carolina. *Not just some boy*, the irritatingly-right voice reminded her, *her boy. Luke.* The only one she'd ever wanted to give herself to completely.

David stepped in and edged her bra straps off her shoulders with his fingers.

He stepped even closer so she could feel his breath against her neck, her shoulders. His lips began to move further down.

"Wait," she said assuredly before she could stop herself.

"What?" David looked up at her, baffled.

"I'm—I'm not doing this, David," Cat backed away. "I can't be with you like this. I mean, I want to—or I wanted to—I. I don't even know what I'm saying anymore. I don't want this."

"What are you saying, Cathleen?" He stepped back. "Not tonight? Or not ever?"

Cat couldn't respond. For what seemed like an eternity, they stood there like that. Half-way undressed. His sad puppy eyes staring at her so pleadingly. Her heart firmly planted elsewhere. Both of them wanting something that neither could give.

"I don't know," came her eventual response.

"Don't you want to be with me?" there was the slightest whine to his voice now.

"I don't know," she repeated.

"Is this about that kid in North Carolina?" his voice grew hard and his eyes narrowed. He bent down to scoop up his pants.

"What—what are you talking about?" Cat's breath caught in her throat. *How on earth did he know about Luke?*

"Your mom," David answered her thoughts. "Your mom told me about him before I asked you out. She wanted me to know why you might be reluctant to open up to me."

"And?" Cat questioned. She sat down on the couch, numbly. She made no move to put her clothes on.

"And, she was right," David tossed her shirt to her. Or more like threw it at her. "You've always been guarded, Cathleen. Sometimes things are perfect between us and other times …. I just don't feel like I know you." He sat beside her and, with a sigh, placed his hand gently on her knee.

"David, I—I'm sorry," Cat faltered. She didn't know what else she could possibly say. "I care about you very much."

"Do you love me?"

Cat paused to search his face. He didn't look hurt, or worried, or even upset. He asked so matter-of-factly that one might think he was asking if she preferred mustard and ketchup on her hot dog.

"Cathleen Rhodes, you agreed to marry me … do you love me?" he asked a second time.

Cat swallowed hard, "Right now, I don't know that, either."

David looked down and nodded.

Cat tried to recover, "I think I could love you. I want to love you. I'm trying, David. I'm trying." Cat reached out to touch his hand and he let her.

"I'm okay with that—for now," he answered softly. He stood and walked to the large window of his apartment. The view of the city was spectacular from his high-rise doorman building.

He buttoned his shirt slowly as Cat waited for him to add to what he had said. He was okay with her not loving him for now? What does that even mean?

"David," she proceeded with caution, "what if I will never love you … would you want to be married to someone who didn't love you back?"

Cat didn't know if he would cry, yell at her, or simply let her walk away. But she had to know what this future might look like. She eyed the door and then her clothes, wondering if she should have put them on already to make a quick get-away, if need be.

"I want you to know," he inhaled deeply. "If you never love me the same way that I love you, I would be okay with that."

"You would be okay with that?" Cat shook her head. She could not comprehend a loveless marriage.

"Yes," David looked at her. "There are hundreds—thousands of couples, even—that are in marriages that are mutually beneficial. They care about each other. It's not ideal. But no one expects life to be perfect."

"My parents do," Cat disagreed. "They have been planning my perfect life for as long as I can remember."

"Well, to your parents, our marriage will be perfect." David shrugged. "You'll be married to me."

Cat fought the urge to roll her eyes. She nodded. She needed to get out. She needed some fresh air. She needed to clear her head. And she *really* needed to put her clothes back on.

"Cathleen," David turned to face her. "We should just go ahead and have sex."

"What?"

"You'll feel more connected to me."

"I'm sorry," Cat stood up from the couch. "Sex is off the table tonight."

"What are you so afraid of?"

Cat wanted to scream, 'Nothing that you could possibly understand!' But instead, she managed to turn to him calmly and said, "David, you've given me a lot to think about tonight. Like how this marriage is mutually beneficial. Or, maybe, about how it's not a big deal if I don't love you. I had no idea that I was just a piece of arm candy to you!"

"Cathleen! No, I'm sorry." David frantically backtracked. "I've had too much wine. Things didn't come out right. I'm sorry. I care about you. I love you. I know you'll love me too … even if it's been slower for you. We really are perfect for each other."

"I know," Cat could agree on that one fact. On paper they did appear like the perfect couple. But was that enough? Cat quickly dressed while David sat looking like a scolded puppy.

"Wait!" he called as she crossed to leave. "What about us? Are we still engaged?"

Cat turned to look at him once more. Everything she thought she had known seemed to fade away in one evening. So much for the perfect match. Maybe there was no such thing. Marrying him would please her parents, and obviously David, but where would Cat be in all of this. Lost, she answered herself. She'd been lost before. The last four years had felt like a fog. She had no desire to be lost again, but at the same time, she lacked the courage to call things off completely. She needed some time to find herself without someone else clouding her view.

"I need some time." And with that, she opened the door to leave. "I'll call you tomorrow, David," she glanced into his eyes once more as she closed the door. They looked cold. A chill ran down her spine.

CHAPTER SIXTEEN

WALKING THE CITY STREETS AT NIGHT HAD NEVER BOTHERED CAT.
Tonight was no exception. The lights twinkled in the puddles left
from the rain and lit the way home to her modest apartment that
was hers and hers alone.

It was hard to believe that an hour ago she'd been standing,
practically naked, in front of her fiancé, and now, she wasn't
entirely sure if they were even still engaged. The cold air cut right
through her blouse and made her thankful that she only had eight
blocks to walk north. If only she didn't have two and a half long
blocks east. She shivered and wrapped her arms around herself.

Cat wasn't sure if it was the biting cold or the fact that David
had brought Luke up, but suddenly her mind was carried back
to another cold, lonely day.

Cat pulled the thin hospital blanket up to her chin and rolled
on her side to face the window. Her parents had gone to gather
all of her things from Mimi's house, refusing to let her return to
say goodbye to Mimi or to pack on her own. She stared blankly
out of her window at the Watauga Medical Center to watch as
the sun dipped lower behind the pine trees on the horizon.

After her initial check at the hospital that morning, they had
no real reason to let her stay. No frostbite, no injuries. *Other*

than a broken heart, Cat said sardonically to herself.

No, her father must have paid them an agreeable sum to keep an eye on her for a few hours. He seemed to specialize in those kinds of arrangements. The nurse had checked in on her every half hour or so and when Cat had refused lunch for the third time, she had only seemed more intent on discovering what on earth could be wrong with this pitiful teenage girl.

The door creaked open, "Excuse me," the young nurse cleared her throat. "Your parents called, Cathleen."

Cat didn't respond.

"They just wanted to make sure you'd be ready to go in about fifteen minutes. They're on their way."

Cat managed a small nod. Her eyes were still glued to the spot in the road where she'd last seen Luke. Sitting in the passenger's seat of his father's pickup truck, he had turned back towards the hospital just as they drove through the intersection. How could he leave her like this? How could he give up on her? Landon had given up and look what happened to him. This was supposed to be different. It was different. It was her happy ending … only now it wasn't.

A new wave of tears emerged and she buried her head into the thin blanket, which now was soaked from a day's worth of crying sessions. Just when Cat was certain there were no tears left, another round would emerge. It wasn't fair. It wasn't right. None of this should be happening.

She and Luke should've woken up on this beautiful snowy day and enjoyed the early morning, cuddled snugly in their shared blanket. Maybe they would've made out. She sighed. Maybe Luke would've painted her like in that *Titanic* movie. She laughed to herself at that thought. No, that would NOT have happened. But now it never would.

More than anything, Cat desired to know what her father had said to Luke. What could he possibly have said that would make him walk away? Cat's thoughts were interrupted by the sound of the nurse clearing her throat again. She hadn't even realized she was still standing there.

"I'm so sorry to bother you," she hesitated. Cat rolled over to face her only to see that she was holding a folded piece of paper in her hand. "He gave this to me. That young man."

Cat sat up quickly. So, he had left her a note hours ago and the nurse was only just now giving it to her?

The nurse continued, "I wasn't going to give it to you. I mean, we all heard your father yelling at the poor kid. I didn't want to make it worse … but he asked me to get it to you somehow … so."

And with that, she quickly walked forward and shoved the crumpled note into Cat's hand before turning abruptly and leaving the room. Cat sat in stunned silence while the second hand of the clock on the wall drummed loudly in her ears. He had left her a note. He cared. He hadn't deserted her completely.

Ever so slowly, as though she might frighten it away, she unfolded the note, wondering what secrets it might hold. Would it give the location of a clandestine meeting place? Would they be running away together this very night? Cat's pulse quickened.

She forgot all hesitation and unfolded the rest of the note in one swift movement. Luke's hasty handwriting stared back at her on a page torn from Southern Living: "Cat, I'll always love you. I'm sorry it had to end this way. Luke"

This was not the message that Cat had been hoping for. In the six seconds that Cat learned she would be receiving a note from him to the time in which she unfolded it, Cat had seen their entire elopement play out in her mind. A few years living together, happily married, hiding out from their parents. Then, returning to Boone, smoothing things over with family, and building their lives together. Preferably, with two little curly-haired boys and a tire swing in the yard. "I'm sorry it had to end this way." That sentence had cut her tire swing mid-flight. Everything came crashing down again.

Cat crumpled the note and threw it across the room with a shout, "Fine!"

If Luke can move on from me so easily, then I sure as hell can move on from him, she told herself. And she would keep telling herself that line. Everyday.

✳ ✳ ✳

Cat shivered again. Thankful to look up and see that she was approaching her apartment, she pulled the key out of her bag.

Who would've thought that David had been a part of this whole "help Cathleen forget about Luke" crusade her mother had been on? Cat was mumbling something about sabotage as she put her key in the door when a familiar, but not-too-friendly, voice interrupted her thoughts from behind.

"Ms. Rhodes," came the monotone voice of her super, Demetri.

Cat sighed and turned to face him. "Yes," she replied with no attempt to hide the impatience in her tone. All she wanted, more than anything at this very moment, was a long steamy bath and her cozy bed. Was that too much to ask?

"We have had too many instances with your alarm," he said flatly. "There can be no more."

"I understand," Cat was so beyond caring at that very moment, but couldn't stop herself from snipping back, "I assume this means that you'll be replacing the alarm in my apartment?"

Demetri didn't respond. He simply narrowed his eyes and walked past Cat, into the building.

"I'll take that as a yes!" Cat called after him.

It was well after midnight when Cat finally slipped between the sheets of her own bed. It was a welcome feeling after the night she'd had. She made a mental checklist of what she had to be thankful for, despite all the things that had happened: a job, a recent reconciliation with a long-lost friend, a sister that cared about her wellbeing, her very own apartment, and, oh, she hadn't had sex with the fiancé she may or may not marry. That alone should count double. Cat smiled to herself before she remembered the crumpled note. I'll always love you. If she was perfectly honest with herself, she knew that her note to him would've said the same. I'll always love you, Luke, she whispered as she closed her eyes.

CHAPTER SEVENTEEN

THOUGH IT HAD TAKEN SEVERAL WEEKS AND FAILED ATTEMPTS, Luke's first date with Gabi was finally going to happen. Luke hated to admit it, but he was 98.7% certain that this date was doomed for failure. First, he'd gotten a stomach bug on the night of their original first date and realized he didn't even have her number in order to cancel. After trying for hours to reach Nicolas, Gabi had been waiting at her apartment for him to arrive all evening. At least she hadn't been stuck waiting at a restaurant somewhere, Nicolas said in his attempts to make Luke feel better. But he felt horrible, nonetheless. Then, Gabi had been stuck on the subway during a power outage when they were supposed to be meeting at Union Square. Luke ended up watching street performers for an hour and a half before he picked up a gyro from a street vendor and walked home. The gyro was great. The feeling of being stood up was not. By the time three hours had passed, Luke was convinced that this was a successful attempt to give him a taste of his own medicine.

'This catty shit is not what I have in mind when it comes to dating,' Luke mumbled to himself as he tried, unsuccessfully, to call Gabi for the fifth time. He tossed his phone onto the nightstand and fell into bed, feeling dejected and annoyed at himself for trying.

He woke up the next morning to seven missed calls and his phone violently vibrating.

"Hello," Luke's muffled voice was barely audible from under his quilt.

"It would be nice if you would try answering your phone once in a while?" Nicolas sounded snippy for so early on a weekend morning.

"What are you talking about?" Luke sat up in bed and leaned over to see his clock—11:43. *How had he managed to sleep until 11:43?*

"Gabi and I have both been calling you all morning! And last night, actually? Did you get the messages?"

Luke rubbed his eyes, "No. I'm sorry. What's up?"

"The power outage uptown. Gabi was on the subway to meet you and the entire grid shut down. She was stuck on the train for hours."

"Oh, man. That sucks!" Luke hated it for Gabi, but felt a sudden rush of gratitude that he hadn't actually been stood up the night before. He didn't think his ego could handle getting stood up as often as he had been lately. And he wasn't an arrogant guy.

"Gabi feels awful! She's been trying to call and apologize but thought you were ignoring her calls."

"No. No, honestly, I was just sound asleep."

Nicolas laughed, "Thank God! I didn't want her to think you were an asshole."

Luke laughed, "Nope. But I definitely felt like an ass last night when I thought I'd been stood up. Again."

They chuckled together.

"Well," Luke said at last, "is it worth trying this date again?"

"Definitely." Nicolas nearly shouted in the receiver. "Third time's a charm, right?"

"Man, I hope so. Well, what about next week?"

"Do you think I keep Gabi's social calendar?" Nicolas responded.

"Yep. You've planned every date so far."

"That's true."

"In which case," Luke paused, "maybe I should plan the next one. The first two sucked."

"Ha. Ha. Unfortunately, you'll have to wait a few weeks."

"Really?"

"Gabi and Paulo leave for Brazil tomorrow. Their Avo, Maria, passed and they're going for the funeral."

"Oh man," Luke pulled on a shirt and turned up the speaker on the phone while he finished getting dressed. "I'm sorry to hear that. And Avo is?"

"Portuguese for Grandma."

"Right," Luke made a mental note to express condolences whenever the future date took place, if it took place.

"They'll be gone for a few weeks," Nicolas continued while Luke began brushing his teeth. "But don't worry. This date will happen, Luke. It will."

Luke spit into the sink.

"Whatever you say …"

"I did say," Nicolas insisted. "Remember—"

"I know," Luke interrupted, "third time's a charm."

"Exactly."

Luke wondered if the flowers were a bit much as he skipped up the stairs to Gabi's Upper West Side brownstone apartment and buzzed for apartment 5NE. Nicolas had bought them, insisting tulips were Gabi's favorite, and that Luke should bring them to make a good first impression. He was beginning to worry that Nicolas would be crushed if things didn't work out with Gabi. It already felt like the expectations were too high and the first date hadn't even happened. Luke took a deep breath and swallowed hard before reaching out to buzz a second time.

"Come on up" the voice came through the intercom, just before he could press the buzzer. And the front door of the building clicked to let him know it had been unlocked.

Too late to back out now, Luke acknowledged inwardly as he crossed the threshold, multi-colored tulips in hand.

He arrived, slightly winded, after running up the four flights of stairs to the fifth floor landing and bent down to catch his breath. He had kept up running since moving to the city, but clearly had not been running up any hills. Luke was still bent over with the tulips when Gabi answered the door.

She looked dazzling, yet casual, in a jean skirt and white and yellow striped tee that accentuated her golden complexion and bronze skin. She smiled at him.

"Those steps are a killer."

"I think I made a mistake by running up them," Luke laughed, straightening up.

"Think you'll make it?"

"Once I catch my breath," Luke returned her smile and reached out to take her hand. "Luke Presnell."

"Gabi Baros," her handshake was firm. "At last we meet."

"No power outages or stomach bugs this time," Luke squeezed her hand before letting go.

"Thank goodness," Gabi stepped to the side to hold the door of her apartment open for him. "Would you like to come in for a minute? I just need to grab some shoes."

She gestured to her bare feet and threw her head back in a

laugh. Luke liked her laugh. It was deep and hearty. Not what you would expect from someone so young and lithe. She pivoted on her tiptoes and danced back inside her apartment where sounds of Latin music drifted into the hallway. Luke was suddenly all too happy to follow.

"You like Shakira?"

"Ummm … sure," Luke shrugged.

"I'm just going to grab my shoes but make yourself at home," Gabi waved as she scurried through the galley kitchen to what appeared to be a tiny bedroom.

"Thanks," Luke called, as he stepped into the bright yellow living room.

The colors of the room struck him instantly. The cheerful yellow walls accentuated a peacock blue couch, on which many multi-hued pillows were arranged. They varied from rich plum, fuchsia, emerald green, a light blue bolster pillow with tassels on the end, and several more bedazzled with sequins or gemstones. The desk, placed directly in front of the open window, had been spray painted teal, and sheer embroidered curtains blew in the wind. The overall effect of the space was vibrant and upbeat and, paired with the Latin music, it felt like somewhere Luke wouldn't mind spending his time.

Gabi appeared behind him in low-top Converse sneakers, ready to go.

"So," Luke held open the door, "where should we go?"

"First, food." Gabi smiled. "I've been chasing around twin kindergarteners all afternoon and I'm starving."

"Whoa! That would be exhausting." Luke shook his head. "I mean, I knew you were a nanny but I didn't know they were twins."

"Yep. And I usually have their eight year old sister, but she has ballet on Tuesdays. So, it was a bit less chaotic today."

"And you're a student?"

"A junior at Columbia," she confirmed. "And you're a painter?"

"Trying to be."

"I'd say you're succeeding from what Nicolas has told me," she winked. "He doesn't offer up compliments that easily."

"We'll see how the show goes this summer," Luke ducked his head modestly. Talking about his art or his profession still felt like bragging. Maybe it would always be difficult for him.

"Is it coming up soon?"

"Well, it was supposed to open in June but the date keeps getting pushed back. First, we were waiting on new electrical for the gallery, then the HVAC system went out, now the lighting designer has a delay on the installation for the foyer. It seems like it's always something."

"Ah," Gabi gave him a knowing smile. "Welcome to the world of renovations in New York City."

"Did you grow up here?"

"I did," Gabi took his elbow as they stepped into the warm sunshine. "And my mother is an interior designer. She mostly does homes on the Upper East Side now, but if you want some recommendations for dependable contractors I'd be happy to send them your way."

"That would be wonderful," Luke exclaimed appreciatively. "I mean, it's not my gallery. But part of my internship is to assist in overseeing the renovations and prep the space for the opening exhibit."

"Well, when that day comes," Gabi beamed up at him. "I want to be there."

"It's a deal."

Luke couldn't believe how well his date with Gabi had gone. She was nice. Normal. And their dinner conversation had lasted for three hours at the tiny, hole in the wall, Peruvian restaurant she had taken him to. Pio Pio. Incredible chicken. Addictive sangria. And, without a doubt, the best date he'd been on in four years.

Luke had messaged Nicolas immediately after leaving Gabi on the front steps of her apartment.

His cell phone was ringing before he reached the subway.

"So," Nicolas shouted over the heavy bass of club music in the background, "best date ever?"

"Pretty damn good," Luke acknowledged. "Nicolas, are you out clubbing on a Tuesday?"

"Never mind what I'm doing?" Nicolas diverted. "What are you doing? Why is your date already over if it was going so well?"

"She has an 8am class," Luke laughed. "And I wasn't about to go upstairs with her after the first date. I did that on the last one. Remember Lulu? Never again."

"Well, tell me that you at least kissed her!"

"I didn't."

"Oh, come on!" Nicolas shouted before repeating their conversation to Paulo who was obviously keen on getting all the details as well.

"But she did kiss me," Luke interrupted Nicolas's side conversation.

"Repeat that, the music's loud. It sounded like you said she kissed you?"

"Just a peck on the cheek." Luke started down the steps to the C train. "Look, I've gotta run. I'm going down into the subway."

"Sure thing."

"Hey, Nicolas," Luke stopped on the stairs before he lost signal, "thanks. She's great."

Luke heard cheering in the background as he hung up the phone.

CHAPTER EIGHTEEN

LUKE CALLED GABI THE VERY NEXT AFTERNOON. HE HAD HEARD about some unwritten rule where waiting three days was expected. But he'd enjoyed himself with Gabi, and he wanted to get to know her better, so why bother waiting? She sounded pleasantly surprised to hear from him. And even more surprised to find he was waiting downstairs with her favorite hazelnut latte. She had mentioned the night before, as they had strolled past the hipster coffee shop on the corner, that they had the best hazelnut lattes. Luke hoped the gesture made him seem sweet and not stalker-ish. When Gabi skipped down the stairs toward him, the look in her eyes told him his gamble paid off.

"Well, aren't you full of surprises?!" she exclaimed.

"I was in the neighborhood," he shrugged.

Gabi squinted her eyes at him, "Lies."

"Well, alright," Luke laughed. "I was not in your neighborhood, but I wanted to be."

"How long do you have?" Gabi glanced at her watch.

"I'm actually done for the day," he smiled. "You?"

"Done with classes. I'm meeting some friends for dinner at 7pm—you should join!" she grabbed his elbow.

"Oh, I don't want to intrude on your dinner plans."

"Not at all. They'd love to meet you," Gabi insisted. "It's actually a group of girls from high school and a few guy friends and significant others. Now I won't be the odd one out."

She winked at him. It was settled.

"Should I run back and change?" Luke glanced down at his athletic pants and Appalachian tee shirt. "I'm not exactly dressed for a dinner date."

"Totally up to you," Gabi shrugged. Though Luke could tell she hesitated before responding. "The place is downtown though, so it would be easy for us to swing by and let you change first."

"That's fine," Luke didn't want to be underdressed in a group of native New Yorkers. "But since we have a few hours, should we take a stroll in the park?"

"That sounds delightful!" Gabi took his elbow and followed his lead towards Central Park.

The afternoon spent soaking in the early summer sunshine while strolling hand in hand came so naturally that Luke was surprised at himself. He hadn't really dated since Cat. Occasionally he attended a mixer in college at Rachel's bidding, but he never let himself open up to anyone. Long dinner conversations and a promenade in the park seemed like something out of a Nicholas Sparks book. Not real life, and certainly not Luke's life.

He supposed his years of avoiding relationships had caught up to him at last. He was tired of dinners alone in his apartment. He missed the idea of being with someone, of knowing someone intimately.

I guess a few bad dates were all it took to change my mind, Luke thought to himself. *Maybe I should thank Rachel after all.*

It was 6:30 when Gabi and Luke walked out of the subway and onto 14th Street.

"I'm just a few blocks from here," Luke led Gabi through the crowd of tourists that had gathered with their tour guide at the top of the stairs.

"How did you snag a West Village studio?" she asked in genuine awe.

"Lucky sublet from someone in the arts community."

"It pays to know people."

The crowds thinned significantly by the time Luke and Gabi had turned onto Bank Street. He pulled the key from his pocket and held the door open so that she could walk in under his arm. It wasn't until they reached the second landing that he realized he was bringing a girl into his apartment for the first time since moving to New York. Unless he counted Rachel, but he didn't.

A wave of nerves hit him and he fumbled the key, dropping it twice before he managed to open the door.

"You need help with that?" Gabi laughed.

"Too much coffee," Luke responded, opening the door. "My hands feel jittery. I—I'm actually new to drinking coffee, believe it or not."

Gabi took both of his hands in hers and steadied them as they stepped in the sun dappled studio apartment.

"Are you sure it's the coffee, Luke?" She lifted his hands to her lips and kissed them.

Luke took a breath. He felt more for Gabi than he had felt in a long time. But he wanted to take things slow, for both of them. He wanted to be respectful of her, but he couldn't deny the intense longing that he felt rising through his body.

"I'm not good at this, Gabi," Luke whispered, as he leaned down to her. "I haven't dated anyone seriously since high school. I— I—," he swallowed, pausing, thinking carefully about how much he was ready to say, "I've never even been with anyone."

Gabi looked up at him with raised eyebrows, "You've never slept with anyone?"

Luke shook his head.

"Not even a drunken hook-up at a party?"

"Nope. Weird, right?"

"Not at all," Gabi kissed his hands again and gave them another squeeze, "I think it makes you even more attractive."

Luke took her chin into his hands and lifted her face for a kiss. In his mind, he envisioned what it would be like if their clothes started flying off and they ended up tangled on the floor, but Gabi's buzzing cell phone interrupted his thoughts and their kiss.

"Um—hello," Gabi spoke breathlessly into the phone. "Yes, we're heading that way! I'm bringing someone. Luke. Yeah, from last night." She winked at him.

Luke took that opportunity to grab some clothes from his armoire closet and change in the bathroom while she wrapped up the conversation.

"Ready?" she asked as he stepped out.

Luke had taken a minute to splash some cold water on his face while in the bathroom. He needed to collect himself again before going to meet Gabi's friends.

"Let's go!" He nodded with enthusiasm and just a bit of nervousness.

They were holding hands as they stepped into The Spotted Pig. Gabi scanned the room, spotted her friends at a rear table and let go of Luke's hand to weave through the crowd, leaving Luke to catch up. She made her way around the table giving quick kisses on both cheeks to each of her friends, male and female, while Luke stood awkwardly by his chair. He suddenly felt uncertain of whether or not he should shake their hands or do the weird European kiss thing. He opted for the firm handshake he always used when meeting someone new.

"Whoa! That's some grip," the young woman closest to him remarked as introductions were made.

"Luke," Gabi gestured to the table. "These are some of my best girl friends from high school: Bridgette, Sade, Naomi, and Evelyn. And this is Sade's boyfriend, Jeremiah, and Evelyn's partner, Devon." Gabi glanced around. "I thought Charlie and Lili were coming?"

Naomi spoke up as they took their seats, "Charlie texted to say she just couldn't make it into the city tonight. And you know Lili is late, as always.'

"True," Gabi handed Luke a menu.

"What is a gastropub?" Luke asked as he scanned the menu.

Everyone laughed.

"I told you he's adorable," Gabi smiled at the group, leaving Luke feeling slightly confused. The sting of being the butt of a joke reminded him of the pettiness of high school. He did not like it.

No one had actually answered his question. After further examination of the menu, it led Luke to the conclusion that a gastropub was just a bar with 'highfalutin food,' as his father would have said. And so, Luke ordered the most extravagant burger he'd ever heard tell of. A Wagyu beef burger, chargrilled, and placed tenderly on a toasted brioche bun, topped with roquefort cheese and caramelized onions, with a side of truffled shoestring frites. As the waiter brought it out with his beer, he thought about taking a picture with his phone to send to his dad but then thought better.

Don't want him to think I've moved to the big city and gotten 'too big for my britches,' Luke thought to himself as he took his first bite.

Ostentatious as it was, he could get used to this gastropub fare. He sat back and tried to join in on the conversation that, for the most part, had left him bewildered. He didn't know any of the high school friends they were talking about. He didn't really care whose parents had rented a yacht for the summer or understand any of the inside jokes that sent the girls into fits of giggles. As sweet and interesting as Gabi had been last night and earlier in the afternoon, she seemed to be someone else entirely around her former classmates. It was then that an adorable blonde appeared at the table, fashionably dressed, but looking a bit disheveled.

"Well, look who decided to show up," Gabi stood up and repeated her cheek-kissing routine with the newly arrived friend.

"I know. I know!" the girl smoothed out her dress. "But I have a really good excuse this time!"

"Sure," Sade mused, "like when you thought you saw Maggie Gyllenhaal and followed some chick all the way to Queens."

"That was years ago," she laughed. "That was when I was still at Spence."

"Shall I go on?" Sade asked.

"No, no," the tardy friend slid into the booth beside Luke. "I get it. I'm late a lot. And I'm Lili." She turned to him and extended her hand.

"Luke."

"Nice to meet you, Luke."

"Did you all go to Spence?" Luke began to do the math in his head. They were all younger than Cat, but it's likely they would have known of her. Suddenly, his chest felt tight with memories and heartache.

The girls nodded and continued their jabs at Lili.

Gabi leaned across him, "He's a friend of mine." She winked at Lili.

"Watch out for Gabi," Lili nodded knowingly at Luke. "She's wild when she's not watching those kiddos."

The table roared with laughter. Luke suddenly felt compelled to run for the door. *What had he gotten himself into?*

"She's kidding you," Gabi whispered so closely to his ear that her breath tickled his neck. "I mean. We all had a lot of fun in school, but that was a long time ago."

Naomi piped up, "But who doesn't get a little crazy in high school? Right?"

Gabi, "Luke didn't!"

They all turned to him.

"Well—I mean—I got a little crazy," Luke spoke hesitantly. *Where was Gabi going with this comment?*

"If you've never had sex then you haven't gotten that crazy," Gabi said pointedly, before downing the last of her second dirty martini.

One of the girls stifled a laugh, while the others looked at each other as though he had three heads and one of them was on fire. Luke felt as though the entire dining room had gone quiet. He cleared his throat and shifted uncomfortably in his seat.

"I think that's really sweet," Evelyn broke the silence.

Luke took a swing from his beer and pulled out his wallet.

"I need to get going," he mumbled as he pulled out a couple of twenties.

"You know," Lili directed her words to Gabi. "Some things are private, Gabi."

Realizing far too late that she had misspoke, Gabi seemed to snap back to reality, "Oh God! Luke, I'm sorry. That just popped out. Honestly, I don't know why I said it."

"I'm going to head out," Luke stood to leave.

"I'm sure you're not the only virgin in this bar, Luke" Bridgette leaned into the table.

"Yeah, man," Jeremiah spoke up. "If anything, it guarantees you could have any girl here. Except for mine." He winked at Sade.

"Nice try, guys," Luke laughed. "Trust me, I fully realize I'm the only virgin on the island of Manhattan."

"Not the only one," Lili took a sip of her beer. "I actually think my sister is still a virgin."

"No way!" Evelyn's hand hit the table. Luke felt the weight of the conversation shift instantly off of him and so he slowly sat back down in his spot. He would stay a little longer, if only to finish off his fries. They practically cost a dollar each.

"That's not possible," Bridgette shook her head.

Naomi agreed, "Cat was the queen bee … I mean, until her senior year. I was certain she had something going on with that boy before he died."

Luke choked on his fry and reached for his beer to wash it down. *Cat? His Cat?*

"Are you okay?" Gabi patted his back.

"Fine. Really." Luke took the final swallow from his beer. "I've really enjoyed meeting you guys, but I'm going to work early in the gallery tomorrow. I need to get back."

Gabi rose from the table as though to leave with him. Luke turned and gave her a quick hug.

"This was fun," he said quickly. "Stay and enjoy the night with your friends."

"But—I—"

"We'll catch up later this week."

Luke tossed his money onto the table and turned quickly to leave. His eyes paused ever so briefly to take Lili in; *was this Cat's beloved little sister?* He had seen a glimpse of her at the hospital that last day he saw Cat, but that moment had become a blur in his mind. This was the first time he really got a good look at her. She shared some of Cat's features but didn't bear a true resemblance. Luke thought if they were standing side by side, one might guess that they were sisters. He smiled at her quickly as he made his way to the door. He needed to leave before he blurted out a hundred things that he couldn't take back.

CHAPTER NINETEEN

WHEN GABI CAME BY THE GALLERY FIRST THING THE NEXT MORNING, Luke had already been working for three hours. With paint smeared on his arms, he'd taken his shirt off and tossed it to the side. Sweat beaded across his face. Her low whistle made him turn on the spot. When he saw it was Gabi, he smiled slightly and turned back to the canvas.

"I know I was awful last night," she began speaking to his back while he worked. "I can't believe I blurted that out to the entire table."

"Yep," Luke agreed and dipped his brush into an indigo hued paint on his palette.

"They were practically strangers to you," Gabi continued. "I can't imagine how embarrassed you must have been. And I was the cause of your embarrassment."

"Uh-huh."

"Luke," Gabi's voice broke. "I have secrets too, you know."

Luke turned and put down his paint brush.

"If I had entrusted someone with something and they revealed it to a table of strangers, I would be furious, too." She bit her lip as tears welled up in her eyes.

"Gabi," Luke sat on the nearby stool and ran his fingers through his hair. "You're right. I'm pissed. But I'm not mad at you. I'm mad at myself for telling you. We barely know each other. I just—I should have known better."

Her tears started rolling freely now. "Please give me another chance, Luke."

Luke glanced down at his paint covered hands. He felt his stomach doing flip flops and not because of Gabi. It was Cat. Hearing her name last night. Sitting beside her sister in a booth. Even if only for a few minutes, he felt in some strange way like he had been close to Cat. To finding her again. He cursed himself inwardly. *How could he have been so stupid? Did he really believe that this huge city, swarming with people, could hide Cat or what he felt for her.* Someone once told him that there's only six or less degrees of separation between all humans. *Well, last night there had only been one.* He was close. Too close.

"Luke, say something."

Luke stood up. He looked at Gabi, who was so beautiful with her long dark hair. So sincere in her apology. He thought of their dinner date. The hours they'd talked. Their walk in the Park. The laughs shared, holding hands, the ease of it all.

"I—of course, Gabi," Luke walked forward and started to open his arms for a hug before stopping himself. "I'm filthy."

"I don't care," she said, wiping her tears. She stood on tiptoe to kiss him and wrapped her arms around him.

Even with Cat on his mind, he held Gabi in his arms, and prayed that this decision to move on was the right one.

The next weekend, Gabi had planned a special outing for them—salsa dancing at her favorite club. Luke insisted, regardless of whether it was salsa dancing or any kind of dancing, he was probably not the right guy to bring along. Nicolas and

Paulo would be joining them and that thought brought Luke some relief. Nicolas would sit with him at the bar while they watched their significant others dance together. The fact that they were siblings only slightly weirded him out.

"Paulo was my first dance partner," Gabi exclaimed happily on the way to the club. "We are going to tear this place up."

"Yes, baby sister," Paulo high fived her; he seemed to share her enthusiasm.

"And we are going to tear up that bar!" Nicolas mimicked Gabi's pitch and jump in his step.

"Yes, my man!" Luke replicated Paulo's high five and the group laughed as they approached the entrance to Bembé.

The atmosphere was livelier than any dance clubs Luke had been to in Boone. But there were no real dance clubs in Boone, so there's that to consider. Gabi had told him on the cab ride out to Brooklyn that Bembé was known as the place to go for salsa dancing in New York City. If you can't go to Latin America … go to Bembé.

Nicolas secured a table with two chairs since the bar was full, and Luke got four margaritas while Paulo and Gabi hit the dance floor. Luke watched them while he waited for their drinks. They had already caught the eye of everyone on the dancefloor, securing the spotlight, quite literally. The spotlight operator in the booth up above was already shining it down on the pair. Luke wondered to himself how often they went dancing together or if they had met earlier in the week to polish up their old routine. Paulo started the dance with a lift and flipped Gabi behind his back. Her five inch rhinestone stilettos shined brilliantly under the disco ball.

Luke sipped his margarita and made his way back to the table with a drink tray in hand.

"I went ahead and got them margaritas," he said, nodding towards Gabi who was already gyrating wildly with Paulo behind her.

"We'll be drinking those," Nicolas informed. "They won't leave the dance floor until we peel them off at 3am."

"Won't they get thirsty or something?" Watching them spin made Luke tired already.

"Oh, they'll run to the bar for water, but then their sweaty little asses will run right back to the dance floor. I've joined them for this a time or ten."

"Well, at least this time you have a drinking buddy."

"Cheers to that!" Nicolas raised his glass to Luke's.

When Luke made one final trip to the bar around 2am, he saw a familiar face. Lili. He turned away, quickly uncertain of whether or not he had caught her eye. She looked to be in deep conversation with a gorgeous leggy blonde.

Luke thought he had been successful in avoiding detection, until he heard her call his name.

"Luke! Hey!" Lili came around the bar and gave him a quick hug. "How are you?"

"Good. How are you?" Luke smiled warmly and willed himself not to think of Cat. He tried to focus his mind on Gabi, who had just dropped into a split on the dance floor, eliciting cheers from the crowd.

Lili turned to see where his attention was directed.

"Ah," Lili nodded. "I should have known that Gabi would drag you out for salsa dancing eventually. Have you danced with her yet?"

"Somehow, I think you already know the answer to that?"

"Yeah," Lili laughed. "I did. Gabi likes to draw a crowd. But she's super fun to be around," Lili corrected herself when Luke's face gave him away. "Don't get me wrong. She's really a sweet and sincere person. She's not all show."

"Thanks," Luke nodded and moved to go around Lili.

"Luke," Lili spoke up, "the other night at the bar … I'm really sorry you were put in that awkward position."

"Thanks, Lili," Luke smiled at her. "Have fun tonight!"

"Oh, I will," Lili glanced back towards her friend at the bar. "But first, I have to find my sister."

Luke tightened his grip on the glasses lest he drop them. His eyes quickly scanned the room.

"Your sister's here with you?" Luke tried to ask nonchalantly.

Lili paused before she responded. Whether or not she noted anything strange about Luke's question, he couldn't tell.

"Yeah, she was dancing with a friend of hers, but then her fiancé showed up and—actually, I'm not sure where they went." Lili craned her head to see where they might have gone.

Luke just nodded. His fingers felt like they might go numb from squeezing the glasses so hard. So, Cat was here. In this very dance club. And with her fiancé. He swallowed again, his throat feeling suddenly dry.

"I'm sorry, I'm keeping you," Lili patted him on the shoulder. "I'm sure I'll find Cat somewhere around here. Have a good night, Luke! And have fun with Gabi!"

Lili turned and headed in the opposite direction and left Luke frozen in his spot. Have fun with Gabi. That's what she had said. Apparently, that's exactly what he should have been doing all along. He couldn't believe that he'd been so fixated on Cat since meeting Lili at the pub. But not only since then. With every date that Rachel had set him up on, he'd been comparing each of those women to Cat. She was on a pedestal in his mind and seemed to be the impossible comparison for every woman. She had become the litmus test for true love and it was time to change that.

Luke moved quickly to his table and set down the glasses with such force that Nicolas jumped. However, before he could say a word, Luke turned and marched onto the dance floor where Gabi was twirling out from Paulo's arm.

True love, Luke thought to himself, as he reached out to catch Gabi's hand. True love is a myth. If it had been real between him and Cat, then she wouldn't be engaged now. She had clearly moved on. And so would he.

Luke leaned down to kiss Gabi's hand. His mouth moved up her arm until he moved behind her to kiss her neck, her chin, and then her mouth. She melted into him on the dance floor.

CHAPTER TWENTY

CAT WAS AN EXPERT AT AVOIDING THINGS. FEELINGS. PEOPLE.
Squirrels. So, it did not surprise her that she found it easy to
avoid David. After he'd shown up unexpectedly during her
girl's night out with Lili and caused a scene, she had hopped
into a cab with him and completely deserted her sister. She felt
awful, but Lili said she'd still had 'the best' time without her.
Cat wasn't sure if she should be offended by this or not.

His persistence had vacillated between terribly sweet and
terribly annoying, and more often, the latter. He had now taken
to sending bouquets of flowers signed, "From your loving
FIANCÉ, David." Ugh. She took his first bouquet of roses to
the office to brighten the hallway because she found them so
difficult to stare at in her kitchen. She took the second bouquet
to her parent's home to grace their foyer. She had, thus far,
managed to elude all of his phone calls since the failed girl's
night outing, and when she had caught a glimpse of him entering her apartment building that very morning, she had
managed a very narrow escape out of the rear door, through an
alleyway, and hid behind a dumpster until the coast was clear.
A smelly, yet successful, escape. Yes, Cat had managed all of
this without getting caught.

It had been eight weeks since she told him that she needed

space. She wasn't missing him exactly, but she was beginning to realize that a decision had to be made on her part. Were they engaged or not?

She still had not taken the ring to be resized as she had promised. It was, at present, safely tucked in the change purse in her Marc Jacobs bag. She would slip it on if she was going to her parents' home, of course. No need to alarm them. Her mother had moved ahead at full-steam in planning the wedding, now barely six months away. Large deposits were being made daily to secure various services. From florists to caterers to the string quartet that would play for the ceremony, it had all been neatly arranged according to her mother's plan and paid for with her father's wallet. She was involved in some of the planning, but clearly not the one making the decisions in the end. Her mother would ask her opinion on things, like the menu, but barely waited on Cat's response before submitting the orders. Cat was a mere observer in the day that was supposed to be hers.

She should care, but somehow could barely muster any excitement about the wedding these days. Lili, of course, had picked up on this. Though her sister lived on campus downtown at NYU during the school-year, she was around enough to know that Cat was not being honest with herself, or anyone else. Cat always knew that Lili was far beyond her in intellect and she had proved it the evening before.

"When are you going to tell her?" Lili asked her quickly, when their mother had stepped out of the room for a moment while they were reviewing flower arrangements.

"Tell her what?" Cat feigned confusion.

"That this isn't happening?" Lili said meaningfully. "You're not going to marry David."

Cat inhaled sharply.

"He's been calling me too, you know," her sister went on.

"What? When?" Cat lowered her voice. Her mother had left the room to take a call but was still standing in view, rearranging the latest bouquet Cat had placed in the foyer. Cat bit her lip. David had been calling Lili, but not her parents. What did that mean? Obviously, he didn't want to strain the relationship he had with her father at work.

"Cat, earth to Cat," Lili waved her hand in front of her face. "You can talk to me. I've always known he wasn't the one for you."

Cat turned her gaze away from their mother, who was still engrossed in her conversation, to Lili. "Why would you say that? Everyone thinks we're perfect for each other." Cat tried to put on a pretense of offense, but it was no use.

"Cat," Lili reached out her hand. "David is a perfectly nice guy. He's handsome, he has a great job, he's everything that our parents want for you. But …" She paused.

"But …" Cat urged her to continue. She needed her to continue.

"But, he's not the one for you."

"Then who is, Lili?" Cat snapped. "If you know so much, then tell me who."

Lili sat, clearly on the verge of speaking again, when their mother walked back in.

"Well, girls!" she sat with a flurry of excitement. "You will not believe who that was." Without waiting on her daughters to respond she continued, "The manager of The Boat House! They were previously booked for December 15th but we got it. We will be having our reception there. Oh, Cathleen, aren't you thrilled?!"

Lili continued her knowing gaze, leaving Cat to put on the show of pure excitement.

"Oh! Oh, wow! That is wonderful news, mom." Cat raised the pitch of her voice to match her mother's, her smile spread wide. She was a pro at this.

Her mother threw her arms around her and Cat returned the embrace with a pat on her back. Lili mouthed 'meet me outside.' Cat nodded her head slightly while her mother clung on.

The early summer sunshine was beaming down, as Lili and Cat picked up their iced coffees and headed towards the Park. So rarely were they both hanging out at their parents' home on a Sunday, but her mother had requested for both of them to be present that afternoon—with Cat as the Bride and Lili as the Maid of Honor, as they had many *important* decisions to make.

"What did David say?" Cat finally asked her sister, as they crossed Central Park West.

"Well," Lili sipped her iced latte. "He asked if I'd spoken to you, if you were upset, if you still wanted to get married … I don't remember all the questions. He sounded pretty desperate, Cat."

"Ugh," Cat groaned. "I know I need to call him. I just told him I needed space."

"Why? What happened?" Lili pressed.

"Nothing," Cat answered. "And a lot of things …" She realized she wasn't making much sense. "We—we haven't had sex yet. And I was going to, but, but I just couldn't."

"Okay," Lili shrugged. "Cat, I already figured you had done that."

"But," Cat stammered, "How? Never mind that. I just—it seems like David is perfectly fine marrying someone who doesn't really love him."

"Of course, you don't love him."

"Of course, I don't," Cat agreed before she could stop herself.

"Because you love the boy from North Carolina."

"I love—wait," Cat stopped. "Lili, you never even met him. How could you possibly know whether or not I loved him."

"You mean still love him," Lili corrected her. "And, you're wrong. I did meet him. Well, kind of. I saw him and dad arguing at the hospital. I just didn't tell you about it."

Cat needed to sit. Four years had passed. Her sister had seen her go through so much inner turmoil and heartache over losing Luke. How could she not have spoken up? Cat lowered herself to a nearby bench and Lili joined.

Cat shook her head in disbelief, "Why now? Why on earth would you tell me now?"

"Cat," Lili's voice was shaky, "For the last five years ... since Landon died ... I've watched everything you've gone through. I wanted so badly to be there for you, to help you, to let you know that I had your back. I saw how awful our parents were treating you. And so often for things that were beyond your control. I'm sorry I didn't stand up for you then."

Cat stared at her little-now-grown sister and knew that perhaps no one, except Luke and Mimi, had ever cared for her more. "I still don't understand why you are choosing to tell me this now."

Lili struggled to continue, "Cat, with all their attention turned on you, I was able to go unnoticed. It was nice not to have them on my back or constantly obsessed with my choices. I saw how hard they made things for you ... I didn't want to find myself in your shoes. That's really no excuse though. I should've told you."

Cat understood that sentiment. So often she had wished herself out of her own shoes, but that never worked.

"Can you forgive me?" Lili squeezed her hand.

"Of course, I forgive you." Cat wrapped her arms around her. "Now, I feel like I need to know what you overheard."

Lili nodded. "You had just gone into the exam room and Dad began yelling at—"

"Luke," Cat whispered. "His name was Luke."

"Right, Luke," Lili paused for a moment. "Well, Dad was yelling at Luke for being so irresponsible with his daughter. It was awful and everyone in the hospital was listening. Mom was trying to get him to lower his voice. Finally, he asked Luke to step outside with him. And I, well, I decided to follow them outside. I kept my distance, following about fifteen feet behind, when they stopped at the edge of the parking lot and dad pulled out his checkbook."

"He what?!" Cat interrupted. It was so like her father to think that he could buy anything, people included.

"Seriously," Lili agreed. "I about died. And clearly Luke felt the same. He tore up the check and said he couldn't be bought. He said that he loved you, Cat. That he wanted to take care of you and make sure you were never hurt again by anyone, but especially mom and dad."

"He said that?" Cat could not imagine anyone standing up to her father so brazenly. But now knowing what Lili had seen, she could picture Luke being so bold.

"He ripped dad a new one, Cat" Lili laughed, throwing her head back, as if she was seeing it again. "I remember being so shocked I forgot to hide myself when dad turned back to go inside the hospital."

"Wait, but that was all?" Cat wanted to replay it all again. "Was there anything else?"

"It was four years ago, Cat," Lili said apologetically. "I wish I could remember everything. What I remember clearly was hearing how earnest Luke was in expressing his feelings for you. He spoke so highly of you and really laid into dad for the way they had treated you after everything you'd been through. But …"

"But …" Cat urged her sister to continue.

"But, then their voices dropped. I couldn't hear what Dad was saying to Luke, but I could see their faces. Luke looked heartbroken, Cat. Or scared, I dunno. Whatever Dad said to him must have scared the shit out of him. That's all I saw before dad grabbed me by the arm and practically dragged me inside, making me promise not to breathe a word."

Cat's mind was reeling. *So, he had cared enough to stand up to her father. That was something. And he proved he couldn't be bought … but why was her father trying to pay him? To stay away? To keep his mouth shut regarding their naked barn escapade? What on earth could he have said that frightened Luke so much that he would end things without discussion.* Nothing she imagined was enough to make him desert her. *No. He was still wrong.* She didn't think she could ever forgive him for that.

Cat turned to look at Lili, who seemed relieved to have the weight of that secret off her chest.

"Thank you," this time Cat squeezed Lili's hand.

Lili nodded, "So, what are you going to do?"

"About what?" Cat couldn't keep her decisions straight in her mind. What was she supposed to be deciding now? Whether or not to marry David? Go find Luke? Pick a different floral arrangement?

Lili smiled and patted her sister's hand before rising, "I know you'll figure it out, Cat. But don't take my word for it … listen to yourself, for once."

Lili turned to walk back towards the avenue.

"Where are you going?" Cat called.

"I would love to stay longer, my dear sister, but I have a hot date tonight," Lili grinned slyly.

"Oh really," Cat was surprised. Her sister never mentioned dating. She was always so engrossed in her studies. "Who's the lucky guy?"

"Uh—girl," Lili said with a wink. "I told you it was nice to fly under the radar." And with that, she turned on her heel and left Cat to stand rooted to her spot on the sidewalk.

"She's freaking brilliant," Cat whispered to herself, remembering the events of the previous evening. How else would her sister manage to date girls unnoticed by their parents?

Cat acknowledged that Lili had a pretty sweet set-up. All of their attention had been turned to herself for so long and Lili's grades had always been top notch. What was there to worry about?

Cat's thoughts were interrupted by the buzzing of her iPhone in her purse. She glanced at it cautiously. She wasn't ready to face David yet. She knew what her answer had to be to his 'Are we still engaged?' question. But she simply wasn't ready for the turmoil it would create in her life. More arguments with her parents. More threats from her father. More tears from her mother. More guilt from Cat. No. She would not submit herself to that quite yet.

The incoming call was from a number she didn't recognize. Telemarketer, perhaps? She took a chance and answered anyway.

"Cathleen Rhodes," she said brightly.

"Hello, Cathleen," said the very professional sounding voice on the other end. "This is Daniel Rothman, calling from the Modern Museum of Art."

Cat was breathless. It had been months since she'd submitted an application and a follow-up email with no response. "Oh, yes. Hello!"

"We have been reviewing your application here and would love to have you come in for an interview with Monique Cadell, our Senior Deputy Director of Exhibitions and Collections. I'm sorry it's taken us so long to give you a call. We've been absolutely buried in applications the last six months and only recently began hiring again."

"Yes, of course," Cat was practically floating as she walked back towards the Children's Museum from her lunch break. "No problem at all. I would love to come in for an interview."

Landing a position at MOMA would truly be a dream come true. Cat's mind was racing with ideas of what she might do if given the opportunity there.

"Great, good to hear that." Daniel's voice was crisp and professional. "How about coming in this Friday at one?"

"Friday at one," Cat stopped quickly and stepped to the inside edge of the sidewalk to pull the day-planner out of her purse and jotted it down. "Yes," she confirmed after ensuring the time was open, "yes, I can do that! Thank you so much."

"We look forward to meeting you then."

Cat waltzed back to the "Grossology" exhibit on cloud nine. Who cared if she had to give a lecture to kindergarteners in the "Belching Zone," she had landed an interview at MOMA.

CHAPTER TWENTY-ONE

SIX OUTFITS. THAT WAS THE MAGIC NUMBER BEFORE SHE FOUND THE perfect ensemble for her MOMA interview. She stepped back to take a look at herself from the full-length mirror she had hung on the inside of her closet door. Professional, yet youthful and stylish, the best balance. Her slim cigarette-legged navy pants from J. Crew, Tory Burch classic bronze flats, and a top she had picked up at a Parisian boutique during "Les Soldes" the previous July. She looked polished. She looked like someone who belonged in marketing at The Modern Museum of Art … at least, that was the goal.

"Now, this says, 'hire me,'" Rachel proclaimed, as Cat did a full turn before the mirror.

The two had easily reconciled, after Cat's outburst the morning of the bridal salon disaster. Rachel, ever the constant friend, had steeled herself to being there for Cat, regardless of any fiancés or feelings for Luke that may or may not need to be dealt with. Rachel had not shown pleasure over Cat's more recent struggle—whether or not she wanted to be engaged— but rather, had assured her that she would be supportive of whatever decision she made.

"You sure?" Cat turned once more. She wanted to look en vogue but still professional.

"Absolutely," Rachel handed her the vintage Chanel clutch from her nightstand to complete the ensemble. "Now, I've got to run to work myself. But text me after the interview!"

"I will!" Cat embraced her friend, before Rachel sprinted out the door.

Cat sighed with relief. Rachel had such a steady presence about her. And she had never steered her wrong. Perhaps Rachel was the one to thank for everything that had unfolded in the recent months. Had she not reconnected with Rachel, her mind wouldn't have been on Luke nearly as much, she wouldn't have realized just how uncertain she was about her feelings for David, the day at the bridal salon probably would've gone perfectly, and she likely would've slept with David by now. Cat pursed up her lips at the thought. The fact that the very thought of sleeping with her fiancé made her wrinkle her nose made her realize she was, in fact, making the right decision by calling things off with him. She would do it. She had to.

Cat glanced at her watch. Though she wasn't quite pressed for time, she didn't have time to spare, either. The only question that loomed was whether to take a towncar or brave the subway. She didn't mind the subway, it was just unpredictable. The type-A side of her wanted to arrive early and smelling fresh, and not like urine, the fragrance of the subway in the summertime. Her type-A side won, she called a car, and arrived twenty minutes early for the interview. Arriving early gave her time to collect her thoughts and sit for a moment to people watch before heading inside the MOMA offices on West 53rd street.

Cat smiled at the family walking past. The mom seemed a little frazzled but happy, as she pushed the stroller that held a toddler making siren sounds and clutching a firetruck in his squishy little boy hands. With one hand pushing the stroller and the other pulling a preschool aged girl that appeared to be avoiding all the cracks in the sidewalk, the threesome passed by

Cat in a blur of noise and excitement. Cat found herself longing for that. It was a new sensation and it hit somewhere deep in her belly. It surprised her actually. She shook her head to try and clear her thoughts, but it remained. The sweet sense of belonging and togetherness. Something that was always lacking in her own family, if she was being honest. Something she had only felt with a few people, all of whom were back in the mountains of North Carolina.

Cat turned her attention to the solid glass wall of doors where she would soon be interviewing. She nodded to herself. *This is it.* And with that, she bolstered herself and walked inside.

"Cathleen," an elegant, statuesque woman walked towards Cat, extending her hand as she approached the chair where Cat had been sitting in the waiting area. Her hair was platinum, her skin the color of nutmeg. She was gorgeous and impeccably dressed. "I'm Monique. I'm so pleased you could come in for an interview. My assistant, Daniel, was very impressed by your resume."

"Thank you, Monique." Cat felt herself relax almost at once in her welcoming presence. "I'm thrilled to be here."

Monique's persona warmed the entire lobby. Cat felt a gravitational pull to her and could tell that those around her felt likewise. Following Monique back through a labyrinth of inner offices, Cat noticed she addressed everyone by name. She was like the sun, the workplace seemed to revolve around her light.

"Charles, I saw that little Daniel learned to ride his bike without training wheels!"

"Selah, I'm going to stop by later to hear how your mom's surgery went."

Between each interaction, Monique would turn her attention to Cat. Asking if she'd taken in any of their current exhibits. *Of course, she had.* Or how she enjoyed her internship in Paris the previous summer. 'C'était magnifique,' Cat had responded enthusiastically. And so, Cat followed, noting with delight how the office seemed to buzz with positive energy. It was a hive of art, vision boards, and activity with Monique as their queen bee. Cat knew, without a doubt, that this is where she wanted to be. By the time the door had closed in Monique's grand corner office, Cat had begun a silent prayer, 'Please help me get this job, Lord. Let me speak with confidence but not appear cocky. Help me to be as articulate as possible … oh, and please don't let me trip and fall on my face. Amen.'

"Cathleen, meet my assistant Daniel."

"We spoke on the phone," Daniel heartily shook Cat's hand.

"So good to meet you in person," Cat responded.

Monique turned to another older gentleman who was seated in the corner, "And this is Mr. Lorenzo. He serves on our Board of Directors."

"Pleased to meet you," Cat began to cross the room to shake his hand when the strap of her clutch caught the arm of a chair, knocking it over and sending Cat sprawling to the ground under the weight of the chair.

"Oh! Oh my gosh. I'm so sorry," Cat scrambled out from under the chair. So much for appearing graceful. Daniel was already by her side, offering her his hand. With her cheeks flushed, she stepped carefully around the chair to shake Mr. Lorenzo's hand.

"Happens all the time," he said with a wink.

Cat laughed, "It will if I work here."

Everyone joined in her laughter. The ice was broken. She hadn't fallen on her face exactly, but knocking over furniture and tumbling to the ground came close. They hadn't kicked her out or even seemed the least bit phased. Any anxiety Cat had felt about the interview melted away with their laughter.

"Cathleen, have a seat," Monique motioned to the chair. "Do you go by Cathleen?"

Cat paused. She did technically go by Cathleen to everyone who knew her these days, except Lili and Rachel. Which made it seem so surreal when she found herself saying, "My friends call me Cat."

They smiled and the questions began. In truth, she felt like she was talking to old friends. They let Cat share about her life-long passion for the museum; her experiences growing up in Manhattan and attending their summer day-camps. They discussed the areas of the arts that most interested her, particularly new artists. Monique, like Cat, had also completed an internship at Musée d'Orsay in Paris, though twenty-some odd years prior. The conversation was easy and moved quickly. Cat couldn't believe it when she glanced at the clock and realized she'd been there for just over an hour.

"Cat," Monique leaned forward in her chair with a serious expression. "I have just one more question."

"I'm ready," Cat leaned forward and matched Monique's expression with a twinkle in her eye.

"When can you start?"

CHAPTER TWENTY-TWO

CAT BEGAN HER NEW POSITION ON JULY 1ST. IT WAS LESS THAN SIX months out from the wedding that her mother was still frantically planning and Cat wasn't planning to attend. She had finally mustered up the courage to tell them that she and David just weren't meant to be. The wedding was off. Cat had planned a family dinner for the end of the week, on Friday night, when she would tell them. Two and a half days to go. *Fifty-two hours,* Cat thought to herself as she grabbed her signature latte on her way to the office. A grande iced vanilla latte with coconut milk—perfect for the summertime.

She was only a few days into her new job and she already felt more "herself" than she had in years. Lili had told her to 'listen to herself' and, for the first time in a long time, she was doing just that. Rachel had told her to "follow her heart" and Cat was determined that she would. Absolutely. Follow her heart straight to breaking it off with David. She was ready to be the real Cat again. It felt so good just to hear people call her Cat around the office. No more pretending, she told herself. *We are done with that shit.*

Cat had also been successful at evading David for nearly ten straight weeks. She took a deep breath. It was time to break the news to him. She didn't think it would come as a surprise, considering the way they had left things at his apartment in April. She would be kind, gentle. She was determined to let him down easy and with class. Her phone beeped. She glanced to see the text from David: 'See you tomorrow for lunch. Love you!'

Cat had messaged him for the first time that very morning to ask him for a quick lunch at Dos Caminos in Midtown on her lunch break. Not a lunch *date*, mind you. Just a quick lunch. Meeting during her break was strategic, she thought. The limited amount of time left less of an opportunity for awkward break-up tension. She had the ring secure in her bag, ready to return. She would no longer be engaged. She would just be Cat. On her own and starting her career. It felt big and scary and right. She was ready.

What Cat was not ready for was the obscene amount of flower arrangements that sat in her office when she stepped in with her latte. Her first thought was that they must belong to someone else.

"What's all this?" Cat called over to Daniel, with whom she shared the office space. They now shared the title of Assistant to the Deputy Director of Exhibitions and Collections.

"Oh, honey," Daniel waved his hand. "These are not mine!"

"Whaaaaat?" Cat's eyes went wide. She put down her things and walked over to the nearest of the dozen arrangements. It couldn't have been David. He didn't know. She hadn't spoken to him in weeks. Unless her parents had told him, which they probably had. She sighed and glanced at the card.

'Looking forward to our date tomorrow. Almost 5 months till our wedding! Always, David'

Cat fought the urge to cuss aloud. Instead, she just let loose in her head. *Oh, shiiiiiiiit.*

"So … who's David? How long have you been engaged? Where is the ring? And, most importantly, am I invited to the wedding?" Daniel crossed to Cat and playfully leaned on her shoulder.

Cat smiled. Daniel was fun, funny, and easy to talk to. She also appreciated the fact that she didn't have to be concerned about him hitting on her.

"Oh, where to begin ..." Cat laughed.

"My, my! What's all this?" Monique stepped into the office and immediately stopped to smell the flowers. She glanced at one of the cards that Cat had not yet read.

"Cat!" she exclaimed. "You're getting married?!"

Cat took a breath and looked from Monique to Daniel and back again. "Alright. It's a long story, but I'll give the CliffsNotes version."

She sat down as the pair scrambled to sit on top of her desk and direct one-hundred and ten percent of their attention to Cat. She couldn't help but laugh.

"Scooch over," Monique prodded Daniel. "My butt is bigger than yours."

"I should've made popcorn," Daniel responded.

"Uh-huh. With lots of butter."

"Oh, I just love movie theatre butter!"

Cat waited, barely able to contain her laughter.

"Okay, shhh!" Monique hushed Daniel. "He can't control himself, Cat. You go right ahead."

"You're the one who mentioned butter."

"Hush!"

"Well," Cat swallowed. "I got engaged in February. We took a break in April. He crashed my girl's night out with my sister last month and made an ass of himself. He was belligerent and I had to take him back to his apartment that night. It was—anyway— tomorrow I'm going to break it off completely and return the ring. My parents will likely disown me. But I'm thankful that I have an amazing sister and now, a job that I love. That's pretty much it."

Monique and Daniel sat quietly for a moment.

"That's a lot to take in," Daniel nodded.

"Do you have the ring with you?" Monique stood up from the desk. "Because I'm going to need to see that."

"I do," Cat reached for the coin purse in her Marc Jacobs bag. It held no coins, only a 2.3 carat diamond. She pulled it out for their inspection.

"Dear god!" Daniel exclaimed.

"Sweet Jesus, I'm blind," Monique yelled out.

At this, several more heads popped into the office. Cat was utterly embarrassed and amused at her colleagues' reactions. She was just getting to know Daniel and Monique, but she was still learning the names of others around the office. She didn't want to be known as that new girl who broke men's hearts. Quickly, she pulled the notes out of all the flower arrangements, tossed them in the trash, and sent the flowers off with the onlookers that had come to see what all the fuss was about. Monique took the biggest arrangement of all.

"Now, Cat," she added with a mischievous grin as she exited the office with her embarrassingly large vase of hydrangea and roses, "You can tell him Monique is single."

"I'll do that," Cat laughed.

Though they had helped her make light of the situation at hand, she knew that breaking it off with David would not be easy. It was a classic case of 'it's not you, it's me.' Only, she expected he would not accept it easily. He was used to getting what he wanted. He was stubborn, but Cat was resolute. She would not be getting married in December, and that was final.

CHAPTER TWENTY-THREE

CAT ARRIVED EARLY AT DOS CAMINOS THE NEXT DAY ONLY TO FIND that David was already waiting for her. And, surprise, surprise, he was holding a small clutch of mini-roses. They were an exotic variety, their petals striped in multi-colors. She sighed.

"David," she forced herself to smile, "You really shouldn't have."

"I wanted to," he said.

He leaned in for a kiss. Cat turned her head at the last moment, so it ended with a kiss on the cheek.

"Can't I kiss my future wife?" he asked woundedly.

"David ..." Cat swallowed hard. "You did kiss me, it was on my cheek. Let's grab a table on the patio."

After they were seated and Cat had her prickly pear margarita in hand, she felt ready to broach the subject of their engagement, or lack thereof. Normally, she would not have a drink on her lunch break, but on this day, she made an exception.

"David," Cat began softly. "I–"

"I forgive you." He interrupted, reaching across the table to take her hands. "Let's put all of this behind us. God, it's so good to see you! You look as beautiful as ever."

He reached across the table to brush a stray hair out of her face when she caught his hand mid-air. Cat felt a familiar sense of heat in the pit of her stomach. This awareness coursed through her veins. This sense of who she was and who she was not. She was not the subservient little flower that she'd been forced to play the last few years. She was capable, intelligent, and she'd be damned if some man tried to make her feel otherwise.

"I did not apologize to you," Cat placed his hand gently down on the table.

David's mouth was slightly ajar.

"I asked you to lunch today because I wanted to thank you—"

"Thank me?" he interrupted a second time.

"Please let me finish," Cat paused.

David's body went rigid. He sat back from where he'd been leaning on the table towards Cat. His spine straightened as he pulled himself to his full height, towering over Cat and the table between them. She imagined this is how he must sit in tense client meetings. His eyes became calculating, unyielding.

"Go ahead," he gestured.

"Thank you for giving me time to think over these past couple of months." Cat had rehearsed this in the mirror that morning. "I didn't realize how much I needed the space until I had it. I didn't realize how much of myself I'd been suppressing until I allowed myself to think and feel again. You are a wonderful person. Successful, smart, thoughtful, generous … I am grateful for the time we spent together and that it has led me back to who I truly am and who I want to be. And right now, I want to be single. You deserve to be happy and get married, if that's what you want in life."

Cat opened her purse and pulled the ring out of its secure location where it had been tucked away since its side show in her office that morning. She slid it towards him without another look.

"So, that's it," he said.

"Yes," Cat affirmed with a nod.

Silence.

The waiter approached the table, "Helllllo! I'm Marco! Who wants to hear the specials?!"

He was bouncy and bright and it took him a moment to read the situation. Cat glanced up at him. David crossed his arms, still glaring at the ring. Marco looked between the solemn couple, his eyes fell upon the ring before he audibly gasped.

"I –I –I'll just give you a minute," he whispered and slowly backed away as though a bomb might go off.

Cat watched him retreat before turning her attention back to David. She fought the urge to say something cliché, like, 'we can still be friends.' That would never happen. Why waste words on meaningless promises or reassurances? She waited politely for him to speak.

"Cathleen," David finally spoke. His voice was not sad, but tense, staccato. "I understand you have been doing some soul searching. I will give you more time. Clearly, that is what you need from me as your fiancé."

"David, I don't think you understand—"

He held up his hand, "Let me finish, please. I allowed your little speech."

Cat fought the urge to throw her ice water at him and storm out. She needed to make sure he understood this was over. Completely over. If that required a lengthier conversation than she hoped, then so be it. She nodded.

"We will be getting married on December 15th. You will come around. You are sensible and I know you will see what a tremendous blow this would be to your family. I am committed to making this arrangement work. It is mutually beneficial to both of us. It will all work out."

"David, it is not beneficial to either of us to be married if that's not what I want."

"Cathleen, you are too tied to your feelings. Think about this, please."

"I have thought about it, David." Cat felt her voice rising, "I have been thinking about it for the last ten weeks. It is over between us."

"Your father is offering me the promotion of a lifetime, Cathleen. A lifetime. But that promotion will never happen if we break-up. Think of someone other than yourself for once!"

Cat lost it.

"Are you freaking kidding me?" Cat shouted as she rose from her chair, drawing glances, giggles, and gasps from surrounding tables. At this moment, she could not care less. "I have been thinking of EVERYONE other than myself for the last four years. Which school I'm supposed to attend? Which guy I'm supposed to date? Who I'm supposed to marry? But you know what David, this is my life. Mine! I am done being a bystander while someone else dictates every decision along the way."

"You're embarrassing yourself," David lowered his voice. "Please sit back down. We can figure this out together. We don't need to make any rash decisions today."

"My decision is made."

"Cathleen, I have to run back to work for a meeting." David rose from his chair and tossed a one-hundred-dollar bill on the table. "Enjoy lunch. We will talk soon and work this out."

"I– I–," Cat stammered over her words. She could not believe what was happening. She held up the ring to him. "Take this, David. Please, just take it."

"Put your ring back on, Cathleen." David leaned down to kiss her on top of the head before walking out of the restaurant and leaving her standing by the table, hand held aloft, ring clutched tightly in her fingers, and feeling utterly ridiculous.

Fine, Cat thought. Just great. How was she supposed to return the ring to him now? It wasn't the sort of thing you could just pop in the mail. She would just have to send it by way of her father. Oh, he would just love that. She left her half-drunk margarita on the table with David's money and pocketed the ring. She hoped the conversation tomorrow night with her parents would go better than today's had. At least she would have Lili by her side. She refused to feel defeated. This was a minor setback, but the fact remained that she was not getting married to David. It's not like they could force her down the aisle to marry a man she didn't love. Could they?

"Honey, I'm home!" Cat jokingly called into the foyer as she popped her head into her parents' lavish four-story townhome on the Upper West Side.

Perfectly positioned near Columbus Avenue, they were only a block and a half from Central Park. It was the only home Cat had ever known, but it always felt too polished to ever be hers. 'Don't touch that!' or 'Play upstairs!' were frequent admonishments from her mother when she was growing up. The house had to be just so. This is also probably why they had to have two maids who worked three days a week throughout her childhood to ensure its pristine condition.

"Cat," Lili walked at lightning speed towards her from the sitting room, taking Cat by surprise. "You won't believe who's here."

"What?" Cat was pulled towards the hallway coat closet by her elbow and shoved inside. "Lili, what the hell?!"

"Shhhh," Lili waved for her to be quiet and leaned her ear towards the door as though listening for something.

Cat had not hidden in the hallway closet since she was a kid—well okay, maybe once or twice as a teen when she snuck out to meet Landon. But, seriously, what were they doing hiding in the closet?

"Lili," Cat breathed. "What is going on?"

"David is here," Lili hissed.

"What?!" Cat gasped. "What is he doing here?"

"Apparently, Dad asked him at work if he was coming to the family dinner you arranged tonight and he said yes." Lili leaned her ear against the door, "I don't hear anyone. I think I can sneak you out without having to see him. Then, you can call me to say you have a stomach bug or something. No one will ever know you were here."

Cat sighed. She appreciated her sister's efforts more than she could express with words. She wrapped Lili into a bear hug and planted a kiss on her cheek.

"You're the best," Cat gave her another squeeze.

"I know," Lili shrugged.

"But I'm not going to accept your offer," Cat said resolutely.

"Wha–why?" Lili pulled away. "Cat, this will be a fight of epic proportions. Our parents try to control your every move and your fiancé doesn't get that it's over. You want to walk into that?"

"I do," Cat nodded. "It's time." Looking at her sister's wide eyes she added, "I'm a big girl, Lili. I need to do this."

Both sisters inhaled sharply together and then laughed.

"Let's do this," Lili said.

Cat turned the knob of the coat closet door and peered out. The coast was clear. She could make a break for it and run out the door like Lili had suggested, but she dismissed that fleeting thought immediately. She would face David. She would conquer David. In her version of the story, she was Goliath and David was going to get the ultimate smackdown. *Boom! Take that, shepherd boy. Take your sling shot and shove it right up your—*

"Cathleen!" her mother's voice interrupted her thoughts. "There you are! We thought we had heard your voice. David's been regaling us with some recent office humor on the back patio. Come join us."

"Oh, how … nice," Cat forced a smile and took her mom's arm.

Cat glanced behind her to see Lili slip out of the closet and give her a double thumbs up. 'You got this,' she mouthed. Cat nodded. Deep breath. She could do this.

CHAPTER TWENTY-FOUR

CAT MADE SMALL TALK WITH HER MOTHER AND FATHER ONCE OUT ON the patio, but she took every opportunity to shoot daggers at David with her eyes. *What the hell was he thinking showing up like this? Should she pull him away from the group for a private chat and send him off so she could break the news to her parents without him around? Should she make a public decree to the entire group so that no one could question whether or not she was clear on the fact that she would not ever be marrying David? Should she tell them during dinner? Before? After?* Lili appeared at her side and handed her a cocktail.

"Thanks," Cat smiled knowingly at her sis. "I so needed this right now."

"Yep," Lili nodded and sipped her own drink. Cat was certain she smelled something other than sparkling water in her glass. She raised an eyebrow and Lili winked, "What? I'm *almost* twenty-one."

"Yeah, right." Cat laughed.

Ping, ping, ping. Her father beamed as he rapped on the side of his wine glass. *Oh, dear God. Not a toast.*

"A toast!" he cried out.

"How lovely," her mother clasped her hands together at her chest.

David caught her eye, as though daring her to ruin everyone's night now.

"Let us all raise a glass to the soon-to-be—"

Ping, ping, ping. Cat rapped loudly on her own glass, diverting everyone's eyes from her father.

"I do hate to interrupt, but I feel like I need to say something first," Cat looked at her parents, as their glasses that were half-raised in celebration slowly returned to their sides. Nervous glances were exchanged between them. David, meanwhile, looked stoic and determined, as though nothing she could say would change his plans.

"I am thankful for each and every one of you," Cat began with determination. "In your own ways, you have each contributed to who I am and the decisions I have made."

Her parents let out a collective sigh of relief.

"And that," Cat pressed on, "that has led me to the most important decision I have made thus far in my life."

Darcie sighed happily, looking between Cat and David, unaware that something was amiss.

"I will not be getting married to David." Cat stated emphatically.

Gasps. Her mother's wine glass fell to the brick patio floor, shattering. No one moved to clean it up.

"What?!" her father leapt to his feet with a shout and red wine sloshed out of his stemless wine glass onto his pleated khaki pants.

Cat raised her voice and spoke clearly and resolutely, "David deserves to marry someone who loves him and that is not me. It has taken me four years to realize and remember who I am and what I want from my life. But in the end, it is *my* life. Mine alone. So tonight, I'm toasting to making big decisions and being true to myself. Cheers!"

"Cheers!" Lili chimed in, amidst the commotion.

Her mother had begun muttering unintelligently to herself

and Cat was only able to catch a few words here and there. 'Should've known … that boy … how could she … ruined.' Cat's father had his hand on David's shoulder as though he was a prized possession he refused to be parted with.

Cat clinked glasses with Lili and took a sip. She turned to see her father charging towards her.

"You apologize this instant to your fiancé!" he shouted with his finger a centimeter from her eyeball.

Cat remained calm and took a step back, "He's not my fiancé. And I have nothing to be sorry for."

"You will apologize and you will be marrying him in December as planned!" her father further advanced, pinning her against the wall.

"Dad—I will no-"

"DO IT!" his voice boomed, making her ears ring. She had not seen him this formidable since the day he dragged her and Luke out of the barn in Boone so many years ago.

The silence seemed to drag on forever. Other than her mother's whimpers and her father's heavy breathing, nothing else could be heard. Cat set her jaw. She would not speak. She would not apologize. The engagement was over.

"So, I'm gay!" Lili piped up cheerfully.

"What?! Warren, did you know this?!" Darcie collected herself to respond and rose to her feet.

Cat's father, Warren, lowered the finger that had been aimed at Cat and shook his head slowly as though in a bad nightmare.

"Yep," Lili smiled. "Gay. Gay, gay, gay. I'm as gay as they come."

All of the attention suddenly shifted from Cat. Her parents' wrath was ready to be unleashed. In a moment, three things happened at once. Darcie crumpled to a heap on the patio floor in tears, David and Warren rushed to help her up, attempting to avoid the shattered glass, and Lili grabbed Cat's hand and yelled, "Get out of here!"

Cat didn't need to be told twice. She bolted through the house, grabbed her purse on the way out, and let the front door slam behind her as she skipped down the steps of the brownstone where she may never be welcome again.

Cat didn't walk home. She couldn't. She felt too alive. Too free. She wanted to run down the streets shouting, 'I'M NOT GETTING MARRIED!' Instead, she pointed her feet in the direction of the Hudson River and started walking. Her heart, still pounding from the adrenaline rush, seemed to drum to the beat of the musician on the corner.

She walked until she reached the dog park on 87th and paused to watch two goldendoodles involved in an energetic game of tag. Or perhaps the male dog was just trying to have his way. *Typical*, Cat thought. She cheered inwardly when the female pup turned and nipped him on the nose. *Serves him right.* Cat strolled on until she reached some benches under a tree, perfectly positioned for people watching. She lowered herself with a sigh of relief and turned to watch a few families pass by. Two parents with kids on their shoulders walked hand in hand. A little boy sitting on a park bench nearby was trying to eat his ice cream as quickly as it was melting in the late June heat, which was proving to be an impossible task.

Cat closed her eyes and let the warm evening sun hit her face. The sun was starting to set and the colors of the sky were fading into each other. Cat couldn't remember the last time she felt so at ease. She pushed herself off the bench and continued walking towards the river.

Walking slowly, leisurely, as though half dreaming, half floating, she let her hands glide along the railing. The sound of the water made her close her eyes briefly while she strolled. Cat was surprised when she stopped for a moment to feel the breeze on her face and found herself standing in the very same spot where she had tossed her worn wire ring into the river the previous October. She had been completely unaware that she was walking to this very spot. Or was she? Was she led by some internal compass, some strange innate pull that directed her steps back to this place? She leaned against the barrier and looked out at the water. What had she been thinking? Well, she knew what she was thinking. She had hoped that by flinging a small copper ring off of this island, the thoughts of Luke would vacate her heart as well. That hadn't happened. It hadn't allowed her to find love and it hadn't led to happy endings with David. *But it did lead you here,* a little voice reminded her. She smiled. It had led her someplace unexpected. Not a happy ending, no, perhaps those were best saved for fairy tales. But a happy new beginning. And that was even better.

A glimmer on the rocks caught her eye as she started to turn away. Cat spun back around and leaned closer. She couldn't quite tell what it was. There was a tangled mass of trash, a plastic bottle, some soggy cardboard, but there was something else. A tiny thing catching the light of the late evening sun and reflecting it back to her. Cat leaned over the barrier trying to ascertain exactly what it was that was drawing her in, completely out of reach, and a good fifteen feet below.

It wasn't possible. It couldn't be the ring. Her ring. But she couldn't walk away. She paced back and forth along the river against the railing that separated the walkway from the water below. She thought of leaving to go buy a fishing rod or something that would help her reach whatever it was that was taunting her. But then again, where would she buy a fishing rod? And if she managed to go find one, it would be dark by the time she returned. Not to mention the fact that she didn't even know how to use a fishing rod, so trying to aim it to catch whatever was down there was pointless.

She heaved a sigh and started to leave. *It's just a bunch of trash, Cat.* She told herself. *There's absolutely nothing of value down there. Certainly nothing worthy of climbing the fence and scaling the slippery rocks that led down to the dark waters of the Hudson River. Oily, grimy, infested waters. Lord knows what is down there.*

Not worth it.

Just keep walking.

But ... what if?

It was that 'what if' that made her turn around just as she was about to cross back over Riverside Drive. It was the 'what if' that caused her to pick up her pace before she changed her mind. Her footsteps quickened along with her heart rate. These are the moments when decisions are made, be they rash or reasonable. She secured her crossbody bag and firmly gripped the railing. She glanced over her shoulder. No one in sight. Thank goodness. Anyone who saw her would surely think she was suicidal.

She quickly lifted herself and flung her right leg over, then her left. She moved a step at a time along the back side of the railing until she was directly above the refuse. The rocks leading down to the water were steep, nearly vertical in their descent to the murky waters below. She couldn't walk down. But, perhaps, she could use them as a ladder. They were jagged in places and not made for climbing. The rocks were covered in spots by wire fencing to hold them in place. It was a dangerous embankment, a retainer of sorts for the park above, and Cat knew she should not be climbing down it.

But she was drawn to—whatever it was. Just a few more feet down. Almost there. She reached the spot and steadied herself so she could dig through the litter. A soggy Papa John's pizza box, a beer bottle, some bits of wet toilet paper. *Bleh. Disgusting.* Cat hoped her tetanus shot was up to date. She would bathe in Clorox when she returned home.

She knew she had seen something. A small shiny bit that had caught her eye and held her heart with the hope that it might just be her ring. She picked through a few more items before she saw it. A small, cheap gold hoop earring. She sighed. She swallowed her disappointment and shook her head. Did she really expect to find her ring nine months after throwing it over the railing? The thought made her laugh. But she was glad she tried … otherwise curiosity would have tortured her. No more wondering, Cat told herself. She would live with no regrets.

She made her move to climb up. This proved more challenging than climbing down had been. Night had fallen while she had examined the trash of the Hudson and now, she felt some small amount of anxiety creeping in. One foot at a time she told herself.

Cat reached upwards with her right hand and moved her foot to another rock. Just as she began to pull herself up, she felt the rock shift ever so slightly, sending the foot she had just shifted her weight to downwards, and scraping her entire right leg against the rocks and rugged wires.

"Ahhh!" she shrieked as she grappled for something to hold onto.

She slid a good ten feet down the embankment before catching herself, mere inches above the water. She leaned her cheek against the cool rocks until her breath steadied. Her heart felt as though it had dropped to her stomach and one glance at the blood trickling down her leg made her nauseous. *Stupid, stupid, stupid.* She closed her eyes to hold back the tears and reminded herself of all the reasons she had to be grateful in this moment. This practice of gratitude grounded her and steadied her racing pulse. Cat opened her eyes and glanced upwards. Now, a good twenty-five feet separated her from the railing and the safety of the park. She would take it slower. She would be fine.

Reaching to the rock above her head, she poised herself to climb but her fingers landed on something small. Something circular. Her breath caught. She pulled it down and nearly fell backwards in surprise. She pulled herself quickly in towards the rocks to steady herself. Tears came quickly to her eyes and felt hot on her cheeks. Though no longer shiny and copper hued, it was unmistakably her ring. The ring Luke had so carefully fashioned from wire some four and a half years ago. She bit her lip and slipped it onto the well-acquainted ring finger of her left hand. Tears flowed freely now as she moved with careful yet sure steps to the railing above.

Disbelief and gratitude. Cat hardly noticed the scrapes along her left leg, as she set out to walk home, until a passerby pointed them out.

"Ma'am, are you okay?" Asked a gentleman who was walking his dog through the park and approached her with distress in his eyes. He gestured to the blood running down her shin.

"Huh? Oh, yes! I'm fine. Really! Thank you," Cat smiled warmly at him while gingerly touching her newfound treasure.

To avoid any additional stares or encounters she hailed a cab on Riverside Drive. All the while, her mind was racing. I'm alive. I'm hurt but I'm oh-so-happy. Her ring was proof that things can endure. Lost things can be found. Old things can feel new. It is never too late to claim the life you were meant to live.

Cat thanked the cab driver and hopped out, as he slowed to a stop in front of her Upper East Side apartment building. The bleeding on her leg had stopped and the pain had dulled. She probably should check into that tetanus shot tomorrow, but tonight she felt whole.

You never know what you will find on the banks of the Hudson: trash, a body part (unlikely … but you never know), or possibly, just maybe, everything you ever hoped for.

CHAPTER TWENTY-FIVE

IN THE DAYS THAT FOLLOWED CAT'S FATEFUL EVENING IN HER PARENT'S home, she became certain of several things. One, she felt like herself again. Free and fiery and finally in tune with who she truly was. Two, her parents continued to make wedding plans as though nothing had changed. No matter how many phone conversations Cat had with her mother, she remained inexplicably convinced that Cat would change her mind. Three, David, though more subtle in his attempts to win her back, was not deterred. He had accepted his promotion from her father and the two of them seemed bent on negotiating with Cat. She began ignoring calls from both her father and from David. Reasonable discussions had not phased their attempts. It reminded Cat of the movie that Luke had made her watch in North Carolina, *The Godfather*. 'I'll make him an offer he can't refuse.' But Cat could refuse and she did so, repeatedly. Perhaps it would take her parents losing all of the money they'd deposited towards this wedding to get the message. That would likely be the case with her father. Money talks. And when you lose it, it shouts.

Two weeks had passed since the night she had lost her fiancé and found her ring. Lili had taken on the brunt of their parent's wrath. With Cat, they came bearing gifts, soft words, and promises of what a beautiful life she and David would have together. Cat would not negotiate and their treatment of Lili made her all the more resolute. Lili had called her panicked the day after the show-down; through lots of shouting and background noise, Cat had made out the gist of the message. Her sister's belongings were being taken out of the townhouse by the cleaning ladies and placed on the sidewalk. Just like that, Lili had become a pariah. Cat became the one her sister could turn to, just as Lili had always been there for her for so many years.

So, she did the only thing that seemed right. She rented a U-Haul truck that very morning and drove it, with extreme caution, through the one-way streets of Manhattan. This ensured many honking horns, but whatever, she hadn't hit any cars or pedestrians. So, she considered it a victory, even if it had taken her fifty-two minutes to make the fifteen-minute drive. Lili stood waiting on the sidewalk, lattes in hand, and an impossibly wide grin.

"This is not how I imagined to find you," Cat laughed as she turned on the flashers and hopped out of the truck.

"Yeah, well," Lili shrugged. "After the initial shock of being permanently exiled, I realized, it's going to be alright."

"Absolutely," Cat smiled and cast a glance to the 3rd floor window of her parent's bedroom. The curtain that was being held slightly open quickly closed. Cat thought she caught a glimpse of her mother's face.

"So, I guess you won't be staying home this summer," Cat lifted a garbage bag that appeared to be filled with Lili's stuffed animal collection, "Come live with me?"

"I thought you'd never ask," Lili winked and they clicked their iced lattes together in celebration. "It will only be until fall semester. Then, I'll be out of your way."

"You know you can stay as long as you need to. Now … let's load up this shit."

Cat tossed the bag containing Mr. Snuffles over her head and into the rear of the U-Haul, before taking a long refreshing sip of her latte.

They were going to be okay.

As July drew to a close, their parents finally reached out to Lili, offering to pay for some ridiculous conversion therapy in Texas. They told her that if she relented and agreed to go, then the townhouse would go to her in their will. Lili hung up on them during that phone call.

Cat was determined that she and Lili would, as they had done in their childhood, create a safe place away from the people that had "raised" them. Due to a slew of nannies and babysitters, Cat had always felt strangely separated from the people she called her parents. But now, with Lili exiled, Cat felt more resolute than ever to set her own course. Not only for herself, but as an example for her sister. They would not be controlled, condemned, and be held captive by expectations. No more of that.

"Please, please come with me!" Lili bounced into the room, taking Cat from her thoughts and making her jump as she stirred the macaroni noodles, sloshing boiling water out of the pot.

"Again, Lili," Cat sighed with a mixture of affection and annoyance. "I love you. But I can NOT go clubbing every Thursday. I have to work tomorrow."

While Cat had thoroughly enjoyed having Lili stay with her, she didn't party like a college student anymore. She had no desire to stay up too late and wake up with a splitting headache the next day.

Cat glanced up at Lili to see her making her all too endearing pouty face.

"It's not working," Cat giggled.

"You know you want to come," Lili leaned her head on Cat's shoulder and wrapped her arms around her big sister, even though Cat was now shorter than Lili by several inches.

"Nope, I'm not going out tonight." Cat patted her head awkwardly while she stirred the noodles. "And neither should you."

Cat already felt closer to Lili than she had since high school. Back then, Cat felt obligated to rescue her little sister from any uncertain situation that might arise. But now, together in Cat's little apartment, it felt like they were rescuing each other. They would often take their cocktails up to the rooftop after Cat got home from work, or go on a run together along the East River through Carl Schurz Park. They called it sister-therapy. Cat was more grateful than ever that they could lean on each other. The realization that Lili would be moving into her dorm downtown at the end of the month left her with a mixture of emotions. Sadness at seeing her go. Relief of having her space to herself again. A twinge of guilt that she was the reason Lili had decided to come out to their parents so abruptly. Joy, knowing Lili had been ready to do so. How are humans capable of feeling so many things at once? But Cat knew she'd be seeing her often. Family dinners once a week they decided; and now, those would include just the two of them. Much more pleasant.

"We won't stay late," Lili continued to appeal.

"You said that last week and I had to peel you away from some Penelope Cruz look-alike at 2am. No way."

"She was gorgeous," Lili sighed as she slumped onto a bar stool. "I reeeeaaaallly don't want to go alone."

"Then, don't go," Cat lifted a noodle out of the pot to check if it was done. Perfectly al dente. She moved to the sink to strain the noodles. "Stay and have my grown-up mac and greens."

"Meh … mac and cheese doesn't sound as appetizing as Penelope."

Cat rolled her eyes as she scraped in the cheeses she had carefully shredded from the cutting board into the saucepan. "This is not just any mac and cheese. This is the mac and greens recipe from Red Rooster in Harlem. It is divine and you must try it."

She stirred in the braised bok choy and collard greens before scooping a sample for her sister onto a salad plate.

"Here, blow," Cat passed it over the counter with a fork. "It's hot."

"I know I should be content to stay here and study for my test in Civil Procedures," Lili lifted a bite to her lips and blew on it. "But I just need to take my mind off of mom and her constant texts. Now she's sending me articles on former lesbians, or women who thought they were lesbians and now are happily married to men since completing their conversion therapy."

"And I supposed they have 2.4 precious children and live in an exquisitely restored 1940's bungalow on Elm Street," said Cat.

"Likely," Lili winked as she put her fork into her mouth. "Oh. My. God."

"I know," Cat stated.

"This is legit, the best thing I've ever tasted," Lili spoke while forking another bite into her mouth.

"More?" Cat asked.

"Um. Yes!" Lili said.

"It's the braised collards and bok choy." Cat spoke with an air of certainty as she served her sister a heaping pile of the mac and greens onto her plate, "They pair perfectly with the cheddar-gruyère-parmesan mix. It is heaven on a plate."

Lili dug in. "I'm impressed!"

"Rachel and I went to that cooking class Monday night. You

know the one I tried to get you to come to, but you were too busy going to that club downtown. What was it? Henrietta Hudson?"

"It was Be Cute and it's in Brooklyn," Lili sighed in appreciation. "This is so good. Seriously, it might be better than sex."

Cat raised an eyebrow and smirked at her sister, "I wouldn't know, remember?"

"Oh Cat," Lili stammered. "I didn't mean. Well, it's actually not as good as sex. Sex is better."

"You're not helping, Lili." Cat turned and helped herself to a bowl full of her gooey, but not-as-good-as-sex, mac and cheese.

"Someday, you are going to find someone you want to be with like that," Lili eyed her big sister closely. "It will be worth the wait, Cat. I promise."

"You know," Cat turned suddenly. "Sometimes, I wish I hadn't waited this long. Now I've built sex up in my mind into something so perfect that it's likely unattainable. What if I've screwed myself over?"

"So, what are you saying? You should just go have sex with any guy for the heck of it so you won't have to worry about waiting for that perfect person?"

"No, of course not." Cat leaned back against the counter. "I don't know. Maybe?"

"Didn't Rachel want to set you up with someone?"

"I told her no. Not yet, anyways." Cat shook her head in disbelief, "Technically, mom is still planning my wedding and Dad is taking David golfing at Southampton Golf Club this weekend. They have completely ignored the fact that this wedding will not be happening."

"Let Rachel set you up, Cat. It could be fun!"

"Even though my ex-fiancé insists we're still engaged?" Cat asked.

"Especially since your ex-fiancé thinks you are still engaged," said Lili.

CHAPTER TWENTY-SIX

CAT PACED THE FLOOR OF HER APARTMENT. SHE WAS WEARING HER sister's way-above-the-knee Proenza Schouler sequined shift and had reluctantly agreed to letting Rachel do her hair and make-up. She couldn't decide if she looked impossibly chic or like she should be standing on a street corner.

"You look positively gamine," Rachel cooed as she straightened Cat's hair and pulled it back into a low pony at the nape of her neck.

"Very Audrey Hepburn," Lili agreed, nodding in approval. "But with sequins."

In the end, Cat had conceded that her ensemble did give off distinct 1960's Parisian vibes, but she would've been more comfortable in something decisively simpler. No matter, this date was meant to be something flirty and fun. It was a means to show David, once and for all, that she was not getting married. Letting him know that she was dating again would certainly end their engagement beyond question.

Cat's intercom buzzed.

"He's here!" Rachel shrieked.

"Buzz him in so I can meet him too," Lili called from the couch.

"Guys," Cat turned to her audience, "this is not really a date. It's an 'I'm not engaged anymore' announcement. I can take a few pics on the date, post them on Facebook, and voila! Once David, mom, and dad see it, that will be it. Done."

"Okay, but can you buzz him in?!" Rachel exclaimed.

Cat pursed her lips and hit the buzzer.

"You'll love him, Lili. He's dreamy. You're gonna wish I'd set *you* up with him," Rachel bounded over to join Lili on the couch.

"Hmmm … does he look like Winona Ryder circa 1996?"

"Uhh … no."

"Then he's not my type," Lili winked.

Rachel paused; her head tilted to the side for a moment. Then, a look of recognition passed over her face as she glanced between Lili and Cat.

"Oh!" she nodded. "Oh. Gotcha. That's cool."

Lili laughed and patted Rachel on the shoulder as she hopped off the couch, "I'm sure I'll think he's dreamy for Cat, though."

A knock at the door sent all the girls scurrying.

"He's here," Rachel leapt up.

"Where's my purse?" Cat spun around.

"Should I open the door?" Lili asked as Cat sprinted past her, back to her bedroom.

Lili turned and opened the door as Rachel approached, her smile wide. Apparently, Rachel knew Jack from work but found him too intellectual for her taste. She assured Cat they'd have an enjoyable evening. Plus, he was an art lover.

As the door opened, Rachel's face filled with confusion while Lili's expressed a look of shock. Cat re-entered the room, adjusting her cross-body bag.

"David!" she nearly shouted, before lowering her voice, "What are you doing here?"

"Why did my buddy from college just message me that he thought he'd been set up on a date with my fiancé?" David's fists were clenched at his sides and his jaw was set as he brushed past Lili and stormed into the apartment.

"Who's your friend from college?" Cat asked.

"Jack. Jack Wallace." David surveyed the room, shooting daggers at Lili and Rachel. "He said he was set up by someone at work and didn't realize it was my fiancé until he saw your name and photo on my Facebook page. It took him a minute to put it together, but when he did, he called me … and I confirmed."

"We are not engaged anymore, Dav-"

"You are my fiancé, damnit!" he screamed.

"I WAS your fiancé," Cat raised her voice to match his. "Get out of my apartment!"

"This isn't funny anymore, Cathleen. Your parents are spending a fortune on this wedding." David barked.

"This is a break up, David. It's not supposed to be funny," Cat retorted. "Now, get the hell out."

David stood immobile. His eyes darting from Cat to Lili to Rachel and back to Cat, hair perfectly coiffed, make-up done. She looked dazzling. It only seemed to further infuriate him.

"This. This is how you plan to cheat on me?" He stepped towards her.

It was then that Cat could smell the scotch on his breath. He reeked of alcohol and jealousy. Cat had seen enough angry men in her lifetime to know danger. She swallowed hard and stepped back.

Working to keep her voice calm and even, she responded slowly, "David, I'm sorry you're having a hard time accepting this. But our relationship is over. I'm not cheating on you. I'm moving on … and you should, too."

Out of the corner of her eye, Cat could see Lili grab Rachel's hand. The glance they shared acknowledged the gravity of this situation. They needed to get this man out of the apartment and quickly, before things could escalate any further.

"David," Lili smiled sweetly, "let's go for a walk."

"I don't want to go on a fucking walk, dyke," he snapped in Lili's direction.

"Whoa," Cat held up her hands, "You're angry with me, David. Not Lili. That language is uncalled for. Please leave."

"I'm not ready to go," he stumbled to the bar stool and sat down at the counter. An open bottle of red wine and Rachel's half empty tumbler sat on the table. He took a swig and refilled it.

"That's fine," Rachel shrugged. "I didn't really want anymore."

"Lettme guess" he slurred. "Rachel?"

Cat cleared her throat, "David, I'm asking you to leave. If you choose not to, then I'm calling the police."

David tipped the glass back and drank until it was empty. He tipped the bottle to pour himself another glass. This time it only filled half way.

Cat hated that it had to come to this. Getting her father's top employee arrested was not something she wanted to discuss with him tomorrow. But perhaps that would be what it would take to end this once and for all. A restraining order. It's hard to marry someone if you can't come within one-hundred yards of them.

"Lili, call 911 for me," Cat spoke calmly, "Rachel, my super, Demetri, is on the first floor. Can you please go down and see if he's available? Let him know we have an unwanted guest in our apartment."

Rachel gave an imperceivable nod before dashing out the door. Lili was already on her phone. Cat watched as David finished the rest of the wine in one long, slow swallow. He picked up the bottle to pour more and, finding it empty, he glanced at Cat before smashing it on the floor.

Lili screamed and Cat jumped back as shards of glass scattered in all directions.

"Get. Out," she whispered. "Now."

David slowly rose from the bar stool. He was unsteady as he approached her. Cat wasn't sure whether or not to run or stand her ground. He stumbled forward a few steps and Cat held up her hands in case he was about to fall into her, but he caught himself and straightened up.

"Your father will be very unhappy to hear about this." he slurred.

Cat shrugged, "I do not live to please my father. Not anymore."

David rolled his eyes before bumping into her shoulder and heading out the door. Lili had just begun speaking to the 911 operator when he slammed the door shut.

Cat sank to the floor, trembling.

"Do—do we still want the police to come?" Lili dropped down to her sister. "You could file a report."

Cat nodded. Tears filled her eyes. This was proving to be harder than she thought it would be. Everything always is.

CHAPTER TWENTY-SEVEN

"YOU FILED CHARGES AGAINST YOUR FIANCÉ?!" HER MOTHER'S VOICE was shrill in the receiver of her cell phone. "How could you do that to David?"

"How could she do that to me?!" her father yelled.

Cat heard her father's voice echoing in the background and rolled her eyes. Of course, everything was always about him.

"Mom," Cat began evenly, "he stormed into my apartment and threw a wine bottle on the floor. He refused to leave when asked. Lili, Rachel, and myself all felt threatened." Cat paused to steady her voice. "What else could I do?"

"Not that!"

"Alright, well, clearly we cannot have this discussion right now," Cat sighed. "I need to go. I'm heading into a meeting with a client."

"Cathleen, you need to apologize to David. He's heartbroken over the way he's been treated."

"She needs to apologize to me!" Cat heard her father's voice followed by the sound of a flushing toilet. She rolled her eyes.

"Alright, we'll talk later," Cat said quickly. Done. She was so done. "I do hope you've cancelled all the wedding arrangements, Mom. I'd hate for you to lose money over this."

And with that she ended the call, straightened her shoulders, and pushed open the double doors to the conference room.

Monique was already making introductions when Cat slipped into the room. Cat inwardly chided herself for not arriving earlier. Even though technically the meeting didn't begin for two more minutes, on time was as good as late in Cat's mind.

"Cat," Monique gestured to the chair beside her. "Gentlemen, allow me to introduce my new assistant, Cat Rhodes. Cat, this is Marc Whitson and Jonathan Plum. They own multiple galleries in Chelsea, Soho, and two in Brooklyn. Is that right?"

"We actually just opened a third in Greenpoint," the taller of the two nodded before stepping forward to take Cat's hand. "I'm Marc. Nice to meet you, Cat."

"Pleasure to meet you, Cat," chimed Jonathan with a smile.

"Pleased to meet you both," Cat beamed. She observed, as they took their seats around the table, that both men were incredibly well dressed. Both were older than herself, but were quite young to own and invest in their own art galleries. She guessed they were in their mid-thirties by the hints of silver that appeared around Jonathan's temples.

"Cat has been invaluable in assisting me with creating new artist exhibitions the last two months." Monique winked at her. "Which is why I'm specifically assigning her to examine the works at your galleries to create our new collection of up and coming artists."

"Cat, we'd love to organize a roundtable discussion with, maybe, a dozen or so of our best," Marc began.

"And most innovative," Jonathan added.

"And most innovative artists at our galleries." Marc concluded.

"I think a round table discussion would be perfect." Cat nodded as she made notes on her MacBook. "I learn so much more about the pieces themselves when I have a chance to sit down with the artists face to face. There's only so much I can discern on my own by examining the art itself."

"We actually have a new exhibit opening at our place down in

Chelsea tomorrow night," Jonathan piped up. "You should come."

"Three new artists will be debuting their collections," Marc nodded, passing the gallery's business card across the table. "We have a great new artist from Harlem doing ceramics."

"You'll love her. And the other two are equally remarkable." Jonathan said.

"Thank you," Cat accepted the card. "I have no plans tomorrow evening, so I'll be there!"

The meeting ended successfully with Cat making a detailed plan of which galleries she would be visiting and when. The roundtable discussion would take place in mid to late August and include at least a dozen new artists. Cat felt certain she could put together an exquisite exhibit of up and coming artists for MOMA by January. And with Daniel working on an integrated technology and interactive social media component, it was sure to be a success. Cat left the meeting feeling energized by her new project and temporarily free of concerns regarding David and weddings that would not be taking place.

CHAPTER TWENTY-EIGHT

DATING GABI HAD BECOME EASIER THAN LUKE HAD IMAGINED. HE found her fun, charming, and devoted to her family. They had gone running in the Park on Sunday, following their outing to the club, and she had invited him to Mass at her church the following week. It was hard to imagine her as a good church girl after he'd seen her dance, however. Gabi had even come down to help him organize for the exhibit earlier that week. She kept him engaged in conversation, was genuinely interested in his art, and checked all the boxes on the normal person evaluation. Though she had a tendency to ignore him when they went out with a group, she was attentive to him one on one. Luke reminded himself that no one would be perfect. Gabi had listened to him go on and on for over an hour at dinner the night before about the progress at the gallery and the multiple delays they'd faced. Luke was thrilled the opening was finally happening. Tonight would be the VIP preview for special guests and the press. All this hard work, the long hours, the cumulative efforts from years of painting in a barn—it would finally be on display for the world to see. Or at least, for New York City.

Gabi would be on his arm when he strolled the red carpet. Luke's mind drifted back to Gabi—her smile, her glowing skin. She was gorgeous, witty, and fun. He chided himself for the faults he continued to find and reminded himself how lucky he was to have found her. His mind had been wandering to Gabi more frequently in the last few weeks. He found himself thinking of her at random times throughout the day. *Like, I shouldn't eat that much garlic, my breath will be heinous and I have a date with Gabi tonight. Or I wonder what Gabi would think of the lighting for this room.* And then, of course, there was the apparent interest from Nicolas and Paulo that this match be successful for him. It was nice to have friends who cared, but he didn't want them caring too much. Rachel had cared too much and things had gone horribly. Speaking of Rachel, he really needed to reach out to her. He had been feeling like a dick for the way he'd behaved back in March. Five months had passed, it was past time to apologize. Besides, at least now he could bring some good news to the conversations regarding his dating life.

He imagined it so easily, 'See Rach, you didn't need to be worried about me after all.'

'You're right, Luke. Gabi's amazing! You didn't need my help after all. I'm sorry,' Rachel would respond.

Luke rolled over to look at the time. 6am. Early. Normally, he would try to get in another hour or two of sleep on the weekend, but he was wide awake and today was the day his exhibit was finally set to open. He might as well get in an early workout before he dropped by the gallery to go over the checklist for the evening's festivities once more with Nicolas. This weekend, with the opening, Luke would practically be living at the gallery. He had promised Nicolas that he would relax a bit this morning and rest up for the exciting evening ahead.

He rolled himself out of bed and jumped into the shower before jumping back out with a yelp. No hot water. This was the third time in the last month. Though he had grown fond of his West

Village neighborhood, he did not care for the old building antics that came with it—rusty pipes, unreliable electrics, and faulty plumbing. Someday, maybe, he would spring for a spacious loft apartment in Soho. He imagined one of those airy, renovated buildings where he could live and paint in the same space.

Fighting discomfort, he forced himself to take a two minute cold shower to wake up, before heading out the door for coffee. Gabi would be up by now he thought, glancing at his watch. He smiled to himself. She was taking all three of her charges to the 92nd Street Y for swim lessons this morning, and heading to the children's museum in the afternoon, before joining him at the gallery this evening.

He remembered his decision to reach out to Rachel and sighed. It was time to reach out. It was early. Perhaps a blessing in disguise. It was unlikely that she would be awake, meaning that he could get off the hook by apologizing to her voicemail.

Luke quickly looked up her number and hit the call button before he could change his mind. One ring. Two.

"Luuuuukkeee!!" her voice sounded chipper for 6:30am on a Saturday.

"Rachel, I didn't-," Luke stammered, "I mean, hey! It's been a while."

"It's good to hear from you."

"What are you doing up so early?"

"Were you hoping to get my voicemail, Luke Presnell?"

"I'm not gonna lie," Luke shook his head. "That was secretly my hope. I—I'm not good at apologizing, Rach."

"I know. It takes a little practice," she said. He could practically hear Rachel smirking through the receiver. "You go right ahead. I'll let you know how you do."

Luke was grateful for Rachel and her transparency. Her buoyant personality lightened him considerably and made apologizing an easy afterthought.

"Rachel, I was wrong to kick you out of my apartment back in April," he started.

"March," she interjected.

"Right," he continued. "I'm sorry I behaved so badly to my oldest friend."

"I'll give that an 8 out of 10," Rachel chirped. "And, I forgive you."

"I wouldn't blame you if you didn't," Luke teased.

"Truly, Luke." Rachel sighed. "I should be the one saying sorry. I was so determined to direct your love life, I really didn't think about the repercussions for you or anyone else."

"All is forgiven." Luke said decisively. "Meet me for coffee?"

"Love to!" she exclaimed.

"I can hop on a train and head your way or we can meet downtown?" he offered.

"Come up here. I want to take you to Agate and Valentina for brunch. Oh, but they won't open till 10am," she said.

"No worries," Luke glanced at his watch, as he crossed 8th Avenue. "I need to run by the gallery anyway. I'll go by there and then meet you for brunch at 10. This will be the second time I've gone out for 'brunch.' I hear it's a big thing here."

"Oh, Luke! Only the second time? You poor, deprived soul," Rachel exclaimed.

"Haha." he joked.

"We will have to make a standing brunch date on Saturdays from here on out!" She added, "See you in a bit!"

Luke felt relief as he ended the call and strolled towards the gallery. Rachel was a part of his past as much as his own family in many ways. He should have known he could never write her off completely; no matter how pissed he had been, and, he wasn't anymore. Apologizing had never been easy for him. Perhaps that was a large part of why he had never sought out Cat. He would have to start with an apology. But practicing with Rachel had been telling. It wasn't as difficult as he'd expected, and he felt lighter. Forgiveness felt like unlocking a door and realizing that he had been the prisoner all along. What would it feel like to seek out Cat? If only to apologize … expecting nothing in return? Surely, it would be even more liberating than this. But, he was seeing Gabi now. He had moved on, hadn't he? And if he'd moved on, then would an apology be necessary at this point?

Questions surfaced and swirled in his mind as he approached the gallery, like a sunken treasure that had been stirred up by the tide and resurfaced after many years. Or a corpse. Who could tell?

That's what my past brings me. This is what I get. Peace in making amends but the knowledge that I've not really made amends until I find Cat.

Do I really want to find Cat? Luke left that question un-answered.

CHAPTER TWENTY-NINE

RACHEL WAS AS EXUBERANT AS EVER DURING THEIR BRUNCH DATE
on the Upper East Side. She insisted that he order a Bloody Mary
for the "full brunch experience" and educated him on the "best"
brunch spots.

Luke had arrived a few minutes early and snagged a table by the
window where he resigned himself to people watching while he
waited on Rachel. Sometimes, he felt like a fish out of water in
New York City, and other times, like in the studio, he felt content.
He glanced at the couple that had just entered, who were both
wearing matching Burberry polos and loafers. He fought the urge
to laugh. A small pomeranian popped its head out of the woman's
quilted leather tote bag and he couldn't resist. From trying to hold
his laughter in, it came out in a loud blast—half snort, half shout.
The couple turned their heads sharply towards him and he tried to
play it off as coughing. Thankfully, Rachel had arrived at that very
moment and rescued him from further embarrassment.

"So," Rachel interrupted his thoughts. "New York. You've been
here, what, like six-ish months now?"

"It was seven last week."

"What do you think?"

"There's no better place to get my art career started," Luke
took a swig of his Bloody Mary, and while lifting the toothpick,
he slid the blue cheese stuffed olive into his mouth. "And there's
no denying the night life is better than Boone."

"Here, here" Rachel agreed, raising her own glass. "But …"

"I didn't say but," he said.

"No," Rachel sat her glass down. "But I saw it in your eyes."

"Nothing gets past you," Luke laughed. "But—I miss the mountains. The space. The privacy. I miss wearing my Carhartt overalls and driving my pickup truck on curvy roads. Hell, I even miss the tourists that drive 15 miles per hour on the Parkway!"

Rachel laughed. "I do not miss that part in the least. The mountains though—those I miss. I think they're a part of you, you know? There are some places that sink into you, you can't shake them off if you try. The mountains are like that."

"They are," Luke nodded. "What about you? New York seems to suit you just fine."

"I think I was born a New Yorker, Luke. I just didn't know it," Rachel said.

"Not the least bit surprised," he said.

"Will you stay here after your internship? How much longer is it?" she asked.

"Five more months. And, I don't know. My lease ends in December, so I have some time before I have to decide whether or not to renew. In my mind, I keep thinking, man, wouldn't it be awesome if I gained enough of a following while here in New York that I could create art from anywhere?" he wondered.

"You could work wherever you feel inspired," she said.

"Exactly," stated Luke.

"Then that's what I'm praying for you, Luke." Rachel reached out and gave him a sisterly squeeze of his hand. "Clarity, inspiration, and peace in knowing exactly where you should be."

"Thanks, Rach," he said.

"I may enjoy my fair share of Bloody Marys now and then … but I still pray," she winked at him.

"Always the preacher's daughter," he teased.

"And all God's people said—" she started.

"Amen!" they said loudly in unison, before doubling in laughter. It was almost like old times, Luke thought with contentment.

Luke and Rachel parted ways on Madison Avenue and 76th Street where she had seen a sale sign in the window of Christian Louboutin. She just had to go see if her employee discount was still active from her internship the year before.

Luke crossed the road and continued walking. He glanced at his watch. Nearly noon and nowhere to go just yet. He supposed he could head back downtown to the gallery, but there was nothing left to do. He would just be waiting around to get dressed for the party and that didn't begin until much later. Gabi was working today for the family she nannied for. She had invited him to meet them at the Manhattan Children's Museum. As much as he enjoyed kids, the Grossology exhibit did not pique his interest. He continued his leisurely stroll until he had arrived at the Metropolitan Museum of Art.

This was not a museum he frequented. In fact, he had not visited it since he had visited the city last fall to interview for his internship. The MOMA was more his speed. But he had nowhere to be that afternoon and losing himself in the works of the masters seemed like the perfect way for a burgeoning artist to kill some time and calm his nerves.

Luke stepped off the curb to cross 5th Avenue just as the light changed. A polished young businessman was walking briskly towards him from the other side. He was halfway across the road when Luke looked up, caught his eye, and then he vanished. Luke cried out in shock. After experiencing a blur in his vision, he shook his head. A delivery truck had slammed into the man. One moment he was there and then—gone. The man hit the pavement and the truck continued halfway towards the next block before it screeched to a stop. The driver got out and ran towards the park, while pedestrians surrounding him began to scream.

Everything seemed to be happening all at once—a child on the sidewalk was crying, traffic came to a halt on all sides of the street, a woman was on her cell phone beside him dialing 9-1-1, while Luke rushed to the center of the road to pull the man to safety. He was barely conscious and Luke realized the truck must have only brushed him, hitting him with the sideview mirror, because his face was bloodied and, at least, two teeth appeared to be missing. Poor guy. His right arm seemed to be dangling unnaturally.

"Hey! Hey—you're gonna be okay." Luke tried to keep his voice calm. "The ambulance is on the way. You're going to be okay. Here. Sit on the curb."

"I need—lie down." the man sputtered, another tooth dropped out of his mouth and he spit it toward the pavement.

"Don't let him fall asleep," the woman who called 9-1-1 appeared at his side. "The operator is saying to keep him awake. Ask him questions."

"Sure, sure," Luke nodded, keeping his hand on the man's shoulder. He turned to the man, whose eyes were starting to close. "Wake up! Don't go to sleep … umm, I'm Luke. What's your name, man?"

"I'm—uh—I'm—," he blinked his eyes rapidly. "I—I—where are my teeth?" He was searching his mouth with his tongue and finding the missing spaces his teeth used to occupy.

"Um—okay," Luke wasn't sure what to do with this revelation. "It's gonna be okay. Here."

He passed him a wad of napkins that a street vendor had just given him, "Press these against that cut on your head. It will help stop the bleeding," Luke said.

The man continued to run his tongue across his lips and missing teeth. Blood dripped down his chin, "My teeth! Where are my teeth? What happened? Where am I?"

Luke realized that the guy was beginning to panic and the police had yet to arrive.

"The ambulance is on the way," Luke forced his voice to stay even. "I promise they will take care of you."

The sirens rose in the background and Luke breathed a sigh of relief.

"Thank you, Lord," Luke whispered under his breath.

The man's eyelids were starting to droop now and Luke turned to the woman who was on the phone with 9-1-1. She shrugged her shoulders in uncertainty.

"How old are you? What's your name?" Luke pressed him, in an effort to keep him awake.

The gentleman closed his eyes and moaned, leaning heavily into the hand Luke still had planted on his shoulder.

"I can't keep him awake," Luke mouthed to her. "He's not answering questions."

"It's okay." She nodded towards the police officers and ambulance arriving on the scene.

Luke stood slowly, only removing his hand when a female EMT took his place. Before he knew it, the stretcher was being lifted into the ambulance and taking the man to Lenox Hill Hospital, only a few blocks away. Luke was given disinfecting wipes for his hands that contained a few splatters of blood and gave his record of the events to the officers. A team of police were searching Central Park for the hit and run suspect and Luke couldn't wait to get back to his apartment and lay down.

The events had been dizzying and he wanted to feel calm and collected before showing his work that very evening. After giving the officer his contact information, he left the scene of the accident and made a beeline for the nearest subway. Taking in the masterpieces at the Met were no longer an option for a relaxing afternoon. Thoughts of passing the time by taking in Rembrandts were dashed as quickly as a mack truck could plow you down.

CHAPTER THIRTY

LUKE FOUGHT WITH HIMSELF AS HE MADE HIS WAY BACK DOWNTOWN towards his quiet Bank Street studio. Something was gnawing at him, and it wasn't the anxiety of the exhibit opening, or the sight of a man getting run over. It wasn't his relationship with Gabi, or his realization this morning that he was desperately missing the Appalachian Mountains. What was it? Perhaps some combination of all these things?

Luke felt jittery and uncertain, like the feeling when you step off a gnarly roller-coaster and still don't have your footing, except without the pleasure of the thrill. He leaned his head back against the window of the subway train and closed his eyes briefly. Around him, passengers were absorbed in their cell phones or conversations, a lady across from him was reading a book. He opened his eyes and took in the scene. A cacophony of sounds invaded his senses: screeching subway wheels, laughter, the beat of a hip hop track from the teen wearing oversized headphones beside him, the obnoxious ramblings of a homeless man making his way through the train car. It was too much. When the car doors opened, Luke bolted off the train.

Ignoring the fact that it was only at 34th Street and he had several stops to go, he skipped up the stairs and out into the throngs of Herald Square before he could think twice. This mob of people, shoulder to shoulder, only added to Luke's sudden panic. He pushed his way through until he was able to break into a run. He sprinted past Penn Station, and did not stop until he reached the Hudson River Greenway. Sinking onto a bench to catch his breath and close his eyes, he did something he had not done in years. He prayed.

"God, What the hell is wrong with me?" he whispered. Perhaps not the best beginning to his prayer, but Luke was nothing, if not honest. "Help me, Jesus. Show me where I need to be. Who I need to be with? Who the hell I am, for that matter? Suddenly, I feel like I'm drowning in noise and people and expectations … I'm not ready for this, God. I'm not capable of doing this alone. I need you, Lord. I need you. Amen."

Luke wiped his eyes before adding, "And, help that dude that got hit by the truck. Amen."

He looked up at the river and tried to steady his breathing. The afternoon had gotten away from him, and before long, he would be donning his new Hugo Boss suit that Gabi had helped him pick out and getting ready for the opening night. He thought about the gallery and the pieces that would be on display. Some even for sale. His heart felt an uncomfortable prick. Luke knew one reason for his unease. He wished he had stood up to Nicolas earlier, he knew it was too late now. If only he could go back to that moment last month and say no. Or better yet, "Hell no."

It was mid-July and the gallery's a.c unit was on the fritz again. Luke had stripped off his shirt and was continuing to paint his final piece for the opening.

"It's going to take forever to dry in the humidity," Nicolas came in with a bottle of water and tossed it to him.

Luke caught it with one hand, "I know. I know … but I'm nearly done."

"I thought you finished it last week?" asked Nicolas

"Nah," Luke stepped back to examine the piece. "I thought I had. But then I woke up this morning and realized that she was still missing something."

"She?" he asked.

Luke smirked, "I know you've heard stranger things than this."

Nicolas laughed, "You have no idea. Well, does she have a name?"

"Hmmm, not yet." Luke bent down to the metallic sand held in a small ceramic container and picked up a small handful before tossing it into the wet paint.

"Interesting effect." Nicolas nodded appreciatively, "I love your use of texture, Luke."

He perched himself on the nearby stool and watched as Luke continued this procedure, two, then three more times.

Luke paused and looked towards his friend, who seemed to be on the verge of bursting.

"You didn't come in to talk about texture, did you?" Luke asked.

"No, I didn't," Nicolas' face looked solemn.

Luke put down his work and wiped his hands with the rag, "This seems serious."

"Not serious, just uncomfortable," Nicolas stated.

"Go ahead," Luke set his jaw, his mind reeling. Had he done anything that would cause him to be fired? Forgotten to lock up? Had a piece of art been stolen while he was working in the studio that had gone unnoticed by him? He couldn't think of anything.

"Luke, you are an incredible artist," Nicolas began. "You've been diligent in prepping for the gallery opening. Your pieces are exceptional. We all feel thankful to have you on board as the intern this year."

"But," his eyes looked down. "Marc and Jonathan wanted me to let you know that …," Nicolas closed his eyes and took a deep breath, as though steadying himself, "They've chosen you as one of the up and coming artists for the new artist exhibition at MOMA!"

A champagne pop behind him caused Luke to jump. Jonathan and Marc rounded the corner and began serving up the bubbly. He clutched his chest in mock-heart attack.

"You bastard!" Luke playfully punched Nicolas in the arm.

"You should've seen the look on your face!" Nicolas howled.

"Classic," Marc nodded. "Cheers!"

"Cheers!" They raised their glasses in chorus.

"To the gallery opening and your continued success," Jonathan chimed. They clinked their glasses together again.

Luke felt positively exuberant. It was too good to be true.

"Now," Nicolas sat down his glass, "let's decide what pieces you're wanting to sell at the opening."

Luke's heart sank. He knew full well that his ability to have a career as an artist required his willingness to sell his paintings, but it was always the hardest part. Especially when he gave so much of himself over to the process of creating, adding to, and perfecting each one, only to let it go so soon afterwards. He nodded to Nicolas.

"Why don't you tell me how many I should set as my goal?" Luke asked.

"It's always nice if you can sell one particular collection," Marc interrupted.

"Yes, a cohesive group that we could arrange separately always does well," Jonathan agreed, refilling his champagne flute.

Luke glanced at all of his pieces. They were semi-arranged against the walls around the room, waiting to be hung. They reflected a jumble of emotions. His art contained mixed media pieces, some used bits of metal, others had textile work added, broken bits of sea glass adorned the edges of one, and his current piece had sand. None of them could be categorized together as a cohesive unit, unless the theme was dissonance.

"Yeah," Luke shook his head, "I don't really see a group that would arrange well for selling. At least, not a harmonious one."

Marc, Jonathan, and Nicolas exchanged a look.

"What?" Luke asked warily.

"What about the pieces you have in the basement?"

Luke didn't respond. Instead, he looked up thoughtfully towards the new light installation in the foyer. He had fought to get that piece, in particular because it complimented the space just right. He turned back to Marc, Jonathan, and Nicolas, all looking at him expectantly. The works in the basement were his favorite pieces. They were works he had completed when he was with Cat; they fit him just right. More than that, they were a part of him. Like the light that filled the foyer, when he looked at that work, he felt full. He wasn't sure he could part with them, now or ever.

"They are the only pieces that would really work to be set aside as a separate auction," Nicolas interrupted his thoughts. "Because—"

"Because they share the same colors and materials," Luke finished his sentence. "I know, Nicolas."

Everyone was silent. Luke continued his quiet contemplation as he sat on the stool with his champagne.

"Luke," Marc offered. "I've noticed on several occasions that you haven't been too inclined to show us your past work, yet you brought it all the way to New York City."

Luke took another sip and listened to his benefactors politely.

"When an artist creates work that is full of so much conflicting emotion," Jonathan paused. "Sometimes it's just better to let it go."

Luke sighed and nodded, relenting, "Maybe you're right."

Nicolas, seeing the window of opportunity, jumped in, "Does it make you happy to look at those pieces?"

"It used to," Luke answered honestly.

"Then," Nicolas's voice raised happily, "let's drop this excess baggage and make you some money!"

Luke laughed. Money was never too far from a New Yorker's mind, he was learning.

"Alright," he nodded. His stomach twisted into a thousand knots upon this agreement. "Let's do this."

Luke leaned his head between his legs and breathed deeply for another minute before he made himself rise from the bench.

It was too late to change his mind on that point. The gallery was ready for the opening night, and that included a silent auction of Luke's favorite pieces. Or former favorite pieces. He wasn't sure anymore. He forced his legs to move. He had a long walk back to his Bank Street apartment. The biggest night of his life was ahead of him.

"I have found the one whom my soul loves."

—SONG OF SOLOMON 3:4

CHAPTER THIRTY-ONE

GLANCING AT HER WATCH ON THE WAY HOME FROM THE GYM THAT afternoon, Cat calculated approximately how long she could give herself to relax and unwind before grabbing a bite to eat and heading downtown to the exhibit.

It was nearly seven o'clock, but the exhibit didn't open until 8pm. The invite Jonathan had given her said that hors d'oeuvres and cocktails would be served. Maybe she could skip dinner and just eat there? No. She didn't want to be stuffing her face when she was on a work outing. She needed to be focused on examining the art, not scoring a free meal. But sipping champagne while browsing? Yes, that was perfectly acceptable.

Cat detoured into the bodega on the corner to grab a quick deli sandwich before she headed up to her apartment to change. Demetri was exiting the building as she arrived and he even held the door open for her. He'd been considerably nicer since Rachel had run downstairs and dragged him out of his apartment to come to their rescue on the fateful night of David's explosive behavior. Even though David had already vacated the building, the girls all thanked him profusely. Cat had been pleasantly surprised when he'd arrived at her apartment at eight o'clock the very next morning to replace her smoke detector. Finally. It had only taken her long-legged Southern friend to bring him around.

Cat finished up her brie and tomato sandwich while she scoured the dress options in her and Lili's closets. Lili was out for the evening and said she would be staying with some friends in Brooklyn for the weekend. Even though Cat loved having her sister around, she was thankful for the momentary reprieve. She couldn't keep up with the college crowd anymore, despite having only graduated seven months prior. Cat shook her head as she thumbed through the options. She was attending the exhibit opening for work, so she wanted to dress accordingly. Yet, it was also an evening event with an artsy crowd and chic was a requirement. Cat held two dresses up against herself as she posed in the mirror. One was a navy Ralph Lauren that hugged her curves and had a keyhole opening in the back, and the other option was a gold and black Marchesa with distinct art deco vibes. Cat opted for the artsier ensemble and even wore her 4-inch Christian Louboutin stilettos to complete her look. It meant she would be required to hail a cab, as there would be no navigating the subways in these red lacquered bottoms. No matter, it would be worth her aching feet. She grabbed a brush for a quick run through her hair, which hung loose over her shoulders. It just didn't work with her dress. She tried a French twist, but it was too old-fashioned. A quick side braid—too youthful. It screamed inexperienced. Eventually, she just gave up and twisted it into one of the messy yet elegant buns of which she was so fond. Perfect. She paused to glance in the mirror one last time, nodded in approval, and skipped out the door.

Cat had the towncar drop her on the corner of 9th Avenue and 23rd Street, as cars were lined up and down the side street waiting to pull up to the gallery. She had no idea the show would draw such a crowd. It boded well that these new artists were already pulling the interests of wealthy Manhattanites. It meant sure success for the new exhibit at the MOMA, not to mention continued opportunities for her. She side-stepped through a few journalists lingering outside the doors and onto a red carpet outside of a beautifully renovated warehouse with a glass façade. It looked like half of Manhattan had turned up for this event. *Whoever the new artists were, they must be good*, Cat thought to herself.

Her phone buzzed and she pulled it out quickly to glance at a voicemail from a number she did not recognize. Cat ignored it; she would listen to it later when she had the time. She shoved it back into her purse. The sign placed conspicuously near the entrance noted that the artists curated for this particular exhibit would be featured in January 2014 at MOMA's Up-and-Coming Artists Exhibit. She felt giddy at the thought of being a part of this project.

Time to celebrate, Cat thought to herself. She took a glass of champagne off of a passing tray as she stepped into the open foyer space. She let her eyes travel upwards to the elaborate lighting installation above. It was a piece of artwork in itself. Making a mental note to find out whether or not the lighting designer would be available for the exhibit at MOMA, she took in the scene. Several paintings were so large that they served as dividers between the rooms. With all the people lining up to view the artwork, Cat couldn't really catch more than a glimpse of them.

She sipped her champagne and glanced around the room, when suddenly a familiar face caught her eye.

"Rachel!" Cat shouted and waved her hand.

Rachel, spotting her over the heads of other women, waved ecstatically and rushed towards her.

"What are you doing here?!" Rachel nearly shouted over the music.

Cat smiled, "Technically, I'm here for work. But you know how I feel about new gallery openings. Wait. What are you doing here?"

Rachel's mouth opened to respond, her eyes wide, then she closed it and shrugged.

"What?" Cat felt certain she must be missing something crucial from her friend's reaction.

"Um, nothing," Rachel blinked. "I'm here at the invitation of an old friend."

"Oh, nice," Cat nodded. She couldn't help feeling a twinge of unease at Rachel's reaction. Either something entirely worrisome or wonderful awaited her this evening. Cat was certain of it.

"Shall we?" Rachel nodded towards the paintings with an unconcealed smirk and extended her arm for Cat to take.

"What do you know that I don't?" Cat asked nervously, following her friend to the closest painting.

"What do you think of this one?" Rachel tilted her head towards the painting once they were close enough.

Cat turned her attention to the artwork in the room for the first time that evening. It struck her. There was a familiarity to it, though she knew she hadn't seen the painting before. The strokes of color were both messy and precise at the same time. Like a strange combination of both impressionism and something Picasso might have drawn. It drew her in. As she took a few steps towards it, she felt the hairs rise on her arms; a shiver went down her spine, and suddenly her breath caught in her throat. Whirling on the spot, Rachel was directly behind and Cat nearly toppled into her.

"Luke," Cat mouthed silently.

Rachel nodded, "When I saw you here, I thought you must have known."

Cat shook her head. Her knees felt weak.

Rachel grabbed her by the elbow and led her to a bench against the wall.

"He's in New York? He's here?" Her eyes darted around the room. It was teeming with people, her heart was pounding so forcefully in her chest that she felt certain it rivaled the bass coming from the speakers in the corner where a small dj booth had been set up.

Rachel nodded and squeezed her hand.

"Are all of these his?" Cat gestured to the paintings around them, as she tried her best to catch her breath. The room felt like it was spinning slightly. Her mind had been so focused on David, getting rid of David, her wedding, cancelling her wedding, and her new job; but this, this was something she had never expected.

"This section of the gallery. It's all his work. He's really the star of the show tonight. Can you believe it? He did it, Cat." Rachel looked around. "I haven't seen him yet, though. With so many people here, you'd be hard pressed to find him in this crowd."

Cat felt her forehead with the back of her palm, she felt clammy.

"Cat, you're white as a ghost." Rachel rubbed her back, "Do you want me to go find a cab to take you home?"

"No!" Cat's strong reaction surprised even her. "I want to see his paintings. I need to see them."

"Do you want to see *him*?" Rachel raised an eyebrow.

"Not tonight," Cat glanced around at all the people.

"I could go find him," Rachel started to crane her neck, look-ing around.

"No," Cat grabbed her hand, "I want him to enjoy his night. I would only ruin it for him. I think I'll just walk through the gallery, take a quick look, and leave. He won't even know I am here. Besides, I have to make some notes for work. I'm curating a new exhibit for MOMA, an up-and-coming artists exhibition. I just never imagined Luke would be one of them."

Rachel stood up with Cat, "I can walk around with you."

"I think I need to do this alone, Rach," Cat smiled weakly at her friend.

It was coming back to her. Every tiny little detail about her time with Luke that she had tried and failed to forget. The way he threw his head back when he laughed, the way he always made her jump when he popped his head into her bedroom window, how angry he would get when she pushed his buttons, the way he always knew when she wasn't being honest with him … or with herself. Without his help, she never would have made it through losing Landon. She never would have had the strength to forgive herself, to move on, to fall in love.

Cat steadied herself as she walked quietly against the wall, observing the paintings from a distance at first. Luke painted with such emotion, he always had. Yet, many of his paintings were filled with emotions that didn't characterize the Luke she knew: anger, frustration, loneliness, and above all sadness. It broke her heart just to look at them. And it left her confused. He seemed like he'd moved on with his life. She had not heard from him since the day he deserted her at the hospital. He had left her, after all. These paintings told a different story. Cat peered around a partition towards the back of the gallery. The paintings back here were different from the ones in the front. Brighter hues, smoother strokes, Cat recognized them immediately as the paintings Luke had drawn while they were together.

Cat looked around the smaller room. A few people mingled

about discussing various paintings, but Luke was nowhere in sight. Cat stepped into the room; she had to bite her lip to keep from getting choked up. She never imagined she would be seeing these paintings again. Then, she saw it … her painting. It hung in the center of the room under a spotlight. The plaque beside it read, "The Last Life of Cat." It had been framed in an ornate golden frame, which made it seem much larger than it already was. Cat stepped back again to admire it. Suddenly, the memories of the day Luke showed it to her came flooding back to her. She remembered how they stood in the barn with their arms wrapped around each other, how they each had taken turns explaining what the painting meant to them. It all seemed very cheesy now, Cat realized, thinking back to that moment. But it had been so real, so genuine, so heartfelt … nothing that sincere could ever really seem cheesy.

Cat wasn't certain how long she stood there taking in the painting before she realized the small red signs that hung beside each painting in this section of the gallery, 'These paintings are for sale by silent auction in the foyer.' Cat's mouth hung open. *How dare he?!* This painting belonged as much to her as it did to Luke. Cat found herself suddenly furious, livid even. She felt like smoke could come out of her ears. She wanted nothing more than to march through this gallery until she found Luke Presnell and then bop him on the nose. Or maybe give him a black eye, or both. *Aaarghhh!* It was infuriating to think that she had been standing here reminiscing about their romance, when all he wanted to do was get rid of the evidence that she had ever existed.

He never really loved you, a voice in Cat's head spoke up. It was the reason he had found it so easy to leave her in the hospital, to never come after her, to sell her painting. Her heart felt crushed all over again. This had been a bad idea. This whole thing had been a bad idea. She never should have walked through the gallery in the first place. She couldn't believe that minutes ago, she had still been entertaining the idea of seeking him out. It was obvious he had moved on.

Cat did an about-face and strode quickly to the foyer. She wanted to get out of this place as quickly as possible. Her eye caught a sign as she reached for the door, "Silent Auction" read the placard hanging down from the table. It was as though Cat's body was magnetically pulled to the table. Before she knew it, she was looking down at, at least, a dozen bids that had been placed on "The Last Life of Cat." As upset as she was about the whole situation, she cringed at the thought of her painting hanging in anyone's home other than her own. They would never be able to appreciate it the way I do, Cat told herself as she picked up the pen. Cat made a mental note of the amount that she would need to move from her savings account into her checking when she returned home. Taking a deep breath, she placed her bid. It was nearly five times higher than the current highest bid, but Cat wanted to ensure that it was hers and no one else's. In the space for the bidder's name and number, she put down her phone number but simply wrote Cathleen for her name, with no last name.

It wasn't until she had fled the building and thrown herself into the nearest cab that she started hyperventilating. *Twenty-five thousand dollars!* Her breath was coming in spasms.

"What the hell was I thinking?" Cat held her head between her knees and muttered angrily to herself when she was finally able to breathe again.

Her panic attack was interrupted by her phone ringing. As she fished it from her purse, she noted nine missed calls from the same number. Who had been trying to reach her?

"Hello, this is Cathleen Rhodes," she spoke with frustration into the receiver.

"Ms. Rhodes, this is Lainey Masterman," the voice spoke calmly. "I'm a nurse at Lenox Hill Hospital. I'm afraid there's been an accident."

CHAPTER THIRTY-TWO

CAT WAS A BALL OF EMOTIONS WHEN SHE ARRIVED AT THE EMERGENCY room of Lenox Hill. Nurse Lainey had not told her who was injured, only a family member was in serious condition and that she needed to come to the emergency room department right away. She texted Lili and her mom and dad on the cab ride up, hoping to rule out who had been hurt. She glanced at her cell phone, still no responses.

Cat felt her eyes brimming with tears and pushed them back. She had not stepped foot in this hospital since she was a teen and had been forced to participate in the Teen Suicide Support Therapy. It brought back a flurry of memories, none of them happy. She struggled to keep her composure as she approached the front desk.

"May I help you?" the young orderly asked, looking up from his sudoku book.

"I received a call that my family member has been injured. Um—Cathleen Rhodes," Cat stammered.

He looked down at his computer screen, "Oh, yes. Room 232. Just take the elevator to the 2nd floor and go to the nurses station down the right hallway. It looks like they went ahead and admitted them, but they are in stable condition."

"Oh, okay," Cat swallowed. "Thank you."

Her pace quickened. She saw the sign for the elevators just ahead. Pressing the up button more times than necessary, she only stopped hitting the button when the doors finally opened. It wouldn't go fast enough. *Why were elevators so unbelievably slow, especially when an emergency arises?* Cat thought to herself.

The doors opened and Cat sprinted out like a racehorse at a starting gate. She could not get to the nurse's desk quick enough. She thought of Lili, going out to a club in Brooklyn that evening. *Had something happened on the way there?* She thought of her mom, whom she had been furious with on the phone yesterday, but if something happened to her now? Cat couldn't let herself think about that. A lump rose in her throat, hard and painful. The tears were building. She willed herself not to blink, knowing they would surely spill over.

"Room 232," she nearly shouted when the older nurse glanced up. "I'm Cathleen Rhodes."

"Oh, they finally got a hold of you!" the nurse exclaimed looking relieved to see her.

"Yes, yes," Cat nodded. "What's happened?"

"Now, I don't know if she told you over the phone, but he's been quite confused since the accident," the nurse continued, coming around the partition to lead Cat down the hallway.

"No, I didn't know," Cat reached out for her elbow. "My father? Was my father in an accident?"

The nurse looked confused, "No, dear. Your fiancé."

"My—" Cat's voice faltered. She couldn't help but feel a small twinge of relief, knowing that her family was okay. "You mean, David?"

"That's right," she looked at the chart on the door, "David Randolph."

"He's not—" Cat stopped short of the doorway and lowered her voice, unsure of how to handle this, "he's not my fiancé."

"What do you mean?" The nurse stepped towards her and

lowered her voice to match Cat's volume. "He had you listed as his in case of emergency, and when we got a hold of someone at his office they told us that you were engaged."

"We were, but, I—" Cat suddenly wanted to bolt. In the corner of her eye, she saw the emergency exit. As much as she wanted to take off running, she knew that she needed to stay, to help sort this out, for the nurses as much as for David. "I think I have the contact information for his parents on my phone. Let me give it to you."

The nurse shook her head, "We already tried their home in Pennsylvania. Their housekeeper said they are on a Viking River Cruise in Europe for the next two weeks. We are still trying to get word to them, but he will need someone to care for him when he is released tomorrow."

Cat rubbed her hand across her forehead. "Have you tried his brother? He lives in Westchester."

"Apparently he is away on business," the nurse nodded gravely. "So you really aren't engaged?"

"Not at all," Cat emphasized. "And he's had a difficult time accepting it. I—I just don't think I can help you."

"Well, I hate to have to tell you this," the nurse checked the chart and peeked in the door before turning back to Cat, "But according to David, he's engaged to you."

"What?!" Cat shouted, before placing a hand over her mouth.

"He's having trouble remembering very much from the last five months or so, it would seem," she glanced at the chart again. "He insisted it was March to the doctor. And since then, he's been asking for his fiancé."

"No, no, no," Cat slid down the wall. "I can't break it off with him again."

"Looks like you're going to have to."

Cat glanced up to see no sympathy on her face.

"He will be discharged tomorrow, Ms. Rhodes." She said sternly, "We have no reason to keep him any longer."

"Isn't memory loss a reason!?" Cat pulled herself back up to standing.

"He has follow up appointments scheduled and he will likely regain his memory in the next few days, maybe weeks."

"Weeks?!"

"Is that you, Cathleen?" a groggy voice called from the hospital room.

"Shit!" Cat cursed under her breath. "Shit, shit, shit."

"Look" the nurse took Cat's elbow firmly. "It will be fine. Just help him out for a few days. Be a good person, make sure he takes his meds, and get him to his appointments. When his brother returns from his business trip, then he can take charge."

Cat felt herself nodding, but inside, she felt entirely unsure and slightly nauseous.

"Wait!" Cat called, as the nurse turned to walk back to the desk. "What even happened to him?"

"He was hit while crossing 5th Avenue. Broken arm, a few cracked ribs, and missing teeth. But he's very lucky to be alive. He's going in for dental surgery first thing in the morning, and then will be sent home tomorrow afternoon with you, Ms. Rhodes. I suggest you go check on him. He'll be glad to see you."

Her heels clicked down the linoleum hallway as Cat gathered her strength and sanity outside his door.

"Cathleen? Cathleen?" a voice whined. "Is that you, baby?"

"I'm not your baby," she mumbled under her breath, as she turned to enter the room. She gathered her courage and spoke up, "You can call me Cathleen, David."

Cat stayed for an hour. She didn't mention to David that they were no longer engaged, but instead, asked him a few questions that she hoped would jog his memory. Nothing seemed to work. He was pitiful, bruised, and evidently in a lot of pain. Regardless of how he'd behaved the other night, nor the fact that she had been contemplating a restraining order against him, she hated seeing him in this condition.

It took all the kindness and goodness she could muster to gently kiss the top of his head before she left. And only because he asked for a kiss. Cat knew that her current situation didn't change the fact that their engagement was over, it only created a small roadblock on her path to freedom. She was truly thankful that he was okay, for she would have felt horrid if he had died tragically while she was bent on hating him. She wanted to help him, to forgive him, and to move on. *Forgiving someone is much easier when their station in life has deteriorated so rapidly*, Cat pondered as she got into the cab to go home. She was to pick him up at 1pm the next day, but the thought of caring for him while he still considered them to be engaged filled her with dread. She would enlist the help of Lili and Rachel. Perhaps they could be convinced to play nurse with her for a few days.

She leaned back in the vinyl seat and closed her eyes. It was then that she remembered the painting at the gallery. By now the show downtown had ended, Cat knew. Tomorrow, she would learn whether or not she was the highest bidder on "The Last Life of Cat." This last life had been full of so many twists and turns already, she thought to herself, what's a few more?

CHAPTER THIRTY-THREE

"THE OPENING WAS A HUGE SUCCESS!" NICHOLAS GAVE LUKE A standing ovation when he walked into the gallery at noon the next day.

"Oh!" Luke held his head in pain, "No clapping. My head is killing me!"

"Still hung-over?" Nicolas laughed.

"And I think I will be until September," Luke shook his head.

"And how were things with Gabi?" Nicolas asked suggestively.

"Oh, that," Luke groaned. "I think we'd both had too much to drink for that."

"Oh," he tilted his head with disappointment. "Too bad. I thought you had something special planned."

Luke shrugged. Truthfully, he had been planning for last night to be THE night. He knew Gabi had been expecting it to be, as well. He thought Gabi might be the one, he at least felt certain he was ready to take the next step. Apparently, the rest of him didn't agree. He played it off on the alcohol; hence, the reason for pretending to be so hung-over today. But it wasn't that, he really hadn't even had more than a couple of glasses of champagne. He wanted to remember the opening of his gallery perfectly, and thus, had decided beforehand to set a limit for himself. Why couldn't he let himself be with Gabi? Was it the stress of the gallery opening? Was it the frustration he felt towards Nicolas for insisting that it was time to sell his old paintings? Or, was it that even after all this time, he still felt like he had saved himself for Cat?

Luke sighed heavily. He did not like the thought of that. Because, if that was true, then his attempts to move forward with Gabi were all in vain.

"We sold all the paintings for the silent auction," Nicolas sang happily, looking at his clipboard.

"What?" Luke gulped, "They all met the minimum bid?"

Luke had purposefully set the minimum higher than what he thought people would really pay in an attempt to save a few of the paintings for himself. Inwardly, he cursed himself for not setting the amount even higher.

"And then some!" Nicolas typed furiously on his calculator before turning it to show Luke the total.

"Seriously?" Luke felt light headed just looking at the total. It would have taken his father five years to earn that amount. He reached his hand out to grab a chair and sit down.

"I've already had them boxed up for delivery," Nicolas made a check on his list. "I think I'm enjoying being your interim gallery manager a little too much," he laughed.

Luke smiled. But it quickly faded as he faced the reality of parting with his paintings. There was one he was particularly reluctant to let go: "The Last Life of Cat."

"Nick," Luke stood up, "If there's one painting I've changed my mind about … could we reimburse whoever purchased it?"

"That wouldn't be very good business practice," Nicolas pursed his lips, but then seeing Luke's expression he softened. "Which painting, Luke?"

"The Last Life of Cat," he stated.

"Oh no," Nicolas shook his head. "No. I just got off the phone with the young woman who purchased it. It was our highest grossing painting of the night. Twenty-five thousand dollars. She's expecting it to be delivered this afternoon."

Luke sighed. It was probably best to let it go.

"I want to deliver it myself," Luke said decisively.

Nicolas nodded towards where the paintings were being loaded on the truck.

"Here's the address," Nicolas quickly jotted it down on a sticky note and handed it to Luke.

Luke grabbed the keys to the truck and headed out the door.

He was entirely unaccustomed to driving in New York City traffic. After a few close calls, he was safely on the FDR highway and heading up along the East River towards the address on the paper. He tried not to think about the fact that he would never see the painting again, or what that painting stood for. Luke tried to simply focus on the fact that they were getting much, much more than they expected. For a painting of a relatively unknown artist to sell for that much money was a rare feat. Luke knew he should be proud of himself. Why did he suddenly feel like it was worth so much more than that?

"Be grateful, damn it!" he scolded himself. "Forget about her, Luke. Forget about Cat."

Luke unloaded the painting onto the dolly and carefully rolled it to the door.

He rang the buzzer once, then twice, before he was buzzed into the building. Looking up the steep staircase, he decided that the elevator was the best option. If the painting would fit. Luke felt like he was making an eight-point turn as he backed up and pivoted with the dolly to cautiously work the canvas into the elevator. Including himself and the dolly, it barely fit. Luke swore under his breath. He should have let the delivery guy handle it. Now, not only was he dealing with the pain of moving the painting, but he feared he wouldn't be able to let it go.

After many failed attempts and questionable maneuvering, Luke arrived at the door. He knocked hastily, wanting nothing more than to get this over with as quickly as possible.

The door opened abruptly, leaving him speechless, and face to face with the one face he never expected to see.

She looked the same in many ways, but slightly older; and Luke was certain she'd never looked as beautiful as she did in this moment, standing barefoot in her charcoal grey sweatpants, tee shirt, her hair in a messy bun. He inhaled to speak and found that the words were lost, caught somewhere in the space between them. There were a thousand things he wanted to say, and yet, in this moment he couldn't recall a single one. Had he not been wheeling an enormous and carefully wrapped canvas, he would have reached out to take her hand or touch her cheek. So, instead, he awkwardly shifted the dolly and the canvas to the other side of his body and stared at her. Cat.

She gasped and jumped back, "They told me a delivery guy was bringing it!" Cat all but shouted at him, as she fought the instinct to slam the door in his face.

Feeling instantly self-conscious that these were the first words she would speak to him after all this time. She'd had a well-rehearsed list in her mind of things she would say to him if they were to ever meet again. They ranged from 'Go to hell!' to 'Make love to me!' She obviously had mixed emotions when it came to how she felt about Luke.

Luke stood there dumbfounded. She could see his mind thinking a million things at once, and still he hadn't said a word. This fact infuriated Cat even further. After all this time and all the pain he put her through, he sells their painting and then shows up on her doorstep to deliver it to her. As though rejecting her five years ago wasn't enough, now he has to reject her again to her face.

"Aghhh!" Cat screamed, turning away from the open door, and stomping into the kitchen.

"What?" Luke was at a complete loss for words, "Wait? How? Wh-What are you doing?"

"Getting a glass of wine," Cat spat at him, as she reached hastily into her cabinet.

"At one in the afternoon?" Luke fought to hide the amusement in his voice.

She glared at him and wretched open the cabinet. Clumsily, she grabbed the stem of the glass so firmly that it broke in her hand.

"Oh, dammit," she gasped as thick, red blood oozed from the cut.

Cat knew it wasn't a deep cut, but the sight of the blood made her queasy. Before she had a chance to think, Luke was at her side, grabbing a dish towel off the counter, running her finger under water and cleaning her wound.

"Ow," Cat closed her eyes and looked the other way.

"You need to make sure there's not any glass in the cut," he said, leaning down to examine her hand closely.

Luke lifted her hand gingerly in his own and plucked a small piece of glass from the crease in her palm. She was shaking, ever so slightly, and he couldn't fight the guilt that washed over him. Too long, it had been too damn long since he'd been in the same room with her and the effect she had on him was exactly the same. She had an invisible force about her, where he was concerned, she drew him in completely. He glanced towards her face, her eyes fixed on the cut. Her expression was a mixture of pain and alarm, whether from the wound or his presence, he wasn't entirely certain.

She could smell him. For the first time in nearly five years, he was holding her hand. She breathed deeply, as if to breathe him in, before remembering that she had decided to hate him for all eternity. Gritting her teeth, Cat tried to pull her hand away.

"Let me go," Cat forced herself to say.

Luke pressed the dish towel to her hand firmly, ignoring her request.

"You can just leave my painting and go. Please." Cat could feel her composure breaking, tears began to well up in her eyes.

Luke looked up from her hand. He stared into her eyes, as though trying to read her. Just this simple action made the tears spill over. He didn't let go of her hand, if anything he was holding her tighter.

"I'm sorry," his voice began to break.

"It's not your fault," Cat wiped her tears and tried to pull away again, "I was being careless."

"I'm not talking about your hand, Cat," Luke dropped her hand, but firmly took her shoulders and turned her to face him.

Cat realized then that he had grown at least an inch or two since high school. She turned her head down to his shoes. She couldn't bear to hear what he had to say. 'Sorry, I stopped loving you.' 'Sorry I want to get rid of all the paintings I made when we were together.' No, she didn't think she could bear it.

"You don't have to apologize, Luke," Cat put on a brave face. "It was a long time ago. You've moved on. I should've expected you would sell the paintings at some point."

Luke shook his head, "Do you think it was easy for me to sell these paintings?"

Cat could feel a little bit of the anger coming back, "You tell me. You sold them all, didn't you?"

Luke nodded.

"Well, then you can leave my painting and let yourself out," Cat stormed around him.

Her intention was to retreat to the bedroom and slam the door with such force that Luke would know just how furious she was with him, but he headed her off before she'd walked five steps.

Spinning her around, Luke tried to pull her close to him and was met with Cat's hand across his cheek. She was surprisingly strong.

"I hate you," Cat began to sob. "I hate you for leaving me. I hate you for making me love you."

"I love you," Luke let her go and stepped cautiously towards her, with his hands raised as though in surrender. "I never stopped loving you."

Tears of affection were rising in Luke's eyes. This reaction was not what Cat had been expecting. It floored her. Was it possible that he had been going through the same agony as she had for all these years? But if that was true, wouldn't he have wanted to find her? *No*, a voice in Cat's head answered, *because he's almost as stubborn as you are.*

Cat couldn't help but smile, "You love me?"

Luke looked up at her and nodded, "You're a hard girl to get over."

"Speak for yourself," Cat laughed and threw her arms around him.

"Except that I'm not a girl," Luke smirked.

"Right," Cat felt a smile break across her face, "Except for that."

With her arms tightly around his shoulders, he lifted her off the ground and spun her around. Then he stopped, and looked into her eyes. Cat could feel his breath on her lips and she felt a tingle go down her spine. He leaned in slowly, it would be the first time they had kissed in nearly five years.

"Wait," Cat breathed, kicking herself for ruining the moment, but knowing she needed to know something first.

"I need to know, Luke," she looked up at him seriously. "I just need to know why."

She knew he understood from the way he slowly put her feet back on the ground, let her go, and ran his fingers through his hair.

"I made a mistake," he looked down, "I thought you would be better off without me. So, I decided to let you go. It was the hardest thing I'd ever done. The only thing worse was trying to go on without you. I'm so sorry for what I did to you, Cat. You know that right?"

Cat wrinkled her forehead at him, something wasn't adding up. "I know you're sorry, Luke. But I know that's not why you left."

He looked at her incredulously.

"I know my dad spoke with you," Cat stepped toward him. "How …"

"Lili told me," Cat closed her eyes at the thought of it. "She had followed the two of you outside."

"He told me," Luke began, but then he stopped himself and began again. "Cat, parents make mistakes. I don't want what I tell you to affect your relationship with your father."

"What relationship?" Cat scoffed. "Nothing you tell me will make me think any worse of him than I already do. He doesn't care about me, Luke. I don't know if he ever has. He only cares about how I make him look."

Luke paused before sitting on the couch, "He said he would disown you. That he wouldn't even claim you for his daughter and that he and your mother would never have a relationship with you from that day forward, if I didn't break all contact with you."

He said it all so calmly that Cat was having difficulty processing the severity of what her father had said.

"Why didn't you tell me this?" Cat shook her head. "You knew the way he'd acted before, when they sent me to North Carolina. You knew I would have chosen you in a heartbeat."

"I know you would have," Luke looked down. "That's why I let you go. You wouldn't have had all the opportunities you've had the last five years if you had stayed in North Carolina for me."

"Screw the opportunities!" Cat shouted, standing up from the couch.

"Cat," Luke stood up and took her hand, "I didn't want to hold you back. But it was more than that. I didn't want you to lose your family because of me. I've lost a parent. I know what it feels like. I didn't want you to have to experience that with both your parents. It might have been easy for you to go without your dad, but you love your mom, Cat. I knew that."

Cat sighed. She couldn't help but think of all the time they had wasted because of words left unsaid and things left unexplained.

"I know now," Cat looked into his eyes, "I know now that I don't want to live without you. We're adults now, Luke. If my father decides to disown me for choosing you instead of ...," she stopped herself short of saying David. "Instead of some blue-blood Wall Street type, then that's his decision. I've made mine."

Luke pulled her close, "Are you sure?"

"Absolutely," Cat said with determination, leaning in for him to kiss her.

"Positive?" Luke said, leaning closer to her teasingly.

"Yes," Cat said adamantly.

Luke leaned closer, so that their lips were mere centimeters apart, "Cause I don't want to kiss you until you're sure."

"Oh," Cat sighed, "Luke, just kiss me dammit."

"I didn't hear you," he leaned his ear to her jokingly.

"KISS …"

And that was the only word she was able to shout before his lips crushed hers. Happily, she wrapped her arms around him. Like their first kiss, she gave a little jump to wrap her legs securely around his hips. She hadn't felt such passion since, well, ever. He was like a drug. A drug she had been deprived of for much too long. She wanted him. All of him. She could sense that they were moving. Opening her eyes, she found that she had been carried to the bedroom. Their mouths came apart long enough for Cat to catch her breath.

Luke's phone began to buzz in his pocket. He fished it out and glanced at it before wincing painfully.

"Who is it?" Cat frowned.

"Umm," Luke brushed his hands through his hair, "Well, it's my girlfriend—I kind of was supposed to meet her for lunch."

"Ah," Cat nodded knowingly, "Would you like to call her back and inform her you're no longer available or should I?"

"I'll take care of it," Luke swallowed hard and dialed her number back.

Cat listened as Luke gave a polite and brief description of his predicament, as she also listened to the sobs coming through from the other end. She would feel bad for the girl, if she wasn't hopelessly in love with Luke herself.

When the conversation was over, Luke took her hand and squeezed it tightly.

"I'm all yours," he said.

"Ditto," she whispered in his ear, kissing his cheek, "Ditto.

Will you—," she felt her breath catch nervously, "Will you make love to me?"

"Yes," Luke said, with some surprise on his face, "Hell, yes."

Cat wasn't sure whose hands were whose, as she started removing whatever articles of clothing she could get her hands on. She could barely breathe.

"Cat," Luke suddenly pulled away from her with a concerned look on his face, "I don't have anything. Do you?"

"You don't?" Cat sat up in shock. She thought it was some sort of rule that guys had to carry those things around. "Why not?"

"Well," Luke blushed, "for one thing, I wasn't expecting to run into you. For another … well, I have never needed to carry them."

"You mean, the girls you've had sex with were on birth control?" Cat asked, feeling disappointed at the thought of him being with someone else.

"No," Luke shook his head. He ran his fingers through his hair the way he always did when he was nervous. "I've never done this before, Cat."

Cat smiled.

"Are you on birth control?" he asked slowly.

"No," Cat shook her head. "I—I haven't done this either, Luke. Ever."

"You're telling me that after all this time, we're still virgins?" Luke laid back on the bed and laughed.

Cat laid back with him and kissed his neck, "You always said we were going to wait."

"Maybe this is a sign," he rolled on to his side and smoothed her curls.

"A sign that you need to go buy condoms?" Cat joked.

"No," Luke leaned in, "A sign that we should just get married."

Cat laughed out loud before realizing that he was indeed

serious. She swallowed hard and looked into his eyes. She knew her answer.

"When?" she asked, swallowing her fear in one gulp.

"Now," Luke sat up with the most determined look on his face. "I've been without you for five years, Cat. I know what I want. I think we should get married today."

"Are you asking?" she said quietly.

"I only wish I had a ring," he slid off her bed and got down on one knee.

"Wait!" Cat jumped up and quickly crossed the room to her dresser where a small jewelry box sat. Tenderly, she opened it and pulled out the twisted wire ring Luke had fashioned for her so many years ago. Since she had found it on the banks of the Hudson, she had kept it in the jewelry box for safe keeping. She didn't wear it out or to work, but she'd gotten in the habit of slipping it on at night. Or when she felt lonely.

"Use this," she said.

"You still have it?" Luke asked.

"I tried to get rid of it," Cat admitted, holding it out in her hand. "But it came back to me. Just like you."

"Cathleen Rhodes," he smiled up at her as he took the ring from the palm of her hand and lowered onto one knee, "will you marry me?"

Cat let all the tears spill over now, "Yes."

Luke swept her up and spun her around.

"I get my money back now, don't I?" Cat laughed when her toes touched the floor once more.

"Huh?" Luke raised an eyebrow.

"The painting," Cat smiled, "You wouldn't make your wife pay for it, would you?"

"Hey now," Luke joked, "That was my biggest sale."

"I'll make it up to you," she winked.

"Alright," Luke laughed. "When you put it that way … we'll call it your wedding present."

"There's nothing I'd rather have," Cat kissed him forcefully, "Except for you."

"Very soon," Luke returned the kiss.

Cat turned to look up at him. Into those amazingly green eyes that always seemed to entrance her. Suddenly, her stomach twisted into knots of nervousness. Everything was finally falling into place and happening so quickly. It was almost too good to be true. The thought of losing him again made her heart catch in her throat.

"Should—should we wait a little longer? I mean—what if we didn't get married today? This is crazy," she stated with a weak smile.

"Pretty much," he nodded, before taking her hand. "Cat, I want to spend my life with you. I want to be your husband. I want to take care of you. I want us to take care of each other." He paused for a moment, "Do you remember when you once told me that you were on your 'last life?'"

"We were in the barn," Cat smiled, remembering it all perfectly. "It was when you showed me my painting."

"How do you want to spend your 'last life'? Do you want to take time to date again? Or do you want to do something a little crazy, risk being deliriously happy for once in your life?" Luke shrugged, "We can be engaged for a month or a year if that's what you want. I don't want you to get married today if you don't want to."

Cat's lip quivered, "I want to be with you. But this is all so … fast."

"I can't tell you what you want, Cat," Luke said standing up.

"What if I've changed the last five years," Cat retorted.

"I'm sure you have changed some," Luke answered honestly. "I've changed, too."

"But," Cat was floundering, "What—what if you find out you don't like some things about me?"

"I know I don't like some things about you, city girl," Luke joked.

"Ugh!" Cat pushed him away in frustration, "I'm serious!"

Luke took both of her hands and faced her, "I chose to love you a long time ago, Cat."

"I chose to love you, too," Cat looked up at him. Cat paused for a moment, thinking, "Choosing to love someone isn't always very romantic, is it?"

"No," Luke shook his head, "It's hard. I've loved you these last five years and they've been the hardest of my life."

"Ditto," Cat said through misty eyes. "Hold my hand."

"By the way," Luke leaned down and whispered in her ear, "You still look—unbelievable."

"You're not so bad yourself," Cat winked, "Country boy."

Cat's phone began ringing violently from the kitchen. The realization of the time and who was calling made Cat shudder a groan.

"What? What's wrong?" Luke pulled back. "Do you need to get that?"

"What time is it?"

He glanced at his watch. "About 1:30. Why?"

"I was supposed to pick someone up from the hospital."

"Who?" asked Luke.

"My fiancé," said Cat.

CHAPTER THIRTY-FOUR

CAT QUICKLY CORRECTED HERSELF, "MY EX-FIANCÉ."

Luke stepped back, "I forgot that you're engaged."

"You knew?" she asked.

"Lili told me," Luke said.

"You know Lili?" Cat sat down. The emotions were overwhelming—finding Luke, accepting a marriage proposal, but knowing that some fifteen or so blocks south, David was waiting on his "fiancé" to pick him up from the hospital and care for him all seemed too much. A reassuring hand found its way to her shoulder. Cat leaned into him and felt some peace.

"Cat," Luke spoke calmly, "We are going to figure this out."

The phone began buzzing in the other room again.

"Should I get that?" he asked.

"No," Cat stood up. "I'll get it." She walked steadily to the kitchen. "Hello. This is Cathleen Rhodes."

"Ms. Rhodes, we have David Randolph waiting to be picked up in the lobby. Are you on your way?"

Cat sighed audibly, "Yes, I'll be right there."

Luke walked into the doorway and watched as she hung up, "What's next?"

"Well," Cat smiled at him. "First, I need to wrap my arms around you one more time before I leave for the hospital."

"Want company?" he asked.

"I think this is going to get complicated," she said.

"It already is. Tell me about your fiancé-" Luke started.

"Ex-fiancé," she corrected him.

"Right, ex-fiancé," he said.

"Well, for starters, he was in an accident yesterday and thinks we're still engaged," she said.

"You're kidding," he said.

"I am most-definitely not kidding. It's been hard enough to break things off with him, and now I have to do it a second time," Cat said.

"Do you want me to stay and wait?" he asked.

"I don't want to leave you," she said.

"It's going to be fine. Although, I think our elopement will have to wait." Luke lifted her off the ground for another soft kiss. "I've waited this long. I can wait a little longer."

✳✳✳

Cat left Luke to hang up her newly acquired artwork while she left to pick up David, his medications, and get him settled in his apartment. Her fingers fumbled as she attempted to text Lili. She gave up and opted for a phone call from the taxi cab.

"This is unreal!" Lili exclaimed, after Cat brought her up to speed on the excitement of the past twenty-four hours.

"So," Cat sighed, "can you help me with David?"

"Ugh, Cat," Lili groaned. "Yes … but just remember this, if you ever doubt how much I love you."

"Oh, Lili," Cat felt a weight lift off her shoulders; at least now she wouldn't have to deal with David on her own. "Thank you! I'll see if Rachel can help us, too."

"Misery loves company," Lili said.

"Exactly," Cat laughed.

The cab turned onto 77th Street. The portico for Lenox Hill Hospital was just ahead and Cat could see David, seated in a wheelchair, with a young nurse just behind him. *Cat, you can do this*, she reminded herself. *Of all the difficult things you've faced in life, this one will seem inconsequential.* She hoped that would be the case.

As the cab slowed to the curb and she reached into her bag to fish out some cash for the driver, she noticed a black town car just ahead. A man and woman stepped out and hurried over to David. Cat narrowed her eyes to see through the tinted glass of the hospital doors. *His parents must have returned on an overnight flight from Europe*, she thought to herself. *What a relief!*

Cat groaned when the woman turned around and pushed his wheelchair through the glass doors. Not David's mother, but her own. Cat had been very intentional about staying busy these last few months, and had not seen her parents in person since the disastrous night on their back patio. She would have to face them sooner or later.

She thanked the cabbie and steeled herself as she stepped from the vehicle.

They all noticed her right away.

Her parents were beaming at her, which Cat found perplexing, since they had not exactly been on friendly terms. This was especially true since she had considered filing a restraining order against David only a week earlier.

"Cathleen, sweetie!" Her mother stretched out a hand to call her over.

"Hello, dear," her father draped an arm over her shoulder.

"Cathleen, I was getting worried," David reached up from his wheelchair and gave her hand a squeeze. "They went ahead and called your parents when they couldn't get a hold of you."

"I was just so happy when the nurse called about my 'future son-in-law,'" her mom quickly corrected herself, "Of course, we were horrified when we heard what had happened to David." She leaned down and gave him a squeeze on his shoulder that was not in a sling. "I'm so glad you called us. Between Cat and us, you will have nothing to worry about."

Cat forced herself to smile at the happy ensemble. She wasn't sure whether she should feel relief at being relieved of her duties, or terrified that her parents seemed to think that this turn of events changed things between her and David.

Her dad took her by the elbow and led her towards the town car, as her mom helped David get settled in the passenger seat, "We'll take him to our place for now."

"That is actually great," Cat agreed. Her heart skipped a beat. Would she be so lucky to pass David's caregiving entirely to her parents, or whomever they hired? Because, let's be honest, they wouldn't be doing it themselves.

"You're coming with us to get him settled," her dad nodded, opening the door of the town car for her. It was more of a statement than a question.

Cat's initial reaction was to refuse, but she thought better. If she went along to see that he was settled, it may give her more wiggle room later to get out of the situation entirely. No need to cause a scene in front of Lenox Hill Hospital.

"I was just going to suggest that very thing," Cat smiled. *Two can play at this game*, she thought conspiratorially to herself. Maybe they would be so preoccupied with nursing their future son-in-law back to health that they wouldn't know she was gone, until they had a new son-in-law to meet.

Once everyone was tucked into the vehicle, wheelchair safe in the trunk, and David's seat leaned back because he was feeling 'a touch woozy', they were on their way.

Darcie lowered her voice and leaned towards Cat, "So, he doesn't remember anything from the last few months?"

"How did you—?" Cat asked.

"The nurse told us when we arrived," she said.

Warren leaned over to interject in the conversation, "Well, the nurse told me and then I let your mother know."

"Right," Darcie nodded.

"We think it's very wise of you to pick up where his memory left off," her father reached to squeeze her hand, and Cat suddenly felt 'a touch woozy' herself. "No need to continue with this ridiculous business of breaking off the engagement. And for no real reason!"

'Dad," Cat began, willing herself to keep her voice low. David's eyes had fluttered shut as they pulled away from the curb and now he was lightly snoring.

"He's right, sweetie," her mom reached her hand across. "David adores you. All of this nonsense, as of late. Well, it's been just that. Pure nonsense."

Cat swallowed. Luke was on the forefront of her mind and getting back to him, to their lives together, was all that mattered in this moment. The sooner she could get away, the better. And there would be little chance of sneaking away quietly, if she confronted all of these issues now. She resigned herself to wait and smiled.

"I'm ready to get married now," she said finally, telling herself that this was, in fact, true. "I just wasn't ready a couple of months ago. But I realized something last night, and it was that realization that makes me feel so confident today about my future."

Her parents smiled at her and then turned to each other, and Cat sat back against the plush leather seat with a sigh. *Things are going to be okay. Everything's going to be okay.* She repeated this statement to herself as they sped past the reservoir in Central Park. She closed her eyes for a moment to remember sweet Landon. It was hard to pass their meeting spot without him coming to mind. Would he be mortified that she was going along with this and planning to sneak away? Would he be proud that she had spoken honestly, even though the words had a completely different meaning to her? He was the master of all things sneaky, Cat smiled to herself. He would be glad she'd found Luke again, Cat acknowledged inwardly. He was always the one for her. And he'd waited for her, after all these years.

CHAPTER THIRTY-FIVE

ONCE BACK AT HER PARENT'S BROWNSTONE, CAT HELPED DAVID slide into the queen bed of the guest bedroom suite on the ground floor. He winced as she adjusted the pillows under his back.

"Do you need your pain medication?" Cat asked. She looked down at David's face, which was bruised and scraped. A few stitches had been placed on the left side of his cheek. His right arm was broken in two places and six of his ribs had been cracked by the impact of the truck. Cat thought back to the man she'd teased in her kitchen months before. The one who showed off his muscles and twirled her around. *He wasn't all bad*, a voice of pity echoed somewhere in her mind. *But he's not the one for you*, a voice of reason spoke up. Cat knew this to be true. She did hope she could let him down easier this time. They'd been through so much in the last few months. Maybe an amicable break-up would be easier for her parents to digest, as well.

"Yes, please," he quietly murmured. The dental repairs had made his lips and cheeks so swollen he couldn't speak clearly, "Thank you."

Cat crushed the pills and stirred them into his smoothie. Gingerly, she placed the silicone straw against his lips. She stole a furtive glance at the clock on the bedside table. It was nearly 5pm. Was Luke still at her apartment? She hadn't had a spare moment to sneak away and call him. He wouldn't be mad. He had told her to take her time getting everything sorted out. She just missed him. Terribly. After being apart for so many years, their minutes together this morning had been intoxicating. It felt like a shot of adrenaline coursing through her body. She felt alive with him. Cat rubbed her palms against her jeans. She realized her palms were suddenly sweating just thinking about him.

"Better?" she asked David.

He nodded and closed his eyes.

"I'll let you rest," she whispered as she tiptoed out of the room.

Glancing to see that her parents were not around, she pulled out her cell phone and quickly looked up the number that Luke had added before she left. She hit send.

One ring. Two. A voicemail recording picked up. She sighed.

"Hey, babe. It's me. Sorry it's taken me so long to call you. I'm at my parent's house. Long story, but I will fill you in later. I love you so much. Bye."

Cat went up to her former bedroom; it was still decorated very much the same as when she was a student at Spence. Her high school paraphernalia was taped or pinned around the bulletin board above her desk. A dried corsage from Junior Winter Formal and the picture of her and Landon were tucked into the corner. He had passed away only a few short months later. She shuddered. Memories she often kept locked away resurfaced as her hands swept across the surfaces of her room. Track meets. Sleepovers. Sneaking out. Getting up to some good trouble. Some things, sweet and silly. Some, serious. *Life is such a mixture of pain and pleasure*, Cat thought to herself. She had experienced her share of the pain. Oftentimes, she was unconvinced that she deserved the pleasures of life after losing Landon. But Luke had taught her otherwise. Luke had rescued her. And in the last few months, she had finally learned how to rescue herself. She had stood up to David and her parents only to find herself in a pseudo-engagement all over again. Cat balled her hands into fists and counted to ten. Deep breath in. Deep breath out. The current situation was only temporary. She would rise to the challenge, just as before.

Her phone buzzed in her pocket and she opened her eyes. Lili.

"Hey!" Cat exclaimed into the phone.

"You sound very happy for someone playing nurse to David-the-devil," Lili said.

"Lili, I have so much to fill you in on. But that will have to wait. I'm at mom and dad's. They wanted to bring David here," Cat said.

"Does this mean I don't have to help with him?" Lili's voice inflected optimistically.

"Yes, that's exactly what it means." Cat laughed, "But I still need your help with something."

"I'm all ears," Lili said.

"Can you meet me in the park in an hour?" Cat asked.

"Sure! I was just about to head uptown," said Lili.

"I'll see if Rachel can join us, too," said Cat.

"Great! See you in a few," said Lili.

Cat hung up the phone and checked her watch. Luke still hadn't returned her call. She tried not to worry, as she headed back downstairs to talk to her parents. She hoped that she could begin discussions that would lead them to the same realization Cat had made. David was not the one for her. She knew this was unlikely, but she had to try.

Her mother was in her small office just off the kitchen when Cat walked in.

"David is sleeping and I gave him his medicine," Cat began, she knew this would be the best way to start.

"You are being so good to him," her mother spun around. "I can't tell you how happy it makes us to see this working out for the two of you again."

"Mom, you know what I said in the car?" Cat leaned against the marble counter. "About wanting to get married. About being ready to get married?"

"Yes," Darcie reached forward and grabbed both of her hands. "And I know this has been such a journey of self-discovery for you. Your father and I have only ever wanted the best for you, Cathleen. The best. And David is truly the best."

"Well, I—" Cat found herself cut off by the sudden buzzing in her pocket. The hope that it might be Luke made Cat jump, "Oh, this might be work, I should—" She gestured to the door and her mother nodded and waved her hands.

"Of course, go, go," Darcie turned happily back to her online shopping. Those sales at Barney's aren't going to buy themselves.

Once Cat was safely through the patio doors, she pulled out her phone. Luke!

"I'm so glad it's you!" Cat practically burst as she answered the phone with a laugh of exuberance.

"Cat—" Luke choked out. "Cat, I had to leave your place. I—I—" His voice broke.

Was he crying? What on earth could be wrong? Cat wished only that she was there to comfort him.

"Luke? What is it?" Cat sat down on the blue ceramic garden stool by the patio doors.

"My dad—god, Cat. I don't know how to say it," Luke choked up again. "He had a heart attack. He's in intensive care at Watauga Medical Center, but they're transferring him to Wake Baptist Medical Center for surgery right away."

"Oh, no," Cat placed her hand to her heart. She felt broken for

Luke. To lose one parent already was hard enough, he just couldn't lose another. He couldn't. "I'm so sorry."

"He's gotta make it through this Cat. He's got to," Luke's voice was emphatic and filled with emotion. "I'm on my way to the airport now. I know we have so many things to discuss. But—"

"No, it's okay. You have to go," Cat assured him.

"I want my dad to see us get married," Luke spoke earnestly. "I know I said we should just run off and do it. But Cat, you deserve more than that. I want to watch you walk down the aisle with everyone there that we care about."

"What about my parents?" she asked.

"The people we don't care about can come, too, if you want," he said.

Cat laughed. Luke always had a way of making a difficult situation seem light.

"Alright," Cat laughed. "Keep me updated, okay?"

"I will," he said.

"I'm praying for him, Luke," she said.

"Thanks, babe," he said.

Babe. She hadn't heard him say that in years. Her heart lifted. She closed her eyes as she got off the phone and whispered a prayer. One for Luke's father. Another of gratitude, that after all the twists and turns these last few years had taken, she had found Luke again. Or maybe, he had found her. Regardless, she never wanted to let this moment, or him, go.

CHAPTER THIRTY-SIX

THE NEXT FEW DAYS FELT LIKE A BLUR AND HAD CAT BOUNCING between work, her apartment, and her parent's brownstone where David was still playing the starring role of pitiful patient. Not that she doubted the severity of his injuries or his memory loss, she had just expected a quicker recovery than this.

Thankfully, Luke's dad had come through his quadruple by-pass surgery successfully and was heading home to the mountains with Luke to care for him for the time being. Stealing away to talk to Luke seemed to be an impossible task, but Cat relished the fact that she had him to talk to again. A week had flown by, and Cat had still not broached the subject of their break-up with David. Everytime she would get up the nerve or find an opportunity in the conversation, they would be interrupted or he would suddenly "need a nap."

Cat knew from accompanying him to the various doctor's appointments that his memory loss seemed to be worse than expected, and the severe concussion did seem to make David more tired than usual. The swelling on the brain was significant enough that his doctor had requested another CT scan at the follow-up appointment ten days after David had been "home" from the hospital.

On this particular day, Cat sat beside him in the waiting room, her fingers drumming nervously on the armrest of the couch. David reached out and stroked her hand, took it gently in his, and lifted it to his mouth for a kiss.

Cat pulled it away quickly and sneezed into her elbow just before his lips could touch her.

"Bless you," he handed her the box of kleenexes from the table beside him.

"Thanks," Cat took one and made a show of sneezing again, just in case he was trying to plant another kiss. She hated this. Oh, how she hated this.

"I hope you're not coming down with something," David said.

"I know," Cat agreed. "I really don't want to be sick during the round-table discussion I have at work tomorrow.

"At the Children's Museum?" he asked.

"No, I've been working at MOMA the last couple of months," Cat had lost count of how many times she'd told him that in the last ten days.

"Oh," David exclaimed enthusiastically, "Cathleen, that's amazing!"

"It's been pretty wonderful," Cat nodded in agreement. It was nice to see that his enthusiasm hadn't waned, regardless of how many times she had told him.

It was this David. The kind, thoughtful David, that had been the one she had convinced herself that she loved. This was the one that took her on impromptu carriage rides or wanted to kiss her hand at a random doctor's office. She found it much more challenging to break his heart. The arrogant, self-righteous David—he was easy to let go of.

"You did it!" he continued. "You landed your dream job! I'm so proud of you. We should go out and celebrate!"

"David, we ordered a celebratory dinner last night for that very reason," Cat laughed.

"We did?" he asked.

"And four days ago, as well," she reminded him.

"Gosh," David absently touched his hands to his temples. "I can't seem to remember anything."

"Do you have any memories of the accident?" she asked.

"Just flashes of pictures, bits of sounds, the face of the guy that helped me out of the road, the flashing lights, you coming into my hospital room, flowers on my bedside table at your parents' house. How many days have I been there now?" his eyes looked panicked.

"Not long," Cat patted his shoulder reassuringly. "They love being able to help you out."

"Good," he sighed. "I'm grateful to them."

"Mr. Randolph," a nurse appeared at the doorway. "The doctor is ready to review your results. Mrs. Randolph you should come listen, as well."

"I'm Ms. Rhodes," Cat smiled, as she helped David up from his chair. He had graduated from a sling and brace to a cast on his right arm, but his ribs were still healing, making it a challenge to get up or down without an extra hand.

"She's not my wife, yet," David winked at her.

Cat felt her stomach turn. She could not continue this charade much longer. She just couldn't continue without feeling like she was cheating on Luke, or David, or both of them. Luke had told her to wait until whenever she thought was best, and she didn't want to tell David right after getting hit by a truck. Talk about getting run over, twice! But the time had finally come. She would let him down as gently as possible and she would do it tonight.

David held her hand as they walked down the maroon carpeted hallway. She glanced over to him and gave it a squeeze. The look on his face was a mixture of nerves and nausea. His grip was so tight, she didn't think she could pull away if she wanted to.

"Are you alright?" she leaned towards him.

"Just anxious," he said nervously.

"You're going to be alright," she said reassuringly. "You have to be."

Dr. Gillian assured David and Cat that his CT scan appeared perfectly normal. The swelling had gone down, as expected, and the memory loss and occasional headaches seemed to be the only remaining symptoms of his brain injury. The fact that he was exhibiting both short and long term memory loss was abnormal, but not out of the realm of possibility. It was expected to return within a few short weeks.

A few weeks. Cat mulled over her decisions on the cab ride back to her parent's brownstone. She turned to observe David, who was staring obliviously out the window at the passing scenery in Central Park.

"David," Cat reached for his shoulder.

"Hmm," he turned to face her. "Hey, thank you for coming with me today."

"Of course," Cat drew a deep breath and prepared herself.

"Do you remember our first date here?" He interrupted her thought.

"I do," she leaned over him, careful not to put any weight on his ribs, to point out the window. "You hailed a carriage ride right over there."

"And then you felt sick," he said.

Cat laughed, "Yeah, I felt terrible for deserting you."

"See, I can remember some things," David smiled sadly. "Just not what happened yesterday."

"What is the last memory you have of us?" she asked.

"What do you mean?" he asked.

"Tell me the last date you remember," Cat prodded. "Then, maybe we can fill in some of the missing pieces."

David paused, his forehead wrinkled in deep thought. "Gosh, I—I don't know. I remember lots of things we did together. But they don't seem to fall in any particular order."

"Do you remember any conversations we had? Or maybe times when we argued?" Cat's voice prodded him further.

"We didn't fight often, did we?" he asked.

Cat didn't respond, but bit her lip in desperation. It would be so much easier if he could remember this on his own.

"Did we?" David's eyes grew wide. "Well, if we did fight, I'm sure it was my fault and I apologize. Truly."

He reached out for her hand and gave it a squeeze before glancing down.

"Where's your ring?" he asked.

"David," Cat sighed.

"You were going to get it sized!" he exclaimed triumphantly. "Ha! See, I remembered something. And I was upset that you weren't wearing it. Is that right?"

"Yes!" Cat felt her spirit lift. He was so close to remembering when they took a break. "Yes, that's right. That's great! Do you remember anything else from that night?"

David paused. Then, turning back to the window, "Things seem fuzzy still. But I do remember that one bit. And that you found a wedding dress. The perfect dress, right honey?"

"Oh, yes," Cat nodded. "The perfect dress."

He had been so close to recalling the time that they had spent apart, and Cat sincerely hoped that he would make the discovery on his own, without her having to break the news to him, again.

If he was indeed beginning to regain his memories, then perhaps she could wait just a bit longer to say anything. It would be better this way, for David, for her parents, and for herself.

CHAPTER THIRTY-SEVEN

SEPTEMBER CAME WITH AUTUMN BREEZES AND NO END IN SIGHT TO the accelerated busyness at Cat's work. Luke had been phoning in for the up-and-coming artists round table discussions, and Cat was certain that she blushed ten shades of pink each time he spoke.

If nothing else, she was discovering that the old adage, "absence makes the heart grow fonder," was certainly true.

Luke continued creating pieces of work for the exhibit while in Boone, where he was caring for his father, and everyone remarked on the sudden shift in his style. It was reminiscent of the paintings Luke had created in his youth, Marc had commented, when Cat dropped by their gallery one day in mid-September to help uncrate the new pieces he'd shipped, but more sophisticated.

Cat stared longingly at one in particular, with its endless strokes and shades of blue, and dotted in some places with tiny pearls. It was truly spectacular.

"You like him, don't you?" Marc's statement jolted Cat back to reality.

"This artist," Marc motioned toward the painting. "His work seems to be what you gravitate towards when you come in the gallery."

"Oh," Cat blushed, careful not to allow a girlish giggle to escape her lips. She cleared her throat and straightened her shoulders before responding in her most professional tone, "His work is very special. You can tell he paints with his heart. That's rare."

"I'll have to introduce you to him when he returns to the city," Marc said, as he turned back to his work of taking inventory of the new pieces.

"I'd like that very much," Cat managed to say without bursting into laughter, before she excused herself to take a phone call.

"Cathleen Rhodes," she spoke upon answering; she hadn't bothered to glance at the caller ID as she had stepped outside.

"Cathleen, dear. It's your mother," Her mother's voice had a frightened edge to it. "There's a problem."

Cat was uncertain of exactly what the problem might be, but knew what it would boil down to—David. She had been trying unsuccessfully to remind him of their breakup for two weeks now, but after each discussion, he would wake up the next day forgetting that the prior day's conversation had even happened.

Each time it had been the same, they would have a heartfelt conversation that ended with David graciously accepting the end of their relationship, and then having to repeat the conversation a few days later.

Cat had finally explained to her parents that she and David would not be getting married. Nevertheless, her father had relentlessly insisted on keeping all the reservations, until David was of the right mind to remember that he was no longer engaged. It was "unfair to David" he had said, to break it off with him when he couldn't be counted on to remember it. *It is unfair to me*, Cat thought to herself to remain engaged for the sake of pity.

David's cast had come off the week prior and he was now living on his own, back at his own apartment. Cat's father had insisted that David's performance at work was "better than ever" and he "hadn't lost his touch." Why, then, could he not remember the events that transpired the past few months, or even days, when his relationship was concerned? Cat was growing weary of it all. She was especially weary of the 7am phone calls to wish his "fiancé" a marvelous day.

"What's wrong now?" Cat felt her temper growing short, even though her mother had been surprisingly supportive of her lately. She almost seemed relieved when David had appeared to accept the break up. She had overheard part of their conversation the night before David had moved back to his apartment. Of course, he had forgotten the conversation by the next morning.

"Your father just called me," her mother paused. "He was so upset to tell me that David will be sent on business to London in late November for some global client acquisition-thing."

"Oh, that's perfect!" Cat exclaimed. "If David's away on business the month we're supposedly getting married, then this break up can finally happen."

"They want to move up the date," her mother's voice dropped to a whisper.

"What?!" Cat exclaimed.

"I know, Cathleen." Darcie's voice soothed. "I know. I can see now how ridiculous this has become for you. I have watched you kindly and lovingly break things off with David several times now."

"Did you tell dad that this is not happening?" Cat fought to keep her voice even.

"I did." Darcie's voice sounded equally panicked. "I told him that you did not love David. That you were not interested in marrying him and that David had clearly accepted that."

"And ..." Cat said.

"And he thinks he knows best, as always," said Darcie.

Cat noted a hint of irritation in her mother's voice that was typically absent.

"This wedding is not happening, mom," said Cat.

"I understand," her mother soothed.

"What can we do?" Cat had walked towards the Hudson while on the phone with her mother and found herself ascending the stairs to the Highline, an above ground park that ran along the western edge of Manhattan from Chelsea to the Meatpacking District.

"I'm going to try to talk some sense into him tonight, but at this point, I think David will have to remember the fact that you've broken up with him."

"Okay," Cat dodged a jogger and sat on an empty bench facing the river. "Okay, I'll work on David."

Her phone buzzed and she glanced at the call ID. David.

"Speak of the devil, he's calling me on the other line," said Cat.

"I'll let you go," said her mom.

"Thanks, mom. And, thank you," Cat said.

David pulled out the chair for Cat as she took her seat at Orsay. The art-nouveau styled French brasserie never disappointed, and Cat figured if she had to break it off with David for the third time this week, she might as well be enjoying some French comfort food, like her favorite—boeuf bourguignon. Maybe she'd even treat herself to the mousse au chocolat for dessert.

"I have been dying to tell you about my day," David smiled brightly at her as he took a seat, his new veneers flashing a brilliant white. Where he'd lost several teeth in the accident, David had taken the opportunity to improve his smile. No one on the

Upper East Side had straighter or whiter teeth than David Randolph, and that's saying something.

Cat leaned forward with interest, but since her mother had already filled her in on his upcoming travels, she was prepared to feign surprise.

"Tim, the former VP, do you remember him? Obnoxiously drunk at the Christmas party last year and spilled wine on your dress?" asked David.

"Oh yes, I remember him." Cat paused. "David! You are remembering more and more. This is exciting."

"Wow," David seemed surprised. "It just came to me. The memory, I, I didn't even have to call it to mind—it's like, I could just see that moment happening again."

"I'm so glad your memory is improving," Cat smiled genuinely at him. "You were saying, about Tim."

"Oh, yes," David nodded, "Anyway, he's been promoted to President of Acquisitions and they've asked me to be the new VP of Global Acquisitions."

"Wow!" Cat's voice carried the authentic excitement she felt for David. And, the knowledge that with a job promotion he would be more likely to accept her break-up and the permanent severing of their engagement. "David, that is incredible. I am so happy for you. This is well deserved."

"The only issue is," he sighed and reached across the table for her hand. "I have to leave in mid-November to go to London for six weeks."

"I think you will love London, David," Cat squeezed his hand.

"But, our wedding-" he began.

"It's not happening, David," she said softly and earnestly. "We've broken it off several times now but you never remember the next day."

"You're kidding," he said.

Cat sat silently.

"You're not kidding," he started.

"I care about you," Cat squeezed his hand again. "In the past two months, since your accident, I've been reminded of the man I thought I could marry."

"Couldn't you still?" His eyes looked at her hopefully.

"I want you to find someone who will love you the way you deserve to be loved. And that's not me," Cat stated earnestly.

He sat back in his chair and eyed her suspiciously, "When did we break off the engagement?"

"Quite some time ago," she answered truthfully. "We took a break in late March and ended things in June."

"Wow," he ran his hands through his hair. "You've been going along with this since August?"

Cat nodded and waved the waiter off as he approached the table.

"I'm sorry," David said finally. "I'm sorry I've put you through this."

"It's hardly your fault." Cat leaned towards him. "You had a traumatic brain injury. You couldn't be expected to recall everything from the past few months. It's been a difficult time for both of us. I'm just thankful to see you recovering."

"Your dad is trying to contact all the wedding vendors to move up the date," he stated.

"So I heard," Cat sighed. "Can you please call him personally to let him know that he will need to cancel?"

"Of course," David nodded. "I'll call him right after dinner."

"Thank you, David," Cat hoped her voice reflected the gratitude she felt. "And I have something for you." She leaned over to her purse and pulled out her Marc Jacobs change purse. Carefully, she unzipped the top and pulled out the flawless princess cut diamond ring that had been tucked into the change purse since March and said, "It is a beautiful ring. You are going to make some girl very lucky someday."

She held it aloft for him to take. He reached forward and lifted her left hand as he took the ring.

"What ring is that?" he motioned to the twisted copper wire she'd slipped back onto her ring finger for the evening.

"Oh, this?" Cat pulled her hand back. "I've had it forever. Since high school actually. It was missing for a while, but I found it again."

"Interesting," David sat back and began examining his menu. His expression had shifted ever so slightly.

Cat cautiously opened her menu. Her heart was pounding; now that her engagement was officially off with David, she was free to move forward with Luke. Finally. She desperately wanted to sneak to the bathroom and text him, but decided it would be prudent to wait, since she was having one last supper with her ex-fiancé.

David and Cat parted ways that evening, with David assuring her that he would be calling her father as soon as he returned to his apartment. He wanted to make the call in private, since her father had become a surrogate father to him in many ways over the last year. Cat felt the weight of expectations crumble at his departure. She was finally free.

Cat walked at a leisurely pace back to her apartment, stopping to buy sunflowers at the corner bodega. She twisted the ring on her hand and reached into her pocket for her phone to call her Luke. Her fiancé.

CHAPTER THIRTY-EIGHT

HER PHONE RANG EARLY THE NEXT DAY. CAT NORMALLY ALLOWED herself to sleep in until 7am on Saturdays, before rolling out of bed, throwing on her favorite pair of Brooks sneakers, and heading on her long weekend run. She glanced at her iPhone. It was her father—she groaned and briefly considered ignoring the call. This would not be good.

"Hello," she made sure her voice was extra groggy, so he would know he had woken her up.

"Well, I hope you're happy—" he began.

"Dad, I know this has been difficult," Cat sat up in her bed and crossed her legs.

"I managed to get everything rebooked for the 1st of November," her dad's voice was triumphant.

"I'm sorry, what?" Cat put her feet on the floor. If she had been half-asleep a moment before, she was now wide-awake and fueled by rage.

"Everything is rebooked," he repeated.

"Did David call you last night?" Cat did her best to keep her voice calm, but her sounds came out in staccato despite her attempt.

"No. Was he supposed to?" he asked.

"He told me he was going to call you last night." Cat was pacing her room. She took several deep breaths. *In thru the nose and out thru the mouth,* she told herself as she closed her eyes and took another breath.

"Well, he didn't," her father sounded nonchalant. "I guess he forgot. You know how his memory has been."

Cat lost it. "YES, I KNOW EXACTLY HOW HIS MEMORY HAS BEEN!!" She shouted so loudly that her next door neighbor banged on the shared wall of her apartment a moment later. She winced.

"Cathleen, is there something you need to say?" her father's voice was terse. He knew exactly what she needed to say. The fact that he was perpetuating this situation and taking advantage of David's memory loss only further infuriated Cat.

"I am not getting married to David. I reminded him of our break up last night—for the ten-thousandth time. I gave his ring back and he accepted it. It is over. OVER!" She shouted the last word, not caring who heard her. The entire building might have felt her rage and she wouldn't have been surprised. She felt it coursing through her veins like something dangerous that had been unleashed and now was beyond containment. She ended the call before he could respond.

This morning, for her run, she headed to the East River. Her normal loop in Central Park didn't seem sufficient for rage-running. She needed to get away from the norm, from her routine, from the never-ending cycle of breaking it off with her fiancé who never seemed to remember.

The island of Manhattan, which on some days felt like her playground, had become her prison. The early morning mist from the river hit her face as she jogged through Carl Schurz Park. She needed to escape. More than anything she wanted Luke—to sit together on a morning like today and have pancakes, to hold hands and wander through the Christmas trees, to simply be.

As steadily as her feet hit the pavement, a plan started forming in her head. Throughout the last month, her focus had been on the up-and-coming artist series. She had been able to meet with and interview each artist in their studio space and watch them work. One of the photographers from MOMA had always accompanied her to document the artist at work in their space. She only had three artists left to meet with, and Luke was one of them. She would have to go to where he was working. And, when she returned, married, her father and David would have no choice but to accept the finality of her decision.

Her heart quickened and she picked up her pace. This was it. This was the moment that Cat made her own decisions and directed her own path. If her life was a story, stretching out before her, Cat had finally taken the pen. In this tale, she would not be some damsel in distress. In her story, the princess saves herself.

Her runtime that morning was a new personal record—5.6 miles in forty-one minutes. She ran all the way to Lili's dorm apartment in the village and didn't stop until she found herself pounding on her sister's door.

"What in the name of all things holy?" Lili's greeting was less enthusiastic for an early Saturday morning.

Cat brushed past her quickly into the apartment, "I've had an epiphany!"

Lili did a double take at Cat in her running shoes, "Did you run here?"

"I'm getting married in North Carolina next month," Cat stated emphatically.

"I'm sorry," Lili shut the door and turned to face her big sister, "Did I miss something? What time is it?"

"Never mind that, Lili." Cat began pacing. "I need to plan a wedding. A wedding that I want. Not mom. Not dad. And certainly, NOT David."

"Can I get coffee before you continue?" Lili stumbled towards her Keurig. "I was out until 3am."

"And whose fault is that?" Cat raised an eyebrow.

"Do you want my help planning this or not?" Lili asked.

"Make me a coffee too, in that case," said Cat.

Once both sisters were seated with coffees in hand, in Lili's small studio space, the planning began in earnest. Cat would spend the next couple of weeks wrapping up her work and interviews for the MOMA exhibit. On Monday, she would fill Monique in on her unique situation and relationship with Luke Presnell and request to take her two week vacation time from the end of October through the first of November. Cat had not used any of her vacation days thus far and did not see this being an issue. Of course, she could also interview her soon-to-be-husband and complete the assignment for work while she was there.

Lili and hopefully Rachel would fly down the week of the wedding to help Cat prepare everything, and she knew Mimi would be more than agreeable to help. There was just one thing gnawing at Cat. Her mother. As strained as their relationship had been over the years, Cat wanted her to be there. With Lili's encouragement, Cat decided she would let her mother in on their project. After a quick call to her mother, she had a girl's brunch planned for 11am that morning. *Two hours from now*, thought Cat, as she glanced at her watch. This was it. Either her mother was in and she would happily go along, or she was not.

Cat only hoped she could be trusted not to tell her father until after the ceremony would take place. He had already swooped down to North Carolina and attempted to ruin her life once before. She would not allow him to do it again.

Cat and Lili ordered their mimosas at Nero in the Meatpacking District and waited for Darcie Rhodes to arrive.

Their mother had always been something of a mystery to Cat. How a farmer's daughter from Western North Carolina had elevated herself to become a Manhattan socialite and ended up with her father remained a mystery. Of course, her parents had regaled them with the tale of their whirlwind romance a time or two. Mom had saved every penny to take a Greyhound bus to New York City in 1986, the day after she graduated high school. Arriving in Port Authority on 42nd Street back then meant walking through a pretty gritty Times Square. Gone was the Toys R Us and the M&M candy store that Cat knew today. It was a sea of peep shows and unsavory characters. Darcie had grit back then, Cat knew she must have, she only wished she could see that side of her mother again. Or, really, for the first time in Cat's life. She longed to see the side of her that had put herself through night school at CUNY and worked two day jobs. How had she become the perfect Upper-West-Side, Junior League blueblood-type? Cat was forever left to wonder.

"Girls!" Darcie exclaimed as she approached the table. "This is such a surprise. I can't remember the last time I had brunch with my two favorite daughters."

Cat and Lili smiled at each other before turning to face their mother.

"Mimosa?" Lili offered.

"Not for me," Darcie declined. "Just a Pelligrino and lime wedges, please," she told the passing server.

"A creature of habit," Cat commented on her mother's signature drink.

"Yes, well," she shrugged, as if to say 'you know me.'

Lili leaned in towards her mother, "How's dad taking the news?"

"Which news would that be?" her mother accepted the glass from the waiter and began squeezing in two wedges of lime. "That Cat is not marrying David or that you're a lesbian?"

"The David news, Mom," Lili rolled her eyes.

Darcie laughed. "I was just teasing. You know … I'm really fine about the whole thing now."

"Really?" Lili looked unconvinced.

"Absolutely," Darcie nodded emphatically at both of her girls. "I've spent too many years pushing you away with my expectations. I'm sorry for the time we've lost. It wasn't worth it … and look where it's gotten us."

"Absolutely nowhere," Cat said flatly.

"Exactly," Darcie agreed. "So, let's make today a day of new beginnings for both of you. To my beautiful daughters," she raised her glass, "may you craft the life you were made for."

The trio raised their glasses in salute.

Cat spent the brunch listening to Lili and her mother exchange news and updates on Lili's pre-law classes, ever increasing in their difficulty and requirements. When it was Cat's turn to give updates, she kept mostly to news of her work and the new task of preparing the exhibit at the MOMA. She wanted to save the Luke update until just the right moment but she wasn't entirely sure how to broach the topic.

"You know, mom, I have to drop by the gallery I was telling

you about," Cat mentioned nonchalantly as they rose from the table. "You should join me."

"That sounds nice," her mother agreed.

Lili gave Cat a thumbs up when Darcie had turned to grab her jacket, "My schedule is wide open this morning. I can come along."

"Great," Cat beamed at both of them. "I'll lead the way."

CHAPTER THIRTY-NINE

"THESE ARE EXQUISITE, CATHLEEN," HER MOTHER REMARKED FOR the second time since entering the Chelsea gallery. "Really impressive."

Luke tried not to think about how snugly his possessions had fit into the back of an old Silverado. He tried to focus on the fact that he was about to accomplish something that for so long he had only dreamed of. He was about to intern at a gallery, a gallery in New York City in fact. He had even been offered the rare opportunity to show his own work in the new artist series the gallery would be doing the coming year.

"I think so, too," Cat nodded. "This artist; he'll be the last one I have to interview for the exhibit."

"The one that you'll be going out of town to meet with?" her mother asked, walking slowly towards another canvas. "I'd be interested in acquiring one of these pieces for our home. This one would be lovely in the dining area. All the shades of blue."

"This is his newest piece. He sent it back from North Carolina where he's been working."

"North Carolina! Really?" Her mother turned towards her. "Where in North Carolina is he?"

"In Boone, actually," Cat took a tentative step in, her eyes never leaving Darcie's face.

"In Boone," her mother lowered her voice, "Cathleen, who is this artist?"

"The man I'm going to marry next month." Cat stepped in and took her mother's hands in hers. "It's Luke, mom. It's always been Luke."

Darcie's eyes filled to the brim and spilled over. "Oh, honey." Her hand reached up and touched Cat's cheek, which was now wet with tears of her own. "I should have known."

"I want you to be there when I walk down the aisle," Cat swallowed back her own tears and reached up to wipe her mother's cheeks. "I'm crafting the life I was made for, just like you said."

Her mother turned to look at the pieces displayed throughout the gallery before clutching her heart and spun back to wrap Cat into a bear hug. Darcie extended one hand and pulled Lili in, who had been sniffling off to the side.

"I would love for nothing more," Darcie kissed each of them on the cheek. "I will figure out what to tell your father … after the wedding, of course."

"Of course," Cat and Lili spoke in unison.

$$\ast\ast\ast$$

Rachel, being someone who had known both Luke and Cat for many years, was beside herself with glee when Cat told her later that day.

"You're getting MARRIED!!" she shouted in the cab when Cat had told her, making their cabbie hit the break suddenly in surprise.

"Ow," Cat rubbed her forehead, which had just slammed against the partition. "Thanks for that Rach."

"Please, ladies," the cab driver shouted back at them. "You should be wearing seatbelts. I am not liable if you are injured."

He tapped the notice on the divider between the seats.

Securing her seatbelt, Rachel turned to Cat, "This is the most," she started fanning her face frantically, "the most, I just, I can't believe—" Rachel burst into tears.

"I know, Rach," Cat laughed and reached to grab Rachel with both of her hands. "I know. This has been a long time coming. It's been surreal. We've been talking almost every night since August, but didn't want to tell anyone until I figured out what to do about David."

"And about David," Rachel grabbed her hand, "Does he have any recollection of your many break ups?"

"None." Cat sighed. "But, he does have the ring and I've decided to write him something that he can tape to his mirror or door or somewhere. You know, just a brief mental check in to start each day. 'I am David Randolph, a successful Vice President of Global Acquisitions at Goldman Sachs. I am NOT engaged. I am overcoming memory loss from a recent accident. Today will be a good day.' You know, the important things."

Rachel laughed, "I like that you build up his self-esteem and squeeze in the reminder that he's not engaged."

"It's the least I can do," Cat shrugged. "But here's where you come in—I want you to help with the wedding if you think you can sneak away from work for a few days?"

"Nothing would make me happier," Rachel agreed with eagerness, "I'm due for a trip home and this is a perfect excuse."

"Wonderful," Cat checked off her mental list. She was one step closer to the wedding and marriage of her own choosing. "And for location?"

"Oh, there are so many great places!" Rachel began running through a list of possible venues.

"Whoa, there!" Cat held up a hand. "I love your zeal, truly.

But I really want something simple. Is there somewhere we can rent a big white tent for the reception? I want to plan everything around Mimi's farmhouse. The wedding, the reception, all of it."

Rachel squeezed her hand, "Now that sounds perfect."

"And I'm still counting on you to make sure it has that hint of New York sophistication," Cat winked.

"Oh girl, I'm on it," Rachel said.

The cab took the pair to the Vera Wang Bridal Salon on Madison Avenue where Cat had famously passed out cold seven months earlier. She had not made an appointment for a full service stylist consultation, but this time, Cat knew she didn't want one. She knew exactly what she wanted. Returning the dress her parent's had purchased for the wedding to David proved to be a bit challenging since Cat had already had the initial fittings, but when she agreed to accepting a mere fifty percent refund in the form of a store credit, the sales clerk was agreeable.

"Alright," Rachel looked longingly through the dresses once inside the store. "You have three thousand dollars to spend on your dress. Where shall we begin?"

"Oh, we're not getting a dress for me," Cat smirked. "We're getting my bridesmaids dresses today."

"No!" Rachel spun towards her.

"Yes," Cat bounced to her friend. "And since you and Lili are to be my bridesmaids, I need your help deciding."

"Oh, Cat!" Rachel threw her arms around her. "But wait," she pulled back to look at her friend suspiciously, "what will you wear?"

"I have something in mind," Cat said secretly.

"Are you going to tell me?" Rachel asked.

"Not yet," Cat winked. "Today we are finding the perfect dress for you!"

"Well, if you insist." Rachel skipped happily to the other side of the store where racks of chiffon dresses stood waiting to be plucked.

"I always thought a fall wedding would be perfect for the mountains," Cat sighed dreamily as she stroked a lace aubergine knee-length shift dress.

"That one is gorgeous," Rachel reached out to take it from Cat. "And the colors are perfect for fall on your grandmother's farm."

"I think so," Cat stood back to examine the color against Rachel's skin. "It's perfect for you, Rach."

"And it's a great color for Lili," Rachel responded as she danced towards the dressing rooms. "We're one step closer, Cat."

She disappeared into the dressing room and Cat allowed herself to sink into the plush velveteen couch. Since that morning, she'd been going nonstop—the high energy, the expectations, the hopes of the future, it was all poised to become a reality. Past experience had told Cat that anything that seemed too good to be true was likely the case. When would these plans come crashing down around her? What if they didn't? What if it all worked out as perfectly as she had planned it in her mind? Would she allow herself to relax and accept happiness without waiting for the other shoe to drop? Did she remember how to do that? Too many questions. Of course she knew how to be happy and accept the moment for the gift that it was. Luke had taught her that, so many years ago. And he would be there by her side, her partner in this new life, to remind her along the way. One day at a time.

Rachel sauntered into the room and twirled in front of Cat, bringing her back from her distant thoughts, "Well?"

"Perfect," Cat sat up, "We're one step closer, Rach."
Rachel lifted her hand and made an invisible check mid-air.

CHAPTER FORTY

MONIQUE AND DANIEL SEEMED CONCERNED WHEN CAT ASKED TO speak to them privately on Monday morning.

"I told you she was too good to be true," Cat heard Daniel whisper to Monique as they stepped in the conference room and she closed the doors behind them. "She probably got an offer at the Met. I told you they pay more."

Cat turned to face them both, "I'm not leaving."

"Whew!" Monique exclaimed. "You had me worried. I did not want the task of replacing you and Daniel cannot finish this exhibit without you."

"Hey!" Daniel feigned offense.

"You know it's true." Monique gave him a knowing glance.

"Yeah, she's right," he agreed.

Cat pursed her lips to keep from laughing at the two of them. She was truly blessed with the most enjoyable co-workers.

"So," Monique folded her hands in her lap and gave Cat her full attention. "What is this about?"

"As you know, I've decided to interview and observe each artist in their workspace prior to the exhibit opening in January," Cat began. "I only have a few more left, but one of them is currently living and working out of their studio space in North Carolina."

"Luke, right?" Daniel nodded.

"Right." Cat could not suppress a smile in her response. It was like fighting a tide, the mention of his name caused her face to spread wide in an ear to ear grin, and there was no use in fighting it.

"I know that smile," Monique nodded. "You're in love with him."

Cat brushed her hair behind her ear and nodded.

"But, you haven't even met him in person yet, have you?" Daniel stood up. "I mean, he missed the first round-table discussion because he had to leave the city and care for his dad in North Carolina."

"You're right," she nodded. "He wasn't at the first discussion, but I have known him for years. It's—well, it's complicated."

"Go ahead," Monique urged.

"I told you we need to buy a popcorn maker for this office." Daniel nudged.

Cat started with seeing the paintings at the gallery and the realization that they belonged to, none other than, her high school sweetheart. This realization, coupled with the fact that Cat had spontaneously decided to drop most of her savings to purchase the painting, resulted in Monique wiping tears from her eyes before Cat had even gotten to the best part of the story.

"And then," Cat continued, handing Monique a box of tissues. "He appeared at my apartment the next morning to deliver the painting."

"He didn't!" Daniel exclaimed.

"He did," Cat insisted.

"This is just like 'An Affair to Remember,'" Monique blew her nose into another tissue.

"What?" Daniel and Cat spoke in unison.

"Don't tell me?" Monique glanced between the two of them, "Cary Grant?"

They shook their heads.

"Deborah Kerr?" she continued. "Seriously. We are having a

movie night when Cat returns from North Carolina."

"And I'm bringing popcorn!" Daniel chimed in.

"Just tell me he swept you off your feet the moment he walked through the door," Monique held her hands over her heart.

"Well, not quite," Cat blushed. "I think I may have slapped him first."

Daniel gasped.

"But, then there was quite a bit of sweeping and kissing," Cat threw her head back. "It's become a blur. I don't know the last time I was this deliriously happy," she admitted. "Never!"

"You may take as much time as you need, Cat." Monique patted her back as they stepped out of the conference room. "Just promise me I can fly down for this wedding."

"I would love that, Monique," Cat hugged her boss in gratitude.

Things were falling into place and Cat promised herself that nothing would alter her plans. Not David. Not even her father.

✶ ✶ ✶

With her pumpkin spice latte in hand, Cat found a bench in Central Park on her lunch break that day and breathed in the moment.

The leaves were changing and the air had just a bit of a chill. She knew that the mountains of North Carolina would soon be washed in a tapestry of colors. She had booked her plane ticket to Charlotte, with Lili, Mom, and Rachel flying down a week later for the wedding.

Cat pulled out her planner and checked off the to do list.

Plan with Lili, Rachel, and Mom. Check.

Find bridesmaids dresses. Check.

Arrange time off. Check.

Book plane tickets. Check.

She glanced down. There was only one more key element left to plan. Cat carefully dialed Mimi's new cell phone number. Guilt settled into the pit of her stomach. She knew the sensation well but this time it was warranted. Since leaving Boone so abruptly her Senior year, she had only seen her grandmother twice. Once at her high school graduation from Emma Williard and then again when she graduated from Columbia. Neither time did she allow herself a one on one conversation with Mimi. It broke her heart not to have seen her more often these past five years, but with thoughts of Mimi came thoughts and memories of Luke and she hadn't wanted to conjure up either. She longed for Mimi and their easy relationship, the way they had teased each other. Mimi always knew when to come cuddle her up with a cup of hot cocoa or when to be stern, which never lasted long. Cat sighed. They had lost touch over the years and Cat knew she was to blame. Mimi had consistently sent cards for birthdays, holidays, or just because. They were always written in her beautiful penmanship—long, drawn out letters with curls at the end. Cat paused before hitting send.

One ring. Two. Three. Cat pulled the phone away, prepared to hang up when she heard the familiar voice through the receiver.

"This is Mimi Wilson," she sounded breathless, Cat was certain she heard a chainsaw running in the background. She closed her eyes. It was likely they were starting to cut Christmas trees and Mimi was hard-pressed to get back to work.

"Hello, is anyone there?" the voice repeated.

Cat cleared her throat, which suddenly felt like sandpaper. "Mi-Mimi, it's Cat."

"Catie-bug!" Mimi's voice held all the joy Cat could've hoped for. If there was underlying disappointment in her or any failures on her part, it did not come through.

"Gosh, it's good to hear your voice!" Cat reached up to find tears streaming down her cheeks. This wash of emotions has been coming more frequently lately.

"You have no idea," Mimi laughed. "I've sure missed you! Wait—is everything okay? Is your mama—"

"Everyone's fine," Cat interrupted. "There's nothing wrong. In fact, for the first time in a long time, everything feels right."

"Tell me more," her grandmother urged her on. From the sound of the slamming screen door, Cat knew she had gone inside the house and was likely pulling up a chair at the kitchen table.

Cat took a breath and closed her eyes, where to begin?

"I'm so happy, Mimi," she began. "So deliriously happy."

Cat found herself spilling out a story that took more twists and turns than she realized, until she spoke them aloud and strung them together for the first time. Each piece of her story was like a building block that, when constructed, created a structure that was strange, yet surprisingly, beautiful. That was the life she was crafting now.

"We're getting married, Mimi," she concluded with a blissful sigh. "And I wanted to ask you a favor."

"Oh Catie-bug!" Mimi exclaimed, the slamming screen door and the familiar creak of the porch swing came through in the background. Cat imagined her grandmother settling into the porch swing where she and Luke had their first real heart to heart. "You don't even have to ask. You just let me know what you need Mimi to do!"

Cat smiled, "May we get married on the farm? It's where I fell in love with him. It feels right that we should say our vows there."

"Nothing would make your old grandma happier!" exclaimed Mimi.

"Thank you, Mimi. And, you're not that old," Cat joked.

Mimi guffawed.

Cat continued, "I'm going to have Rachel help me set up everything and contact vendors. We want to keep it very small. Only a dozen or so folks if that's okay with you."

"Will your parents be coming, Catie?" Mimi asked.

"Mom will. We haven't told dad yet. I think—well, I think it will be better to wait."

"Well, I don't blame you one bit for that. You know I support whatever you decide," Mimi stated.

"I know, Mimi," Cat rose from the bench and strolled toward the pond. "And, actually, there's one more thing I wanted to ask."

"Anything," Mimi said.

"Do you remember when I helped you clean out the attic and we found your wedding dress?" Cat asked.

"I do. And yes, you may wear it. You will look just perfect," Mimi said.

Cat sat down at the water's edge and began to drop autumn leaves into the water, watching them float away one by one, as her grandmother reminisced about her own wedding back in 1968. Cat closed her eyes and envisioned her wedding day. The dress her grandmother wore was timeless, with sheer lace sleeves, a fitted silk bodice, and an A-line skirt. She could almost hear the swish of the dress as she walked down the aisle. Only two weeks and a million prayers stood between now and her big day. She whispered another prayer for good measure.

CHAPTER FORTY-ONE

CAT WATCHED LUKE'S FACE INTENTLY AS THEY SPED UP THE MOUNTAIN on Highway 321. Since he had picked her up at the airport, she couldn't take her eyes off of him. They had been talking non-stop. There was so much to say. So much to plan. It felt like old times, yet completely new at the same time, and Cat wondered how that was possible.

The sharp incline and twists along the road reminded Cat that she neglected to take her medicine for motion sickness. It'd been so long since she'd had the need. Cat leaned towards the window and rolled it down quickly to inhale a few quick gulps of cool air.

"Uh oh," he said knowingly. "This feels a little too familiar, Cat."

"I know," she smiled weakly. "Are you thinking of the day we met?"

"I'm thinking I'm going to pull over at this overlook," he smiled, handing her a plastic bag from under the seat. "This truck may be old, but I don't want it smelling like vomit."

She hopped out of the car and stood to face the mountain view, while Luke waited for her queasiness to subside.

He rubbed her shoulders while she leaned back against him. She could feel his chest rise and fall. He breathed in deeply.

She turned back to meet his eyes, "Are you smelling my hair, Luke Presnell?"

"Would you think it was weird if I said yes?" he asked.

"Nope," She leaned up to nip at his ear and whispered, "I want to smell you, too."

"That actually does sound a little weird," he laughed. "Come on, weirdo. Let's go."

Luke walked around to the passenger side to open the door for her. She had forgotten his predilection for old fashioned gestures like that. It made her love him even more, if that was possible. Cat realized with delight that it was these moments she had to look forward to. The thrill of falling in love with him again. The exaltation of the little moments that make connections meaningful and lasting. The excitement of remembering all the little things she loved and discovering all the new ones. Nearly five years had passed since their night together in the barn. There was so much to learn about the time they had lost. Without a second of hesitation, Cat leaned onto her tiptoes to kiss him fully on the mouth as she climbed into the truck. Lingering just long enough for their lips to part.

He paused for a moment before closing her door, "We could park here a little longer if you like?"

"Nah," Cat winked. "I just wanted to give you a little taste of what you have to look forward to."

"You like to tease me, Cathleen Rhodes," Luke leaned in and kissed her deeply.

Her hands went automatically to his hair. She felt him take her face in his hands and then move down her shoulders and to her waist.

He pulled back quickly, "I can tease, too."

And with that, he stepped back and shut the door of the truck, leaving her breathless.

"That was mean," she smirked at him as he buckled himself back up in the driver's seat.

She had never seen him so elated. She was certain that her face must look something similar.

Her phone began to vibrate against her.

"It's Rachel," she smiled, "I'm going to let her know we are almost home."

"Of course," Luke stoked her cheek.

"Hey, Rach," Cat answered bubbly.

"Well, hi there, sunshine," Rachel laughed. "Do you have the groom with you?"

"No, he didn't pick me up at the airport," Cat made her voice sound anxious. "I don't know where he is, Rachel!"

"What!?" Rachel yelled. Cat could hear something break in the background.

"Good Lord, Rachel!" Cat laughed. "I'm totally kidding. Luke is right here. Say hi, Luke."

"Hi, Luke!" he shouted beside her.

Cat had to hold the phone away from her ear because of the loud whooping that was coming through. She couldn't hear all of Rachel's words, but thought she caught the jist of it. It was something to the effect of, "You're getting married! AHHH!"

"Look, Rach. I'll give you a call as soon as we get settled at Mimi's house. I can't wait to see you in one week!"

"Ahhhhh," Rachel let out another shriek before hanging up the phone.

"You girls are too much," Luke shook his head. "I don't know what I'll do when we have little girls shrieking and running around the house.

Cat felt her heart skip a beat as she reached out to touch his cheek, "I always imagined two little mischievous boys tracking mud into the house and bringing home toads."

"That sounds exciting, too," Luke laughed. "As long as they're not bringing home squirrels. Am I right?"

"Eeeek!" Cat shuddered. "Absolutely."

Her hand went from his cheek to his shoulder and down his arms. She bit her lip and let her hands move into his lap and back and forth along his thigh.

"You haven't changed, Cat," Luke cleared his throat and winked at her. "I would tell you to scoot closer but there's not a seatbelt in the middle and—"

"And?" Cat unbuckled and scooted closer. She leaned in and breathed softly in his ear, "You don't want me to stop do you?"

"Oh, Cat," Luke hesitated. "Cat, you're gonna make me wreck."

In a flash, Cat saw a movement out of the corner of her eye and Luke slammed on the brake. His right arm stretched out to pin her to the seat as the truck spun around, but Cat still felt the impact of her head hitting the dashboard before everything went black.

"And, tell me exactly why your fiancé was unbuckled?" Cat heard the responding officer asking Luke as her eyes flickered open.

Luke looked towards her cautiously and seemed to search for his words, the shared glance between them made the cop raise one eyebrow.

"I'm just gonna put that she was looking for something," the officer jotted on his accident report, before looking up at them with a wink. "This happens more often than you'd think."

"Uh, thanks," Luke leaned towards Cat and kissed her on the forehead. "You, okay?"

"Yeah," Cat leaned up. "But my head is pounding."

"The ambulance is on the way," Luke pulled back to take a better look at her.

"Thankfully, the officer was passing as the deer jumped into the woods or he would've written me a citation for distracted driving."

"I'm so sorry," Cat squeezed his hand. "That was completely my fault."

"And the deer's," Luke added.

"Yes, but I wouldn't have hit my head if I was sitting in my seat and not putting my tongue in your ear."

"Well," Luke laughed. "That is true."

"I really don't need the ambulance," Cat insisted. A feeling of panic rose in her chest. The last time she was at the Watauga Medical Center was when Luke had left her alone and with a broken heart. She did not want to return to that place until she had a more positive excuse—like childbirth.

"You sure?" he asked.

"Positive," she insisted. "Just an Advil."

"Alright," Luke nodded. "They'll probably still want to check you out. But we can refuse to transfer to the hospital. I do want them to take a look at you, though," he added protectively.

"Alright, honey," Cat leaned into him and breathed him in. She had forgotten how he smelled. It made her miss him, even though he was sitting right beside her. *How is that even possible?* Cat wondered.

It was nearly dark when they pulled up the gravel drive in front of Mimi's house. Cat could tell she'd been doing extensive yard work around the farmhouse. Though Mimi had always loved to garden, the additions of terraced flower beds and hanging baskets around the porch only added to the already charming picture-perfect farmhouse.

"It's changed," Cat said finally. "But, not, at the same time."

"Jim loves to garden almost as much as Mimi," Luke nodded to the flower pots spilling over with fall colors.

"Jim!" Cat exclaimed, "I can't believe I hadn't even asked Mimi about Jim!"

She hopped out of the truck to see Mimi running from the porch towards her.

"Mimi!" Cat ran to her grandmother and found herself covered in grandmotherly kisses and the warmest embrace. A great big bear hug, as Mimi would call it. "Mimi, the farm looks beautiful! Just gorgeous."

"Let me look at you," Mimi pulled back and whistled. "You've found the most beautiful bride," she looked at Luke. "He's lucky," she winked at Cat.

"Yes, I am," Luke agreed and walked into Mimi's open arms. Cat felt herself pulled in again.

After the hugging had subsided, Cat noticed Jim hanging by the door. He gave an awkward wave and smiled.

"Hey, Jim!" Cat called. "Mimi," Cat lowered her voice as she and Luke gathered her bags from the truck. "I can't believe you didn't mention that you and Jim are still together. I'm so sorry I didn't even ask!"

"Not to worry," Mimi grabbed a bag to help.

"Did y'all?" Cat looked at her grandmother before asking, "Did y'all get married?"

"Married?" Mimi laughed, "Why, no, darlin.' We didn't get married. I promise I woulda told ya if we did."

Cat smiled, "I just wanted to make sure I hadn't missed anything."

"Naw," Mimi shook her head, before raising her voice, "We're just living in sin. Right, Jim?"

"That's right honey," Jim laughed and came to take Cat's bags out of her hands. "And loving every minute of it."

Nope, the farmhouse hadn't changed much. But, Mimi seemed to have lightened up a bit about some things. Cat and Luke exchanged glances and stifled some laughter as they crossed the threshold to the home that held so many memories for both of them. Cat couldn't wait to make some more.

CHAPTER FORTY-TWO

CAT SPENT THE NEXT WEEK FUSSING OVER DECORATIONS WITH MIMI, getting Mimi's old wedding dress taken in to fit her perfectly, and picking out a few arrangements at the florist.

"I really do want to keep things simple," Cat insisted for the third time that morning, as she followed Mimi around the local Harris Teeter so Mimi could gather the ingredients for her 'famous wedding punch.'

"Oh I know, honey," Mimi nodded, adding 6 cans of crushed pineapple to the cart. "But folks love punch at a wedding."

"There will only be a dozen folks there," Cat continued. "How many cups of punch do you expect each person to drink?"

Mimi laughed. "Alright, Catie-bug. Alright. I'll try not to get too much. What's next on your list?"

"The cake," Cat scrutinized her to-do list. "I'll head over to the bakery and get that ordered."

"Will they have time to make you a wedding cake? Your wedding is days away," Mimi's eyes widened in alarm.

"It will be fine, Mimi," Cat patted her arm. "Besides, I don't want a big cake. Just a couple of smaller cakes that are all different flavors. Luke thought that would be more fun."

Mimi relaxed and put her hand to her chest, "You'll have to forgive your ole Mimi. You know I've never helped plan a wedding before."

"You didn't help mom plan hers?" Cat watched a surprised

look cross Mimi's face.

"No, no I did not," Mimi began examining her grocery list and turned away. "Now, where would those maraschino cherries be?"

Cat reached up to the top shelf and handed her a jar. "Mimi? What happened between you and mom when she was younger? No one has ever really talked about it."

"Catie, you'd better get over to the bakery and order your cakes," Mimi changed the subject. "I'll meet you at the checkout counter."

Cat tried to suppress her questions as she walked away from her grandmother. Perhaps now was not the best time to open old wounds.

Though the plans for the wedding were falling into place as best as they could with so little time to plan, both she and Luke realized a mere day before the event that they had neglected to find someone to officiate their big day.

"How is it possible that we've been planning a wedding with no one to conduct the ceremony?" Luke said for the third time that morning.

Cat huffed at him while setting up the folding chairs under the tent, "You say that as though this is my fault. I thought that was something the groom's family arranged?!"

"As though I would know!" Luke quipped back. "I'm not the one with the wedding planning experience."

Cat fumed, the stress of planning a wedding without much assistance had gotten to them both, clearly. It didn't help that her mother, Lili, and Rachel had to push back their arrival until today, the day before the wedding. Lili had an exam that couldn't be missed, Rachel's boss was giving her a hard time. And, of course, her mother was having a difficult time escaping from her father for the weekend without raising suspicions. They had already been dodging questions and calls from David for the last three weeks.

"I wasn't involved in the wedding planning, remember," Cat snapped. "Everyone was going along without me. How was I supposed to know about hiring the minister?!"

She felt the heat rising in her cheeks and tears about to brim over. In her anger, she tossed down the chair she was holding and stomped towards Mimi's barn.

"Hey!" Luke called, "Cat! Come back. Shit."

Cat heard the last word muttered under his breath. She heard his footsteps coming up behind her.

"Luke," she sniffed without turning to face him. "I adore you, but you really piss me off sometimes."

"Cat, I'm sorry." Luke stepped right behind her and placed his hands on her shoulders. "I know there's been so much to take care of, and that Mimi's wanting to make this a bigger affair than you'd planned, and I'm still helping care for my dad and—I—I'm sorry I snapped. It's been a stressful time for all of us."

Cat nodded and turned in place to wrap her arms around his shoulders, "It will be worth it in the end. If we have to, we'll go to the courthouse to get married, and the ceremony here will just be for ourselves. And that's fine, too. I just want to be your wife."

"One more day." Luke leaned down, "All this craziness will be over in one more day. No more ignoring calls."

"No more having co-workers lie when David calls the office," Cat said.

"No more pretending," Luke concluded. "We can just be together. And if your dad has a fit, well then, he'll just have to get over it."

Cat laughed. There was no telling what her father's reaction would be. Maybe she would just let her mom break the news to him. He'd come around eventually … hopefully by the time he had grandchildren.

"Catie! Luke!" Mimi's voice called to them from the porch.

"Over here!" Cat called back and the pair jogged towards the porch to meet her.

"Well," Mimi clapped her hands. "That was Rachel's daddy on the phone. He said he would be happy to officiate the ceremony tomorrow."

"Oh, thank goodness!" Cat grabbed Luke's hand and gave it a squeeze.

"I left him a message this morning," Luke rubbed Cat's shoulders. "But I didn't want to say anything until I heard back."

"You just like giving me a hard time about it," Cat elbowed him gently.

"Yeah, pretty much," he reached for her ribs. Cat jumped back with a laugh.

"You two," Mimi clucked her tongue. "Seems like yesterday you were both in high school trying to sneak around without ole Mimi finding out."

"Yes," Cat laughed. "But that didn't work at all."

"Oh," Mimi sat on the porch swing and patted for Luke and Cat to join her. "I knew you two were in love the day you met."

Luke gave her an incredulous look, "Cat, couldn't stand me when she met me!"

"That's not true," Cat insisted. "Luke said I was a stuck up bitch."

"Did you really say that, Luke Presnell?" Mimi's eyes widened.

Luke gave Cat a look that spoke volumes before turning to Mimi, "I may have said that, but I didn't mean it. Cat just knew how to push my buttons."

"And I think you still enjoy it," Cat winked at him.

"Like I said," Mimi patted them both on the knee. "Love at first sight. You should always marry someone that drives you a little bit crazy, I say. Better to have a marriage full of passion than be boring."

"I'm not going to argue with that," Luke looked over to Cat.

"You two have been setting up for the wedding all morning," Mimi glanced over to the field where the white tent was erected with chairs and a few tables underneath. "Why don't you take a break? Everything's pretty much done and I have to leave for the airport in a bit to pick everyone up. You two should relax."

"Cat doesn't know how to relax," Luke joked.

"Hey!" Cat reacted before shrugging, "Actually, he's right."

They laughed easily, as the porch swing rocked back and forth in the October breeze. Mimi gasped as she glanced at her watch and jumped from the swing.

"Land sakes alive!" she exclaimed. "I'm gonna be late if I don't get going. You two … have fun."

Cat and Luke exchanged a glance as Mimi dashed to her SUV and sped down the gravel driveway.

"What do you think she meant by 'have fun'?" Cat scooted over to Luke.

"I think she knows how stressed you've been about the wedding and wants you to relax a little bit," he brushed the hair behind her ear and leaned down to kiss her cheek.

"Oh," Cat slumped. "I thought it was more exciting than that."

"You think your grandmother was telling us to go have sex while she picks your family up from the airport?" Luke kissed down her neck.

"Wishful thinking," Cat sighed. "But we could go inside and 'relax' if you wanted to."

Luke's hands moved to Cat's face as she maneuvered herself until she was sitting on his lap. She returned his kisses with fervor and felt the muscles in his arms tense as he pulled her closer.

"Mmmmm, Luke," Cat sighed. "Want to go inside where we could be more comfortable?"

Luke was kissing down her neck but stopped suddenly to look straight into her eyes. "I have a better idea."

"Tell me."

"Let's go ride four-wheelers," Luke suggested.

"Huh?" she asked.

"I brought both of my four-wheelers over here last week, and I haven't taken you riding yet," he stated.

"That's because I don't know how to ride," Cat was suddenly annoyed. Here she was practically straddling him and he was thinking about riding ATVs. *What is wrong with men?*

"I'll teach you," Luke took her hands and scooted her off of him so he could stand up. "Come on. Go grab your jacket and I'll get the helmets from my truck.

Cat watched him leap down from the porch and stride confidently towards his truck as though this was the best idea in the world.

"I'd better not break my neck before our wedding day!" Cat called after him.

"Come on, city girl!" Luke looked back at her teasingly. "You're on your last life, remember? Time to live a little!"

✳ ✳ ✳

"Isn't there some part of you that thinks this is a very bad idea?" Cat eyed her fiancé suspiciously as he put gas into the four-wheelers.

"You will be perfectly fine," Luke reached forward to brush strands of hair from Cat's face. "Besides, where I want to take you is somewhere the truck can't get to, even in 4-wheel drive."

Luke handed her a helmet and showed her, once more, how to change gears on the four wheeler before hopping on his own. Cat tried to pay close attention but ATVs and vehicles in general had always eluded her.

"Wait, wait," Cat called him back over. "What's the throttle again?"

"It's like the gas pedal," Luke hopped back off and pointed to the lever on her handlebar, "you use your thumb, like this. Engage the clutch and let off the throttle at the same time. And then, change the gear, right there, by your left foot."

"Okay," Cat nodded, though entirely uncertain. "And then, let off the clutch and hit the throttle again. Is that right?"

"You got it!" Luke whacked her on the back. "Let's go."

"I'm going to kill myself on this thing," Cat muttered to herself, as Luke revved his up.

"Just follow me!" he called above the noise. "Don't be scared, Cat." He laughed at the look on her face. "We'll get back before Mimi gets back from the airport if we get going now."

"Alright, but remember, you owe me for this," Cat teased. "This city girl didn't sign up for ATV adventures."

"Oh come on, New York!" Luke revved the engine and shot up the hill, through the Christmas trees.

Cat was tentative as she got started, which began with her jerking forward several times before she actually started going. Aside from the bumpy start, Cat found that she enjoyed the thrill of riding in the open air. Her hair whipped around the nape of her neck where it fell below her helmet. Next time she would remember to pull it back, she thought to herself as she spit out another mouthful of hair.

Though they had started out at Mimi's farmhouse, they crossed the boundary lines at the creek and had continued onto land that Cat hadn't ventured onto in the past. An old logging road led up the mountain, and it seemed to continue up as far as Cat could see. The road was washed out in several spots, bumpy and overgrown with underbrush from years of not being used.

Cat gripped the handlebars tighter as she hit another deep dip in the road. She felt her jaw clench. Luke glanced back and nodded to her. Was that meant as an encouragement or an 'oh good, you're still there'? Cat wasn't sure. She tried to smile at him, but it came out more as a grimace.

"Not much farther!" she heard him call back above the wind.

The trees were in full color at the top of the mountain, Cat noticed, with delight. This likely meant perfect fall colors extending into the valley for their wedding tomorrow evening. She looked up to the treetops and the golden leaves that seemed to wave as she sped by, and then glanced back down at Luke who was stopped just ahead, waving frantically for her to stop.

Cat squeezed the brake on the handlebar and stomped on the foot brake at the same time. Mud pushed out towards Luke and covered the front of his jeans as he jumped backwards. The four wheeler came to a stop, inches from Luke and his ATV.

"Whoa, whoa," Luke lowered his hands. "What were you doing back there, babe? Taking in the sights?"

"Sorry," Cat said sheepishly, as she slid off the four-wheeler. "I was looking at the leaves."

"Typical tourist," Luke kissed her on the forehead as he pulled off her helmet. "I thought for a minute there that you were set to run me over."

"Well, I thought about it," she teased before looking down at her feet that had sunk several inches down into the muck. "I'm glad you made me wear these old boots."

"Yep," Luke pulled her to stand on dry leaves. "Still drying out from the rain last week. Well, come on. I have something I want you to see." He took her hand and pulled her off the logging trail and into the woods.

"What is the elevation up here?" Cat huffed after they'd been walking for several minutes. "I swear I'm going to need an oxygen tank," she laughed. Her head felt light, but she was fairly certain it had nothing to do with the altitude and everything to do with the man holding her hand.

"Alright," Luke stopped. "Now I'm going to cover your eyes before we go any farther."

"Did you buy me a pony and put a big pink bow on it, Luke?" she asked.

"Yep, and hid it on top of a mountain," he stepped behind her and covered her eyes with his hands. "Just step slowly," he whispered in her ear.

Cat bit her lip and stepped forward one foot in front of the other for about twenty paces until they came to a stop.

"Alright," he uncovered them. "This is what I wanted you to see."

Cat blinked into the bright sunlight and found herself on a small knoll overlooking the most picturesque view of the valley below. The Blue Ridge Mountains extended in the horizon, misty shapes, and shades of blue. The colors of autumn cascaded over the ridges, some craigy nearing the summit of Grandfather Mountain, some gently folding into river bottoms and steep ravines. From the clearing where they stood, Cat could see the edge of her grandmother's farm and the gravel road that led to the highway. A few other farm houses and pastures could be spotted in the distance. Cat shaded her eyes and squinted towards a hay field that had to be several miles away.

"Is that the field where we loaded the hay in high school?" Cat pointed.

"The very same," Luke wrapped his arms around her from behind and moved her hair to the side to kiss her neck softly.

"Mmm," Cat leaned into his kisses and closed her eyes. She turned her lips to meet his and reached her hand to his face, his hair. She felt breathless and in love. A smile crept across her lips and interrupted his kisses, "Have I told you how much I love you?"

"Not in the last hour," Luke kissed the tip of her nose.

"Oh good," she laughed. "In that case, I want you to know that I'm hopelessly, head over heels, in love with you."

"Thanks," he shrugged.

"Hey!" Cat poked his ribs.

Luke leaned down to scoop her up into his arms and spun around, "And I love you. Is that better?"

"Acceptable," she squeezed his face against hers. She let her eyes wander back to the view, the woods around them, then to Luke. "This view is incredible, Luke. Thank you for bringing me here."

"You're welcome," he carefully set her feet down. "Being back here. Well, I knew I'd been missing the mountains. But I had no idea how much I missed them until I came back home."

"Well," Cat said thoughtfully. "What if we moved here?"

"Cat," he squeezed her hand, "that would effectively end your career at MOMA. I mean, I can work from anywhere. But you can't … at least, not in your dream job."

"But what if my dreams changed, Luke?" Cat allowed herself to say the words slowly. Though she hadn't mentioned it or admitted it to anyone, not even to herself, she had been longing the last two months for a life she hadn't envisioned since high school. She wanted simplicity, and family, and children, and the mountains, and most of all Luke.

"I would never ask you to give up what you love doing," Luke took her face in his hands and studied her face as though the answers might somehow appear.

"You don't have to ask," Cat took his hands. "If this is something that I want, then I get to decide. I want you, Luke."

She reached up to him, "I want you, and a family, and these mountains, and this view. Well, maybe not this exact view, but you know what I mean."

"What if you could have this exact view?" Luke turned her shoulders to face out to the mountains again.

"What?" She looked back up at him quickly. "Luke, who owns this land?"

"We do," he stated.

"We do?!" Cat felt her heart flutter with elation.

"I had to put some of the money from auctioning off my paintings to good use, didn't I?" he asked.

"Oh my goodness, Luke" Cat leapt up on him without warning, knocking him off balance for a split second, but he recovered before they both could topple to the ground.

"I bought it last month," he hoisted her up and held her closely against him. "I've been dying to tell you, but I had to do it in person. It's twenty acres in all. We border Mimi's land to the south and my dad's land to the southwest so there's two possible access roads for building the driveway."

"It's perfect," Cat kissed him twice and then a third time for good measure. "It's beyond perfect."

Luke lowered himself to the ground, careful to keep one hand firmly around Cat's waist. Cat wrapped her legs tightly around him as her fingers found themselves tangled in his hair. She tried to kiss him in a way that would express every ounce of emotion she was feeling but that just didn't seem possible.

When she opened her eyes and pulled back, his eyes met hers.

"Luke Presnell, you sneaky thing, was this all a ploy to lure me into a mountaintop make-out session?" Cat grinned at him knowingly.

"You got me," he laughed. "But I figure, since we're already up here, a mountaintop make-out session wouldn't hurt anyone."

"Well, I can't argue with that." Cat moved her body closer to him and pushed his back down to the ground. "Since no one can see us up here, I might as well take my clothes off."

"What?" Luke's eyes shot open. "Are you serious?"

"No," Cat laughed. "I just wanted to see what you'd say." Leaning down, she nibbled on his lower lip, "One more day, babe."

Luke glanced at his watch, "Twenty-four hours and thirty-six minutes to be exact. The countdown is on," he pressed his lips against hers as the sun slipped lower on the horizon.

Cat was elated as they returned from their expedition up the mountain, though they may have stayed up there a bit longer than intended as Cat noted that it was dusk by the time they climbed the porch steps. Luckily, they had arrived back home before Mimi had returned from the airport with Lili, Mom, and Rachel.

If nothing else, the time alone had reconfirmed all of the feelings Cat had felt five years prior. She was crazy about Luke. *Over the moon, can't keep my hands off of him, crazy*, Cat thought to herself with a smile.

"What's that smile about?" Luke held the screen door open for her and pinched her butt playfully as she walked by.

"Ha!" Cat jumped. "It's about that!" She swatted his hand playfully. "It's about how you just can't keep your hands off me."

"Moi?" Luke looked affronted. "Look who's talking, Miss I'm-gonna-take-my-clothes-off."

"Yeah, but I didn't," Cat leaned back against the kitchen counter and pulled him in. She knew if they kept this up, it would be hard to wait one more day let alone one minute. But they had already waited five years, and a little voice in her head told her that waiting five years was plenty long enough.

"I wouldn't have minded, you know," Luke lifted her to sit on the counter facing him.

"I still could," Cat lowered her voice and slid her hands down his back and under his shirt.

Luke cleared his throat. "You sure?"

"How long till they get back?" Cat whispered back. "And, why are we whispering?"

"Heck, if I know," Luke pulled his shirt off and tossed it to the side. "Your turn."

Cat obliged. He stepped back to look at her.

"Would it be insensitive for me to whistle?" he asked.

"Haha!" Cat tossed her hair back and struck a pose, feeling oddly empowered and self-conscious at the same time. "Maybe … but I think it would be sweet."

Luke let out a whistle just as headlights flashed through the screen door.

"Whoops!" Cat hopped down and scooped up her shirt. She tossed Luke his and he caught it with one hand.

"This feels strangely familiar," Luke glanced towards her as he pulled his shirt back on over his head. "Remember last time?"

"With the biscuits and the flour," Cat shook her head. "I thought Mimi was going to kill you."

"So did I," he said knowingly.

They were still laughing when Rachel and Lili burst through the door.

"We're here!" Lili cried, hugging first Luke then Cat.

"Let the bachelorette party begin!" Rachel sang out. "Bye, Luke. Good to see you! Don't you worry. We'll take good care of her."

Rachel leaned onto her toes to whisper something in Lukes's ear before bouncing over to Cat.

"What were you saying to Luke?" Cat raised an eyebrow.

"Just offering my congratulations," Rachel smiled, "And seeing if you guys had already had sex."

"You asked him that?!" Cat shrieked, blushing. "Oh my goodness, how embarrassing … but, seriously, I can't wait."

"And now I have the answer," Rachel laughed.

"What?" Cat laughed. "You didn't really ask him that? You are sneaky Rachel McKinney."

"Yes, I am," she smiled. "But enough of that. This is your bachelorette party and we've got to get you ready!"

"What do you think, babe?" Luke glanced at Cat with a grin.

"I know nothing about a bachelorette party, Rachel," Cat eyed Rachel with amusement. That girl was always up to something.

"I know," Rachel pulled a plastic tiara out of her bag and placed it on Cat's head with a flourish, "Surprise!"

"Ta da!" Lili pulled a silk pageant banner out of her bag and put it over Cat's head. Cat looked down.

"Lili, this says 'Manhattan's Pretty Princess Pageant,'" Cat burst into laughter. "This is from when you were in the 4th grade."

"Yes, well, we will have to make do. Won't we?" Lili rolled her eyes. "I'm working on short notice here. Rachel only decided we should have a bachelorette party about twenty minutes before we left for the airport."

"Really, girls," Cat reached out to hug them both. "I'm happy with a girl's night in with pizza and a movie."

"All the Right Moves?" Rachel raised an eyebrow.

"No," Cat held her hands up. "I've already seen Tom Cruises' penis once and that was enough for me. Thank you very much."

"I feel like I've missed something here," Luke looked between them.

"High school," Cat and Rachel said in unison before doubling over in laughter.

"Alright, honey," Luke stepped in to wrap Cat in his arms. "I want you to go out with the girls and have a great time." He leaned down and lifted her up slightly to kiss her.

Cat was expecting a sweet, short kiss in front of Lili and Rachel, but Luke lingered, letting her lips part, and his hands run through her hair and down her back. When they broke apart, Lili and Rachel were both whooping and Mimi and her mother stood in the doorway with their mouths agape and luggage in their arms.

"Uh—that was some kiss," Lili commented, while Cat's cheeks went red.

"Heck yeah it was!" Rachel nodded. "Someday I want someone to kiss me like that."

"Me, too!" Lili, Mimi, and Darcie said simultaneously.

Luke flushed and stepped forward to Mimi and Darcie, "Let me get those for you."

"Thank you, Luke," Mimi handed over the bags she was carrying.

"Mrs. Rhodes," Luke shifted the bags under his arms and extended his hand. "I'm honored to be marrying your daughter."

"Call me Darcie," she took his hand in both of hers and

pulled him into a hug. "I wish I'd formally met you years ago, Luke. I should have." She looked up to him and then to Cat, "My daughter is a lucky lady to have someone who cares so deeply about her."

"Yes, clearly from that kiss, he cares very, very deeply," Lili smirked.

The laughter that ensued between the women in the kitchen was Luke's cue to take the bags upstairs, say his goodbyes, and duck out quickly. As the screen door slammed, he heard Rachel call out, "I hope you rest up before your wedding night!"

"Oh, they won't get any sleep!" Mimi's voice carried through the screen door.

He knew Cat's cheeks had to be five shades of red by now. Less than one day till he could make good on all of his past promises to Cat. One more day.

CHAPTER FORTY-THREE

CAT WAS ONLY SLIGHTLY TIPSY WHEN SHE CAME THROUGH THE SCREEN door at 3am, while holding Lili up with Rachel's help.

"Can we both agree that the shots at the end were a bad idea?" Cat whispered to Rachel, who could not contain her giggles.

"So, so bad," Rachel dropped her bag on the floor and bent to pick it up, while letting Lili fall sideways. "Whoa there, Lil!"

"Are we home?" Lili looked around the dark kitchen suspiciously, "This isn't my apartment."

"Oh, she is so far gone," Cat shook her head and pulled out a chair for Lili to sit in. "Stay here," she over-enunciated her words to Lili, as though talking to a small child.

Cat went to the sink and filled up three large glasses of water, one for each of them. She moved quickly to the cabinet where Mimi always kept her medicine and opened it slowly. It was well-known that one had to be prepared when opening Mimi's cabinets, anything could fall out. She caught the Advil as it fell off the second shelf and twisted it open in one move.

"Okay, ladies," Cat gave each of them two extra strength Advil. "I need you girls to be on your best game tomorrow because we are making hors d'oeuvres for the reception first thing in the morning. Tomorrow is my wedding day and we can't appear to be hung over."

"Ay ay, captain!" Rachel laughed from where she still sat on the floor gathering up the contents of her purse.

"Cat, did you have your clothes off?" Lili lifted her head from the table.

"What? My clothes are on," Cat looked down at her fully clothed self. "Wow, Lili. You are so far gone."

"No, no, no!" Lili slurred. "Not now. I mean when we got here this evening. I thought I saw shadows of shirts being put back on."

"Oh, interesting!" Rachel leaned back on the fridge and pointed up at Cat with enthusiasm. "Spill it!"

Cat pursed her lips and paused, "Maybe." Her smile widened. "Alright, yes. Yes, we were, you know, just making out."

"Were you, like, having sex on this table?" Lili pushed back from the table and looked at it closely as though it might divulge Cat's secrets.

"Absolutely not!" she exclaimed.

"On this floor?" Rachel lifted her hands quickly off the linoleum. "Ewww, tell me that's not why this floor is sticky."

"Gross, you guys." Cat pulled Rachel up. "No, we were not having sex in this kitchen. We haven't. But," Cat sighed. "I. Can't. Wait."

"Only one more day," Lili held up one finger.

"No," Rachel corrected her. "Fourteen hours." She reached out and put Lili's one finger down, which led Lili to proceed to count to herself again.

"Okay, girls," Cat shook her head at both of them. "This was fun. But now it's time for you both to go to bed. And me. Up you go."

It took some amount of effort to get Rachel and Lili settled on the couch bed and the air mattress Mimi had set up for them in the living room. Cat was supposed to be sharing the queen bed upstairs with her mother. Mimi and Jim were sound asleep in Mimi's room down the hall. She could hear the soft sounds of snoring coming from their door.

Cat tucked the quilt around Rachel and stooped to pull Lili's other shoe off, since only one heel had been taken off before she had climbed under the covers on the air mattress.

Then, she stepped back to shake her head at both of them, already passed out, and sprawled across their beds. Cat chuckled to herself before tiptoeing back to the kitchen to pour herself one more glass of water. Strangely, she felt wide awake and with perfect mental clarity. She wanted to go somewhere, or do something, or talk to someone. She wanted to see Luke. *And why not*, a little voice said. *You're a grown up now. You can go over to your fiancé's house if you damn well please.* Cat smiled to herself as she took the keys to the farm truck off the hook on the wall and quietly opened the screen door.

She had only been over to Luke's house twice in high school. Once to pick up his cross country clothes before a meet and another with Mimi to pick him up before work. Neither time had she actually gone inside. Cat wasn't sure if she remembered how to get there, let alone in the dark. And when she arrived, what would she do? Throw rocks at his window? She didn't even know which window was his. She bit her lip as she turned onto the highway. Either this idea was completely romantic or it would be the absolute stupidest thing she'd ever done. *Well, not the stupidest*, Cat thought to herself. She'd made her fair share of stupid mistakes in the past. David being one of them.

David. She hadn't really thought about him since arriving at Mimi's. Other than his missed calls, he'd been out of sight and out of mind, just as Cat preferred. In the past month, she'd seen him several times, each time more firmly reminding him that they were no longer engaged. Each time to reassure and coddle when he was inevitably heartbroken. She'd missed sixteen calls since arriving in North Carolina and hadn't bothered to return them. Now, her focus was on Luke and her wedding and their future together. Now, for once, Cat was putting her own desires first.

And what she desired now was Luke. She pulled to a stop where the road forked, uncertain for a moment which way to turn. Headlights were coming towards her from the left fork. She couldn't stay in the middle of the road. She needed to make a decision.

Cat put on her blinker and turned left towards the oncoming truck. She was seventy-nine percent sure this was the way to Luke's. As the truck coming towards her slowed at the stop sign, she recognized both it and the driver. Luke. *What was he doing? Where was he going? And at three thirty in the morning…*

Rolling down her window, Cat leaned her head out, "Hey, handsome!" she called to a beaming Luke. "Going my way?"

"Babe!" he exclaimed. "Where are you going?"

"I was actually trying to find your house," Cat admitted, before shrugging, "But I couldn't remember which way to go."

"And I was coming to make sure you girls had gotten home safe and sound." Luke hurried to add. "I know you are capable of fully taking care of yourselves, but—"

"I love that you care," Cat interrupted. "I love you, Luke."

"Where to now?" he laughed. "We can't very well sit in the middle of the road. Though, I doubt anyone will come along."

"Let's go to the barn," Cat leaned out the window. "I haven't seen it since I've been back. I know you were taking me there sometime. You might as well show me now."

"Alrighty, then. I'm going to turn around and then you can follow me."

"Sounds like a plan," Cat nodded to him.

Her heart skipped a beat. She didn't need to wait fourteen

more hours for Luke. She was going to be with him the rest of her life and she wanted the rest of her life to start right away. She had to take deep breaths to calm herself as she turned onto the dirt road and pulled to a stop in front of the familiar old barn. In the moonlight, she could see Luke smile as he came around to open the door for her.

"You've done so much work here!" Cat exclaimed as they walked past the old tack room where they had spent the night together so many years ago. "Did you pay for the renovations yourself?"

"Dad paid for most of it," Luke slid open the next set of barn doors, revealing a kitchenette and small dining area.

"I love this!" Cat exclaimed, wandering to the opposite side of the barn where several walls had been removed to create a large living space.

A gas stove had been added in the corner and the rock work around it made it appear as though it had always been there. The bare floors had been upgraded to polished concrete, giving the space an industrial and hipster feel. Luke took a remote off the coffee table and aimed it at the fireplace. The space erupted in the flickering glow of the fire.

"This is the perfect rustic get-away," Cat moved towards him. "And very romantic."

"He's been renting it as an Airbnb," Luke nodded. "He's already paid for the cost of the renovations."

"Do you think we could stay here?" Cat wrapped her arms around him.

"You mean after the wedding?" he asked.

"And tonight," Cat looked up to see his expression.

Luke paused and leaned down to kiss her softly. "Yes, if that's what you want."

"You're what I want, Luke," Cat said definitively. "And I don't need to wait one more minute for it to be official. I've waited five years to give myself to you."

"Can you wait five more minutes?" Luke held up his hand. "I have something for you. I'll be right back."

"I'll give you two minutes," Cat winked, as he sprinted out the door.

She turned to survey the space. The high exposed beams of the barn roof made her eyes drift upward. She noticed the stairs to the hay loft had been redone in wrought iron and a railing had been added around the top. She moved to the banister and let her hand slide up the polished wood as she ascended the staircase. The firelight from below flickered through the rails and cast shadows around the loft, which had been transformed to a magnificent master bedroom space. The elegant king-sized bed had a headboard and footboard that looked like it had been made from twisted laurel branches, a faux fur rug was on the hardwood floors at her feet. A painting, she recognized as Luke's, hung above the bed. Cat moved to the chaise lounge and stretched out. She closed her eyes for just a moment to rest them.

Luke touched her face softly and she jerked awake. Cat smiled up at him. Taking her left hand he knelt down slowly.

"I was saving this to put on your hand on our wedding day, well, later today," he slid a simple, yet classic engagement ring onto her finger. "It was my mother's."

Cat sat up and looked down at her hand. It was simple, yet simple was exactly what Cat had longed for after the complexities of the last few years. Gold band, round cut, and shining brilliantly in the firelight from below.

"It's perfect, Luke." Cat knelt down with him to take his face in her hands.

"I want to say my vows to you, Cat," Luke kissed her deeply and pulled back to look into her eyes. "Don't worry. I'll say them again. But, I want you to hear them now."

Cat just nodded. She felt like any words that would come out from her would cause tears to come out as well.

"Cathleen Rhodes," he began. "You have meant more to me than you'll ever know. You always said that I rescued you when you needed a friend the most. But, in truth, I think you rescued me. Or maybe we rescued each other. Either way, I needed you. God knew that I needed you. I needed you to push me, to love me, to remind me of what I was capable of."

Cat felt the tears and she laughed in spite of herself. Of course, she would be the one to blubber during her wedding vows. Luke laughed and reached to wipe the tears from her cheeks.

He continued, "I want to spend the rest of our lives rescuing each other, loving each other, and driving each other crazy."

"Yes," Cat kissed each of his cheeks, "that is inevitable."

"And I know every day won't be perfect. I will fail and falter from time to time. But," Luke stood up and pulled Cat up with him, "I will love you with all my heart, if you'll have me."

"I've always been yours," Cat whispered. "Always." Cat paused, "I haven't written my vows yet, Luke. I wish I had something beautiful already memorized to tell you."

"That doesn't matter to me, babe," Luke pulled her in for a kiss but she stopped him.

"I do," she began. "I do promise to be honest, to always be there for you, to be your wife, your lover, your best friend, and to remind you everyday of who you are and what you are capable of … and," her voice choked up. "And I'm so thankful for you. I love you,

Luke Presnell, and—"

"And?" Luke raised an eyebrow when he noticed the smirk on Cat's face.

"Now, I have one more thing to say," she held up her hand. "Will you make love to me? NOW!"

"Ummm," Luke pretended to consider that proposition as he pulled his shirt off. "Hell, yes." And with that, he bent down to scoop her up and carried her towards the bed.

The firelight flickered from below, illuminating their every move. When the sky began to lighten on the horizon, two shadows were still moving in the darkness.

CHAPTER FORTY-FOUR

CAT LAID STILL WITH HER EYES CLOSED. SHE WAS SO CERTAIN THAT
to open them would be to make her beautiful dream disappear.
Wanting to hold on to every detail of that perfect dream, she
breathed in deeply as though to breathe in every moment, every
touch, every new sensation she had experienced in that vision.
Suddenly, she felt tender fingertips brush stray waves of hair from
her face. Cat peeked her left eye open only to allow the tiniest bit
of light in. She caught a glimpse of a jaw bone covered with a bit
of stubble, leading to a neck with a distinct Adam's apple. Cat
opened her left eye a bit wider and let it take in more—a firm
muscular chest and abdomen, and leading down … she smiled,
looking back up and opening both eyes to meet Luke's gaze.

"See something you like?" he laughed, as Cat kept glancing
down at his naked body on top of the sheets.

Cat blushed, "I didn't get a really good look last night … it
was dark."

Luke laughed and leaned in to gently kiss her lips.

"I thought it was all a dream," Cat smiled.

"Nope," Luke kissed her again. "Good morning … my love."

Cat smiled brightly, "Good morning, my love! Happy wedding
day." She returned his kisses fervently, "I want to wake up like
this every morning."

She was deliriously happy and exhausted. It was exactly the
way she was certain she should feel.

Cat laughed, "I have to say, I knew it would be amazing, but I had NO idea that that level of amazing, unbelievable, OMG-I-am-in-heaven, even existed."

"Well," Luke lowered his voice, "Thank you, thank you very much."

"Hey," Cat joked, "That means I was wonderful too, right?"

Luke looked at her sincerely, "You were unbelievable. In fact, you were so unbelievable … I think I would like a replay."

Cat pounced on him with her best tiger imitation. They rolled across the bed until Luke pinned her down.

"How's it going, Cat?" Luke kissed her neck, "This last life of yours, is it everything you hoped it would be?"

Cat feigned a solemn expression and spoke quietly, "I'm afraid I have to inform you that Cat doesn't have any lives left."

"She doesn't?" Luke put on a shocked face to play along.

"No," Cat shook her head, "She died and went to heaven last night."

"Twice, if I remember correctly," Luke slid his hands down her body.

"Take me there again?" Cat asked.

A sudden knock from downstairs jolted them both. Cat pulled the covers up to her chin.

Cat looked at Luke. "Would that be your dad?"

"I doubt it," Luke shrugged. "Probably, Rachel coming to track you down."

Cat laughed, "I should have told them I was coming to find you last night, but honestly they wouldn't have remembered."

"Stay here," Luke kissed the top of her head and pulled on his sweatpants. "I'll go get the door. Be right back!"

Cat propped up the pillows and leaned back against them. Holding up her left hand, she examined the ring Luke slipped on her finger last night. Their fireside vows were more meaningful to her than if they had gotten married in the most ornate cathedral in front of a whole host of people. They had committed themselves to each other. For better or worse. Till death do us part.

"I will kill you if I find my daughter in there again," her father's voice rang out clearly from down below. Cat bolted towards her clothes and managed to get herself mostly dressed before footsteps rang out on the stairs.

"And I'm looking for my fiancé," another voice called out. Cat heard some scuffling from down below.

No! David's here, too? Cat's mind was whirring, but her resilience overcame the fear of being found half naked in a barn again. No longer was she some naive high schooler, incapable of standing up against her parent's wishes. She was a woman who had made her choice and she had chosen Luke.

"Mr. Rhodes, we will have to discuss this later. Please leave," Luke's voice was equally as determined as her father's.

The three men reached the landing just as Cat stood up from slipping on her clothes.

"Good morning," Cat said cheerily. Regardless of what the situation was at this very moment, she had been having a very good morning indeed up until this point.

She continued as she watched her father and David's eyes take in the situation, the unmade bed. Luke's shirt and shoes on the floor. "Dad," Cat took a confident step forward. "I'm sure you remember Luke. David, this is my fiancé."

"I am your fiancé!" David shouted at her. He turned to Luke, "I'm her fiancé!"

Luke shrugged, "Clearly, that's not the case."

"Wait a minute—" David held a finger up towards Luke. "You. You were there when the truck hit me?"

Luke was taken aback, "That was you?"

David turned to Cat, "Did you know this?"

Cat shook her head in genuine surprise, "I didn't."

Her father also seemed temporarily rendered speechless by this new found fact.

"Did you know I was engaged to Cat?" David stepped towards him menacingly. "Did you arrange for that truck to hit me?" David's eyes were flashing dangerously between her and Luke, "Were you in on this plan, Cathleen?"

"David, you sound insane." Cat said pointedly. "No one planned for you to get hurt."

"You did," David snapped. "You hurt me over and over again."

"What are you talking about?" she felt anger rising.

Out of the corner of her eye, Cat could see Luke's jaw tightening. His fists were clenching and unclenching in an effort to control himself. Cat knew that look.

"You broke up with me repeatedly. You didn't even care that I was an invalid. You just continued your attempts to end our relationship," David's eyes narrowed as he stepped towards her. Luke came forward quickly to put Cat just behind him. David took another step, ignoring Luke's stare, his eyes fixed wildly on Cat, "I thought you would get tired of breaking my heart over and over again. But no—you wouldn't stop, would you?! You are supposed to marry me."

"So, you were faking it the whole time? The memory loss was just some charade to keep me trapped in an engagement I didn't want?" Cat was livid. She could see from the surprised expression on her father's face that he was fighting against his own preference towards David. "How could you, David? Do you know how desperate that makes you seem?"

"I waited for you, Cathleen," he pointed to the bed. "I waited and waited. We were engaged for a year and you wouldn't sleep with me."

"We broke up in June, David—," Cat stepped around Luke to face David head on.

His voice rose over her to drown her out, "And then, you come down here to give it up in a barn like some common whore—"

His last word was cut short when both her father and Luke stepped towards David with their fists raised. Luke made contact first and David hit the ground hard. Cat worried that the loft was not structurally sound enough to endure a fist fight with three grown men. Her father looked at Luke and Cat and then David out cold on the floor before slowly lowering his fist.

"I—," her father stammered. "I had no idea he was capable of leading us on like that."

"I should have," Cat nodded towards him. She shook her head. "Dad," Cat stepped forward and showed her father the ring on her finger. "I want you to meet my fiancé, Luke. I believe in starting over with new introductions, don't you?"

Her father's face softened, he turned to Luke, the man he'd just watched defend his daughter's honor, "Luke, I'm Warren Rhodes. I hope you can forgive me for—everything." His shoulders slumped. "I'm sorry for this morning and for what I did in the past. I'm so sorry, Cathleen." Her father turned his gaze to her before looking back to Luke.

"Let's just start again, sir." Luke reached forward to shake his hand. "I want you to know that Cat means the world to me. I will give her everything I am capable of. This is the future that she's chosen. Though, I know it may not be what you had in mind."

"I should have realized by now that Cathleen is old enough to choose for herself," he cleared his throat and glanced down at

David, "Will you help me carry him to the car? I need to get him on a plane back to New York."

"Thank you," Cat stepped forward to place her hand on her father's shoulder in gratitude.

For the first time in a long time, he was behaving like a father she could respect. It may have taken many years for him to realize his mistakes, and there had been so many mistakes and misunderstandings in the last few years, but perhaps now he was trying to make things right. If there was any time to begin again, Cat knew this was the time.

Jim had agreed to take a bruised and whiny David to the Charlotte airport so that Warren could stay for the wedding that evening. Cat felt like that gesture, both from Jim and her father, was worthy of celebration alone.

"Well, well," Lili said knowingly as she rose from the kitchen table when Luke and Cat climbed the porch steps hand in hand.

"I thought it was bad luck for the groom to see the bride on her wedding day," Rachel teased.

"Not if you wake up beside him," Cat looked lovingly up at Luke. "Right, babe?"

"That's what I've been told," Luke nodded and rolled up his sleeves.

Cat noticed when Lili held out her hand and Rachel pulled a twenty dollar bill from her purse and slapped it into her palm. She let out a chuckle and shook her head at her dearest friend and her sister. Somehow, she was not the least bit surprised by their little bet.

Luke raised his eyebrows, "Alright, ladies. Put me to work. I hear we have some hors d'oeuvres to make."

Lili handed each of them aprons off the hooks on the wall.

"I've been making the filling for stuffed mushrooms," Lili gestured to the contents of her mixing bowl.

"And I'm supervising," Rachel raised her glass of champagne in salute. "You know you don't want me helping."

Cat laughed, "This is probably true."

Luke picked up the recipe for crab cakes that was on the counter and examined the instructions, "I can take care of this."

"What should I do?" Cat looked at the to-do list to see what remained on the list.

"You could see where mom and Mimi went off to," Lili looked over her shoulder. "They went down to the tent to set out flower arrangements ages ago."

"I'll be right back then," Cat leaned on her tiptoes to kiss Luke on the cheek for perhaps the hundredth time that day and smiled. "Don't miss me too much!"

Luke returned her kiss, "I'll try."

"Oh, you guys," Rachel gushed, placing her hand over her heart. "Y'all are the sweetest."

"Little too sweet for me," Lili made gagging sounds as Cat skipped out the door.

The sky was overcast and it was cooler than had been predicted, but none of that could change the overwhelming joy Cat was feeling. She practically floated across the lawn and down the hill to the tent, where the reception was to take place. She stopped short when she heard raised voices coming from the barn.

"Mom," Cat's mother sounded weary. "I'm not going to explain myself again. It was years ago. It is over and done."

"But, that doesn't change the fact that it broke my heart, Darcie," Mimi's voice echoed back.

Cat slowly stepped towards the barn's entrance, careful to keep in the shadows outside the doorway. She knew she was too old to be eavesdropping, but this particular conversation sounded like questions she'd frequently asked her mother growing up and never received answers to.

"Would you feel better if I apologized?" Darcie asked.

"I've never asked for an apology," Mimi snipped. "Just an explanation. My only daughter left for New York City, cut off all ties with us, and then started dating some uppity New Yorker. Next thing I knew, you were married and expecting a baby. I just don't know why you shut us out to begin with?"

"You wouldn't understand," Darcie sighed. "Your life was wrapped up in farming and Pop. You never had to change your accent just to get a job. I was barely surviving in the city when I met Warren. Barely surviving."

"You could have done anything with your life, Darcie," Mimi's voice carried the invisible weight of disappointment. "You were first in your class. You had a college scholarship. You threw it all away to chase some dream in New York City. And you didn't speak to us … for almost ten years, Darcie. I didn't even know if you were alive."

Cat found herself covering her mouth as she listened. She tried to breathe as quietly as possible, certain they heard her gasp at her mother's words. Barely surviving. From the stories Cat had been told, which hadn't been much, her mother was working successfully as an administrative assistant when she started dating her father. This, clearly, was not the case.

"Mom," Darcie sighed. "I made so many terrible choices. Back then, I just needed money to pay rent and buy food. None of my dance auditions were panning out. It was humiliating. I—I was ashamed to call you. Ashamed to come home."

"You know I would've welcomed you home and—," Mimi began.

"—I know you would've been disappointed," Darcie cut her off. "You can't say that you wouldn't have. I know you. You and Pop had high standards and I always lived up to them. But during that time in my life, I failed. I just failed and I couldn't come home until I made something of myself."

"You mean until Warren had made something of you," Cat heard her grandmother rise from the chair and walk slowly towards the door of the barn.

"That's unfair," Darcie sounded defeated, and Cat pressed her back against the outside wall of the barn to remain unseen.

In leaning back against the wall, Cat knocked over a few pallets that had been carefully tipped on their end just beside her. Of course, her focus had been entirely on Mimi and she hadn't even realized the pallets were there until they were falling over like dominos.

Mimi and Darcie jumped at the same time.

"Alright, Catie-bug," Mimi sighed. "I thought I saw your shadow."

Cat rolled her eyes, she felt like a child with her hand caught in the cookie jar. "Oh, hi!" She chirped brightly as she rounded the corner into the barn, "I was just coming to see if y'all needed any help."

"Mmm-hmm," Mimi nodded slowly, unconvinced. "And how much of our conversation did you hear?"

Cat looked past Mimi to her mother where she remained seated with her arms crossed. Thankfully, she appeared more amused than annoyed.

"I heard some of it," Cat shrugged. "Well, most of it."

"So I suspected," Mimi nodded.

"Cathleen, come sit by me," her mother patted the seat beside her. "I should have told you this a long time ago. It would've helped you understand … me and my relationship with my parents, as well as your father. I just—," her mother sighed deeply and looked into Cat's eyes. "I just never wanted you to think less of me."

"Mom, how could I?" Cat patted her mother's knee. "You were always so perfect growing up. It would've been hard to think of you as anything less than flawless."

"Perhaps, because I was trying to make up for the not-so-perfect past," Darcie looked from Mimi to Cat and back again before sighing once more. "Sit down, Mom. Now is as good a time as any to make peace with the past. After all, Cathleen did say this was a time for new beginnings."

Cat squeezed her mom's hand.

"When I arrived in New York in the late-eighties it was a very different place, as you know. I tried to find work dancing. I auditioned for the Rockettes. I went to open calls for Broadway shows. But nothing was panning out, so I took the only job I could get—waitressing. My roommate Penny, at the time, finally got a gig dancing at a nightclub and told me she could get me a job there, too. So, I went for the audition. Turns out this nightclub was actually more like a stripclub."

She paused to examine Cat and Mimi's faces, but they seemed nonplussed. Cat shrugged to her mother as if to say, 'so?'

Darcie continued her story with her volume rising slightly, "This was such a travesty to me. To have been first in my high school class, to have received a full scholarship—"

Cat interrupted, "Where did you receive a scholarship to?"

"Appalachian," Darcie smiled meekly at her daughter.

Cat nodded. Of course, Appalachian was where she had intended to go before her parents had swooped in her senior year of high school and dashed any chances of a future with Luke.

"Well, to have thrown all of that away to end up—," Darcie's voice caught and covered her face in her hands and shook her head as if to shake away the bad memories.

"So," Cat questioned, "where does dad come into this equation?

"Well," Darcie reached out for her daughter's hand, "he rescued me from that life. You see, lots of professionals came to the club for drinks after work. And your father—," she paused.

"My father?" Cat urged her to continue.

Darcie bit her lip. At that moment, Cat recognized so much of herself in her mother's expression. "I'm just so ashamed," her mother's voice quivered. "I don't know if I can continue this story."

"Mom, you're forgetting that Flashdance is, like, one of my favorite movies," Cat laughed. "You lived out all of my stripper dreams."

Mimi let out a cackle of laughter.

Darcie smiled at both of them, "Alright. Well, I didn't meet your father while working as an administrative assistant. I met him while I was dancing. He came in occasionally with a bunch of men from his office. But, Warren was different. I enjoyed spending time with him. We actually had conversations, went out to dinner, and started dating. Then, I found out I was pregnant with you."

Cat tried to plaster a fixed expression on her face.

"Obviously, I couldn't keep working at the nightclub," Darcie sighed. "When Warren proposed, I promised myself I would be the absolute perfect wife he deserved. No more dance auditions. No big dreams. I devoted myself to you and then Lili and his career aspirations. I never questioned his decisions or choices until we had to deal with what happened with you after Landon died. That was the first time I saw something different in him. It was the first time I wished I had more of a backbone to stand up to him, for you, for myself. I've been so ashamed of myself these last five years. Cathleen, can you ever forgive me?"

Cat wrapped her mother in the biggest embrace and turned to pull Mimi in, too. "I love you both, you know that right?"

"And you don't think less of me?" Cat's mother pulled away.

"Mom," Cat looked into her mother's eyes. "I slept with Luke last night. No one in this barn is an angel."

Sounds of laughter rang from the barn as relationships were repaired. Mothers reunited with their daughters.

CHAPTER FORTY-FIVE

THE WEDDING GUESTS WERE SEATED JUST AS SNOWFLAKES STARTED to fall from the sky. Cat glanced out of the screen porch door and stepped back to glance in the mirror one last time. Nothing that led to this day had been easy. Not one element of reuniting with Luke had come without an equal amount of resistance. From David. From her family. Even from Cat, herself. It had been hard to trust again. To lean in to love again. But it had been worth it. All of the tears, all of the pain. Each moment of uncertainty had been matched by a revelation that this was what she, Cathleen Rhodes, wanted in her life. Her last life, she thought with a smile.

"You ready, sweetie?" Her father touched her shoulder.

Cat nodded to him.

Darcie brushed a stray wave of hair behind Cat's ear. Rachel had taken charge of Cat's hair and makeup for the wedding, which was a relief to Cat. One less thing to concern herself with and she knew that Rachel would do an impeccable job, as always. Her friend had fashioned Cat's hair into a series of braids that wrapped into a chic updo. Rachel had informed her that she had seen the updo in Vogue and had been practicing on herself for three weeks. This did not surprise Cat in the least.

"We'll go ahead and take our seats," Darcie kissed her daughter's cheek and took Warren's elbow to walk onto the porch.

"Thank you, both," Cat called after them. They turned to smile at their daughter. It was a smile of love and pride that Cat hadn't genuinely felt or seen from her parents in so long. And this time, it felt different. It didn't feel as though it was attached to any achievement or expectations. It wasn't because she was marrying a Wall Street businessman nor was it because she was marrying a successful artist. It had nothing to do with a job promotion or exceptional grades. It was simply because they loved her. Maybe they always had. But now, they respected her, and her choices, and that was worth so much more to Cat. She watched her parents walk down the lawn as the violinist began to play and flakes of snow landed on the porch steps.

"I have something for you to wear," Mimi emerged from her room. "It was my mother's mink stole. I thought, well, with the snow coming down you might want it."

Cat let her grandmother drape it over her shoulders. "It's perfect, Mimi. Thank you."

"You are a vision, my little Catie-bug," Mimi leaned in to kiss her granddaughter's forehead. "You ready?"

Cat took her grandmother's hand in her own, "Let's do this."

As Cat stepped slowly across the lawn, which was now collecting a dusting of snow, she let her eyes drift up to meet the man that stood waiting for her. Guests seated around them seemed to melt into her peripheral vision; she was transfixed on him alone.

He was waiting for her, just as she had waited for him. The butterflies in her stomach had nothing to do with her wedding night ahead and everything to do with the man she was going to spend the rest of her life with. When he reached out to take her hand from Mimi, Cat pressed herself into him for a long lingering kiss.

"I haven't quite gotten to that part yet," Mr. McKinney cleared his throat.

Cheers from their friends and family erupted behind them, but Cat only saw Luke. Just as it should be.

Luke squeezed Cat's hand before he stood to his feet. Glancing around the tent at the small gathering of friends and family that had assembled for their wedding day, he tapped lightly on his champagne glass. The guests' laughter and conversations quieted, as smiling eyes locked on Luke and his new partner in life. Cat rose to her feet to stand beside him. They locked eyes before he turned back to those gathered at the reception.

"Cat and I are overwhelmed by the support you've shown us," Luke began. And though he hadn't felt nervous at all until that point, he suddenly found a lump in the place where his voice normally resided. He cleared his throat once more and took a pre-emptive sip of his champagne, "I—I don't know what else to say but thank you."

He glanced over to his father, who was seated with Cat's parents at a nearby round table, "thank you," he repeated.

When his father tipped his cowboy hat towards Luke, he choked up, and his next words were a mix of nervous laughter and tears, "I'm not usually such a mess." He reached up to wipe his eyes but Cat beat him to it.

"I'm the mess—," she laughed. Lifting onto her tiptoes, she kissed a tear from his cheek. Luke squeezed her hand again.

Cat took it as her cue to continue their wedding toast, "We've always known that what we had was special. But losing some-thing, someone so dear, and then finding them again. That was when I knew just how precious Luke is to me. It's easy to romanticize a high school love affair, to wonder if I imagined things—but this," Cat looked up to meet his eyes that were still brimming over with tears.

Luke laughed and shrugged as if to say, 'what is wrong with me?'

Cat couldn't resist planting another kiss, this time squarely on his lips. She lingered there before pulling away, keeping her eyes on his. Looking into those impossibly emerald green eyes, she was as captivated now as she had been when she first locked eyes with him all those years ago.

"But this is real," she nodded in conclusion.

He nodded back in affirmation.

Cat turned back to the gathering under the tent, twinkle lights now illuminating faces, many of which were wiping their own tears away.

"We are grateful to share this moment with each of you," Cat swallowed back her emotion, if only for the sake of finishing their toast, "but, above all, we are grateful to have each other."

Luke gathered himself together enough to say, "here, here!"

Glasses clinked, hearts were full, and two lovers leaned in for a long embrace.

Cat was quite comfortably wrapped in Luke's arms on the dance floor when she noticed her father milling off to the side, stealing glances every so often in her direction.

Of course, Cat chided herself, she had completely forgotten about planning a father-daughter dance. Truly, she had not expected him to be present and therefore the thought hadn't even entered her mind.

Luke followed her gaze and glanced back down, "Do you think he wants to dance?"

"I've never seen my father dance," Cat laughed then paused, "maybe?"

"Do you want to dance with him?"

"I think I actually do," Cat lowered her voice, "Nothing about today has been expected. From waking up beside you—"

Luke continued her sentence, "—to David and your father pounding on the door—"

Cat shook her head, "That, especially—"

"It doesn't have to be planned out to be perfect, Cat."

"Can we get that embroidered on a pillow?"

"Sure," Luke kissed her head, then her hand, before walking with her to where Darcie and Warren sat together, a blanket now draped around both of them. "You look warm," Luke smiled down.

"Babe," Cat squeezed his hand, "why don't you warm up with my mom for a few. Dad, want to dance?"

"I would love to," her father rose to his feet and shook Luke's hand before escorting Cat back onto the dance floor.

Cat could tell the evening would be winding down soon. The snow was falling steadily and the air had grown colder with nightfall despite the outdoor heaters they had stationed around the tent. Rachel's brilliant idea of an outdoor s'mores station by the firepit had been a huge hit. Cat could see the illuminated silhouettes of Lili, Rachel, and Mimi huddled by the fire.

"I know I've apologized already," her father began.

"Yes," Cat nodded. "You have. Thank you for your apology."

"But it doesn't seem adequate," he continued.

Cat couldn't think of the best way to respond and so she resigned herself to a slight nod.

"I am sorry, Cathleen," he repeated. "I would like to make it up to you in some way."

"Dad," Cat stopped him before he could continue, "While Luke and I appreciate your apology, I don't think that now would be the best time to offer any monetary recompense. I hope you understand."

"Because I offered Luke money when—"

"Exactly." Cat offered her father a smile.

"What if I offer something else?"

"Like?" Cat tilted her head.

"My blessing," her father smiled. "My complete support and hope that you will know nothing but love and acceptance from me from this point on … Lili too," he added.

"That is worth more than you'll ever know," Cat leaned in to kiss his cheek and saw that her mother was leaning her head on Luke's shoulder as they watched on.

The night suddenly felt warm.

CHAPTER FORTY-SIX

"ROOM SERVICE," LUKE LAUGHED AS HE CLIMBED THE STEPS TO THE BARN loft, carefully balancing the pancakes and the champagne glasses on the wooden tray he carried, "I made us breakfast in bed."

"Sounds wonderful," Cat started to get up.

"You stay," he winked. "Allow me to serve you."

"Oh, well then" Cat fell back onto her pillows, "I could get used to this every morning."

Luke smirked at her as he brought in a stack of blueberry pancakes.

"Oh, yum," Cat's stomach growled, "I'm famished."

"Yeah, me too," Luke fixed a plate for himself. "I need to refuel after last night."

"Ha!" Cat laughed, "You do, do you?"

"But I mean—" Luke bent down to kiss her neck suggestively, "we could save this for later." He gestured to the tray.

"But I haven't finished my pancakes," Cat said with her mouth full.

"You can have pancakes any day," Luke took the tray back.

"But I can have you any day now, too," Cat teased.

"Hey," Luke pulled her up. "Put a coat on. I want to show you something."

"But the pancakes—," Cat took one more bite before grabbing her sweater and jeans, pulling them on quickly, and following Luke down the stairs.

Once outside, Cat could see what he had wanted to reveal to her. A perfect winter wonderland waited for her outside.

"Oh, wow!" Cat looked out across the field, the Christmas trees of Mimi's farm sparkled in the distance. Each one appeared like a miniature ice-covered tree in a snow globe. "This is incredible."

"I thought you'd like it," Luke wrapped his arms around her.

"I can't help but think of the last time we were snowed in at this barn," Cat leaned into her new husband and let her head rest against his shoulder. "This is exactly what I needed. A chance to replace those memories with beautiful ones."

"Those were beautiful memories too, Cat." Luke said definitively. "Just because something was sad or difficult doesn't make it any less beautiful."

Cat looked up at him. "When did you get to be so wise?"

He smiled and kissed her softly.

"Sometimes this life is messy," he kissed her again. "But I wouldn't trade any of it, not even the messy parts. They brought me back to you."

Cat reached up to find his face in her warm hands, "I have found the one whom my soul loves," she whispered in his ear.

"Shakespeare?" Luke tilted his head.

"My favorite Bible verse," Cat's smile spread so wide she was certain it might freeze there in the winter air. "It has been, since I met you."

If Cat had but one life left, then this was the one she chose, without hesitation or regrets. The messy, the beautiful, the challenging moments, like Luke said, they had brought them back together. It may have taken nine lives, she smiled to herself as she moved in to kiss her husband once more, but at last she could proudly proclaim that she knew who she was and who Cat loved.